Praise for *New York Times*
bestselling author
BEVERLY BARTON

"Smart, sexy and scary as hell. Beverly Barton
just keeps getting better and better."
—*New York Times* bestselling author Lisa Jackson
on *The Fifth Victim*

"With its sultry Southern setting and well-drawn
characters, this richly textured tale ranks among
the best the genre has to offer."
—*Publishers Weekly* on *What She Doesn't Know*

"Get ready for spectacular adventure and great
romance.... Ms. Barton goes beyond the usual
formula with masterful plotting and sharp
characterization to provide thrilling reading."
—*Romantic Times BOOKreviews* on
Gabriel Hawk's Lady

"A riveting page turner!"
—*The Best Reviews* on *On Her Guard*

"Searing emotional intensity that tugs
at every heartstring."
—*New York Times* bestselling author
Linda Howard on *In the Arms of a Hero*

"Beverly Barton knows just how to make
our blood run hot."
—*Romantic Times BOOKreviews* on
Murdock's Last Stand

BEVERLY BARTON

has been in love with romance since her grandfather gave her an illustrated book of *Beauty and the Beast*. An avid reader since childhood, Beverly wrote her first book at the age of nine. After marriage to her own "hero" and the births of her daughter and son, Beverly chose to be a full-time homemaker, aka wife, mother, friend and volunteer. The author of over fifty books, Beverly is a member of Romance Writers of America and helped found the Heart of Dixie chapter in Alabama. She has won numerous awards and has made the Waldenbooks and *USA TODAY* bestseller lists.

BEVERLY BARTON

RAINTREE: SANCTUARY

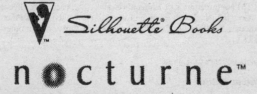

Silhouette Books

nocturne™

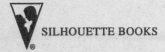

SILHOUETTE BOOKS

ISBN-13: 978-0-373-61766-1
ISBN-10:   0-373-61766-6

RAINTREE: SANCTUARY

Copyright © 2007 by Beverly Beaver

www.silhouettenocturne.com

Printed in U.S.A.

Dear Reader,

Inevitably, writers talk to other writers about writing. And occasionally, when writers are close friends, they share ideas, and in rare instances they are so mentally and emotionally in sync that they create a story together that intrigues each of them. This is what happened when once upon a time Linda Winstead Jones's, Linda Howard's and Beverly Barton's fertile imaginations gave birth to two ancient "more than human" clans who have been at war with each other for thousands of years.

As with most mythological tales, the struggle is one of good against evil. Two hundred years ago, a clan of good wizards, the Raintree, battled a clan of evil wizards, the Ansara, and won the war but allowed many of their defeated enemies to live. What if now, two centuries later, the evil clan has grown in strength and power, hiding away in secret, preparing for the day they can seek revenge and wipe every Raintree from the face of the earth? But what if, in true legendary style, the Raintree princess falls in love with the leader of the enemy clan, the Ansara dranir?

In the two previous Raintree novels, you met Dranir Dante and Prince Gideon, who each reached a pivotal point in his life—meeting the woman destined to be his mate and coming to a chilling realization that his clan's very existence is in grave danger. Let me introduce you to Gideon's sister, Mercy, the keeper of the home place, the guardian of all that is Raintree, the woman who possesses the secret that can either save her ancient race or doom it to extinction.

I hope you find our mystical, magical Raintree and Ansara world of good and evil wizards as fascinating as we did.

Yours,

Beverly Barton

To my dear friend Leslie Wainger, an extraordinary, insightful editor who appreciates unique ideas, encourages individual creativity and inspires her writers to learn, grow and spread their wings.

To my Raintree cocreators, Linda Winstead Jones and Linda Howard, two of the most talented writers I know and friends not only of the heart but also of the soul.

Prologue

On this extraordinary June day, only a week away from the summer solstice, Cael Ansara watched and waited as the conclave gathered in their private meeting chambers here at Beauport. He and he alone knew just how momentous this day would be for the Ansara and the future of their people. Two hundred years ago, his clan had lost *The Battle* with their sworn enemy and been all but annihilated. The few who survived had found solace here on the island of Terrebonne and, generation by generation, had grown in strength and numbers. Like the proverbial Phoenix, the Ansara had risen from the ashes, stronger and more powerful than ever.

One by one, the members of the high council came together this Sunday morning as they did once a month, speaking quietly among themselves, comparing notes on the family's various widespread enterprises as they waited for the Dranir to arrive. Judah Ansara, the all-powerful ruler who was respected and feared in equal measure, had inherited his title from his father. From *their* father.

What would the noble council say, what would they think, how would they react, when they learned that the Dranir of the Ansara was dead? As soon as word came in that Judah had been killed, Cael knew he would have to act fast in order to take control and secure what was rightfully his. Naturally, he would pretend to be as shocked as everyone else, and would make a great show of mourning his younger half brother's brutal murder.

I will even swear vengeance on Judah's behalf, promising to hunt down and kill the person responsible for his death.

Cael smiled, the corners of his mouth curving ever so slightly. Even if several members of the clan suspected him of being behind Judah's murder, no one would ever be able to prove that he had sent a skilled warrior to eliminate the only obstacle in his path to ultimate power. Nor would they be able to prove that he had been the one to bestow a spell of ultimate strength and cunning on that warrior so that he would be equal, if not superior, to his opponent. All would soon learn that Judah the Invincible had been defeated.

At long last, after a lifetime of being the bastard son, of waiting and plotting and planning, he would soon take his place as the Dranir. Was he not the elder son of Dranir Hadar? Was he not as powerful as his younger brother, Judah, perhaps even more so? Was he not better suited to lead the great Ansara clan? Was it not his destiny to destroy their enemy, to wipe every single Raintree from the face of the earth?

Judah claimed that the time was not right for an attack, for all-out war, that the Ansara clan was not ready. At the last council meeting, Cael had confronted his brother.

"We are a mighty people, our powers strong. Why do we wait? Are you afraid to face the Raintree, my brother?" Cael had asked. "If so, step aside and I will lead our people to victory."

At the very moment he had confronted his brother, Cael had already made his plans and had been preparing assignments for the Ansara who looked to him for guidance. He had endowed each young warrior with protective spells. First, the most fearsome of his followers—Stein—would kill Judah. Then Greynell would strike a deadly blow to the very heart of the Raintree, in their home place, the land that had been the family's sanctuary for generations. After that, Tabby would eliminate the Raintree seer, Echo, to prevent her from "seeing" what devastating tragedies awaited her clan.

Unfortunately, only one member of the council had agreed with Cael. One of twelve. Alexandria, the most beautiful and powerful female member of the royal family and third in line for the throne, was his first cousin. She had once been Judah's faithful supporter, but when Cael promised her a place at his side if he were to become the Dranir, she had secretly switched allegiances. What did it matter that he had no intention of sharing his power with anyone, not even Alexandria? Once he ruled the Ansara, no one would dare defy him.

"It is unlike Judah to be late," Alexandria said to the others now.

"I am sure there is a good reason." Claude Ansara, another cousin, had been Judah's closest confidante since they were boys. Claude was second in line to the throne, right after Cael himself, his now deceased father a younger brother to Cael and Judah's father.

Rumblings rose from the others, some concerned by Judah's tardiness, others speculating that undoubtedly there had been an emergency of some sort of which they were not aware. The Dranir had never been late for a council meeting.

Why has there been no telephone call? Cael wondered. *Why hasn't the news of Judah's death been made known?* Stein had been given orders to disappear immediately after killing Judah, and not to resurface until Cael was irrefutably in charge of the Ansara and could give him permission to return to fight the Raintree. Soon. On the day of the summer solstice.

Once the Raintree had been destroyed, the Ansara would rule the world. And *he* would rule the Ansara.

Suddenly the chamber doors burst open as if a mighty wind had ripped them from their golden hinges. A dark, snarling creature, his icy gray eyes surveying the room, stormed into their midst. Clad in black boots, black pants, a bloodstained white shirt and ripped black vest, Judah Ansara arrived, growling like the ferocious beast he was. The wall of windows facing the ocean rattled from the force of his rage.

Cael felt the blood drain from his face, and his heart stopped for one terrifying moment when he realized that Judah had survived the assassination attempt. He had been able to defeat a warrior fighting under a spell created by Cael's incredibly powerful magic, which meant that Judah's powers were undoubtedly far greater than Cael had realized. But that wasn't of key importance right now. Even the fact that Stein was dead was unimportant in the wake of a far greater concern. What Cael needed to know was whether Stein had lived long enough to betray him?

"Lord Judah." Alexandria rushed to his side but stopped short of touching him. "What has happened? You look as if you've been in a battle."

Whirling to face her, Judah narrowed his gaze and glared at her through sharp, shadowed slits. "Someone within my own clan wishes me dead." His voice reverberated with the throaty intensity of a man barely controlling his anger. "The warrior Stein came into my bedchambers at dawn and attempted to murder me in my sleep. The woman who shared my bed was his accomplice and had thought to drug me last night. But they were both fools to think I would not sense danger and act accordingly, despite the strong magical spell that had been placed on Stein. I switched drinks with the lady, so she was the one sleeping soundly, while I was dressed and ready for battle when Stein slipped in through the secret passage to my quarters that only you, the council, even know exists."

Cael realized that he must speak, must react with outrage, least suspicion fall immediately upon him. "Are you implying that someone on the council…?"

"I imply nothing." Judah speared Cael with his deadly glare. "But rest assured, brother, that I will discover the identity of the person who sent Stein to do his dirty work, and when the time is right, I will have my revenge." As Judah rubbed his bloody shoulder, a fresh red stain appeared on his shirt.

"My God, you're still bleeding." Claude went to Judah, his gaze thoroughly scanning Judah's big body for signs of other injuries.

"A few knife wounds. Nothing more," Judah said. "Stein was a remarkable opponent. Whoever chose him, chose well. Only a handful of Ansara warriors have battle skills that equal mine. Stein came close."

"No one has your level of abilities," Councilman Bartholomew said, as he and the other council members surrounded Judah. "You are superior in every way."

"If your battle with Stein was at dawn, why are you still bloody and disheveled?" Alexandria asked. "Couldn't you have bathed and changed clothes before the meeting?"

Judah laughed, the sound deep, coarse and mirthless. "Once my men disposed of Stein's body and the body of his accomplice, the whore Drusilla, I intended to bathe and make myself presentable, but a telephone call from the United States—from North Carolina—interrupted my plans. What I learned from the conversation required immediate action. I spoke directly with Varian, the head of the Ansara team assigned to monitor the Raintree sancuary."

The council members murmured loudly, and then elderly Councilwoman Sidra spoke for the others. "Tell us, my lord, was the call concerning the Raintree?"

Judah nodded; then again cast his gaze directly on Cael. "Your protégé, Greynell, is in North Carolina."

"I swear to you—"

"Do not swear a lie!"

Cael trembled with fear, all the while hating himself for cowering in the wake of his brother's fury. Squaring his shoulders and looking Judah directly in the eyes, Cael faced the Dranir's wrath. He reminded himself that he was an equal, that he was the elder son and deserved to rule the Ansara, that the failure of his most recent plot to dethrone his brother did not mean that he was not destined to rule. Regardless of what Judah said or did, he could not stop the inevitable. Not now. It was too late.

"Did you know that Greynell had gone to North Carolina?" Judah demanded.

"I knew," Cael admitted. "But I didn't send him. He acted on his own."

Judah growled. "And you know what his mission is, don't you?"

Cael wished that he could destroy his brother here and now and be done with it. But he dared not act. When Judah died, his blood should not be on Cael's hands.

"Yes, my lord, I know that some of the young warriors grow restless. They don't want to wait to wage war on the

Raintree. A few have taken it upon themselves to act now instead of waiting until you tell them the time is right."

Judah swore vehemently. The windows shivered and cracked. Fireballs rained down from the ceiling. The marble floor beneath their feet shook, and the walls trembled.

Claude placed his meaty hand on Judah's shoulder and spoke softly to him. The shaking council chambers settled suddenly, the fires burning throughout the room died down, and the broken glass windowpanes jangled loudly as they fell out and hit the floor.

Judah breathed heavily. "Greynell is on a mission to penetrate the Raintree home place, their sanctuary."

Cael swallowed hard.

"Who is his target?" Judah demanded.

Did he lie and swear he did not know? Or did he confess? Cael could feel Judah probing his mind, searching for a way to penetrate the barrier he barely managed to keep in place. If he himself were not so powerful, he could never withstand his brother's brutal psychic force.

"Mercy Raintree." Cael spoke the name with reverence. The woman might be a Raintree, but her abilities were legendary among the Ansara as well as her own people. She was the most powerful empath living today.

Judah's nostrils flared. "Mercy Raintree," he said, his voice deadly calm and chillingly restrained, "is mine. I claimed her. She is my kill."

Chapter 1

Sidonia busied herself with breakfast preparations as she did every morning, moving slowly about the big kitchen. Like the other rooms in the old house, the kitchen had been constructed two hundred years ago, when the Raintree first settled in the hills of North Carolina. Shortly after *The Battle*. Dante and Ancelin Raintree had claimed nine hundred and ninety-nine acres of wilderness, establishing a home place for the Raintree clan, a safe haven where they could recuperate and rebuild after the ravaging war with the Ansara. Over the years, the house had been remodeled numerous times, but some things never changed around here, such as honor, duty and the love of family.

The main house sat atop one of the foothills, surrounded by the forest, with spring-fed streams, ancient trees and an abundance of wildlife. Originally built of wood and rock, the house had been bricked a hundred years ago and wings added to the original structure. Two dozen cottages dotted the landscape within the boundaries of the safe haven, some occupied by relatives, many empty a good part of the time but kept ready for visiting members of the Raintree clan. Family was always welcome.

Sidonia, a distant relative of the royal family, had come to work for them when she'd been a girl of eighteen, brought into the household of Dranir Julian when his wife, Vivienne, was carrying their first child. Young Prince Michael had been an only child for many years, and he had bonded with Sidonia so much that she became like a second mother to him. It was only natural that when he grew to manhood, married and became a father, he chose her to be the nanny for his own children. And when her Michael and his beloved Catherine had been brutally murdered seventeen years ago, it had fallen to her to look after the royal siblings—Dante, Gideon and Mercy.

Dante now lived in Reno, Nevada, owned a gambling casino and was still single, despite knowing full well he was expected to produce an heir. As the Dranir, he oversaw the Raintree clan and handled the clan's finances, having almost doubled the family's vast wealth during the past ten years. His younger brother, Gideon, lived in Wilmington and worked as a police detective. Gideon, too, was single and had made it perfectly clear to one and all that he did not intend to marry and most certainly would never father a child. Mercy remained at the Sanctuary as its keeper. Like her great-aunt Gillian before her, Mercy had been born a powerful empath, and so it fell to her to be the family's guardian, the caretaker of all things Raintree.

The nine hundred and ninety-nine acre refuge lay on a fault

line, and whenever there were any shifts in the earth, any small tremors or minor earthquakes, those forces of nature simply spread out and went around the shielded sanctuary. But the Raintree absorbed the energy produced by the earth's numerous little hiccups. Long ago, a triad of royal Raintrees had placed a cloak of protection about the land, and, yearly, Mercy and her brothers renewed that ancient spell on the day of the Vernal Equinox in early spring. Only someone possessing magic power equal to or greater than the Raintree royals could ever penetrate the invisible barrier that shielded the sanctuary from outsiders.

Sidonia shivered as she recalled the frightening tales of the Ansara and the legend of *The Battle* that had wiped the evil warrior clan from the face of the earth. All except a handful who had escaped, never to be heard from again.

Rolling out biscuit dough, Sidonia pretended not to see the small child tiptoeing into the room. Perhaps it was the weakness of approaching old age—after all, she was eighty-five now—but she loved this little girl with a devotion that was almost sinful. Princess Eve Raintree, a beautiful, charming, precocious imp, had stolen Sidonia's heart the first moment she laid eyes on her. Princess Mercy had given birth at home, in her bedroom upstairs, only she and Sidonia present, as Mercy had wished. Her labor had been hard, but not difficult. Her child had come into the world a perfect specimen of feminine beauty, with her mother's golden hair and delicate features. And with the bewitching green Raintree eyes, a dominant hereditary characteristic that marked the ones who possessed such eyes as true Raintrees.

Sidonia refused to think about that other small but significant hereditary mark the child possessed, a mark known only to her and to Mercy. That one detail set Eve apart from all others and made her special in a way that must be kept secret, even from Dante and Gideon.

Eve crept up behind Sidonia, who held her breath, waiting to see what devilish trick the little one would conjure up this morning. Suddenly the rolling pin flew out of Sidonia's hands and danced through the air, landing with a thud in the middle of the kitchen floor. Gasping as if she were truly startled, Sidonia whipped around and held her hand over her heart.

"You scared me half to death, little princess."

Eve giggled, the sound like sweet music. "It's something new I've just learned to do. Mother says it's called lev-i-ta-tion. I think I will be very good at it, don't you?"

After wiping off her hands on her floral apron, Sidonia reached down and tapped Eve on the nose. "I believe you will be very good at many things, but you must learn to control your powers and always use them wisely."

"That's what Mother says."

"Your mother is a very wise woman." Yes, Mercy *was* wise. And good and kind and loving. And the most powerful empath in the world. She could feel another's pain, remove it from them and heal them. But the price she paid in personal agony often depleted her energy for hours, even days.

"She's very pretty, too," Eve said. "And so am I."

Sidonia chuckled. It was not a bad thing to know your strong points. "Yes, you and your mother are both beautiful."

Mercy was as beautiful inside as out, but Sidonia feared that might not be true of her precious little Eve. She was a good child, with a good heart, but there had been a few times when her temper had flared uncontrollably, and it was at those times Sidonia and Mercy had witnessed the incredible, untutored power Eve possessed.

"Where is Mother? Isn't she eating breakfast with me this morning?" Eve asked as she crawled up onto a stool at the granite-topped bar separating the kitchen from the breakfast room.

"She has gone up to Amadahy Pointe to meditate. I expect her home soon." Sidonia returned to her task. She picked up the rolling pin, washed it off, then used it to spread the dough into a half-inch-thick circle.

"Is something bothering my mother? Is something wrong?" Eve asked, with a wisdom far beyond her years.

Sidonia hesitated, then, knowing Eve had the ability to read her thoughts if she chose to do so, said, "To my knowledge, nothing is wrong. Mercy simply felt the need to mediate."

Sidonia cut the dough and placed each raw biscuit in the rectangular pan, then popped them into the hot oven to bake.

"May I have a glass of apple juice while I wait for Mother?" Eve glanced at the refrigerator.

"Yes, of course you may."

Suddenly the refrigerator door swung open, and the pitcher of juice lifted up and floated out of the refrigerator and across the room. Eve's tinkling girlish giggles jingled about the room.

Sidonia grabbed the pitcher midair and set it on the bar. "You're a little showoff."

"Mother said that practice makes perfect, and that if I don't practice my skills, I won't master them." Eve sighed heavily. Dramatically. The child had a flair for melodrama. "Mother frowned when she told me that. I believe she worries about me. She thinks I have amazing powers."

"Yes, we know, your mother and I. And we both worry, because you are so young and unable to direct your powers. That is why Mercy told you that you must practice. It was no different with your mother and your uncles. They had to learn to control their powers."

"But I am different. I'm not like Mother and Uncle Dante and Uncle Gideon."

Sidonia gasped. Was it possible the child knew the secret of her conception? Sidonia shook her head to dislodge such foolish thoughts. Eve might be talented far beyond any of the other Raintree children, might excel in talents even adults in the clan would envy, but she was still only a child. She might read other people's thoughts, but she did not always understand the words she heard inside her little head.

"Of course, you're different. You're a member of the royal family. Your uncle is the Dranir, and your mother is the greatest empath in the world."

Eve shook her head. Her long blond curls danced about her shoulders. "I am more than Raintree."

A shiver of pure, unadulterated fear quivered through Sidonia. The child sensed the truth, even if she did not know what that truth was. Sidonia removed a glass from the cupboard, lifted the pitcher and poured the apple juice for Eve. She set the glass in front of the child. "Yes, you are more than Raintree. You are very, very special, my precious."

More special than you will ever know, if your mother and I can protect you by keeping your secret.

Mercy Raintree sat on the firm, grassy ground, her eyes closed, her hands resting in her lap. Whenever she was troubled, she came to Amadahy Pointe to meditate, to collect her thoughts and renew her strength. The sunshine covered her like an invisible robe, wrapping her in light and warmth. The spring breeze caressed her tenderly, like a lover's soft touch. With her eyes closed and her soul open to the positive energy she drew from this holy place, this sanctuary within a sanctuary, she focused on what was most important to her.

Family.

Mercy sensed impending danger. But from whom or from what, she did not know. Although her greatest talents lay in being an empath and a healer, she possessed latent precognitive powers, less erratic than her cousin Echo's, but not as strong. She had also been cursed with the ability to sense the emotional and physical condition of others from a distance. *Clairempathy.* As a child, she'd found her various empathic talents maddening, but gradually, year by year, she had learned to control them. And now, despite both Dante and Gideon blocking her from intercepting their thoughts and emotions, she could still manage to pick up something on the outer fringes of each brother's individual consciousness.

Dante and Gideon were in trouble. But she did not know why. Perhaps it was nothing more than stress from their chosen professions. Or it could even be problems in their personal lives.

If her brothers thought she could help them, they would ask her to intervene. This knowledge reassured her that their problems were within the realm of human reality and not of a supernatural nature. Her brothers were, as they had pointed out to her on numerous occasions, grown men, perfectly capable of taking care of themselves without the assistance of their baby sister.

Past experience had taught her that when their souls needed replenishing, their spirits nurtured, her brothers came home, here to the Raintree land, deep in the North Carolina mountains. The home place was protected by a powerful magic that had been established by their ancestors two centuries ago after *The Battle*. Within the boundaries of these secure acres, no living creature could intrude without alerting the resident guardian. Mercy Raintree was that guardian, protector of the home place, as her great-aunt Gillian had been until her death at a hundred and nineteen, and like Gillian's mother, Vesta, the first keeper of the sanctuary in the early eighteen hundreds.

Taking a deep, cleansing breath, Mercy opened her eyes and looked at the valley below, spread out before her like a banquet feast. Late springtime in the mountains. An endless blue sky that went on forever. Towering green trees, the ancient, the old and the young growing together, reaching heavenward. Verdant life, thick and rich and sweet to the senses. A multitude of wild flowers blooming in abundance, their perfume tantalizing, their colors pleasing to the eye.

Mercy wasn't sure exactly what was wrong with her, but she felt a nagging sense of unease that had nothing to do with her brothers or with anyone in the Raintree tribe. No, the restlessness was within her, a yearning she was forced to control because of who she was, because of her duty to her family and to her people. Whenever these strange emotions unsettled her, she climbed the mountain to this sacred peak and mediated until the uncertainty subsided. But today, for some unknown reason, the anxiety clung to her.

Was it a warning?

Seven years ago, she had allowed that hunger inside her to lead her into dangerous territory, into a world she had been ill prepared for, into a relationship that had altered her life. She would not—could not—succumb to fear. And except for brief visits to Dante and Gideon, she would not leave the safety of the Raintree sanctuary. Not ever again.

Pax Greynell knew no fear. Why should he? He was young, strong, brave. A highly trained warrior. And he was an Ansara. The blood of the royal family flowed in his veins, as it did in Cael's, and like the true Ansara Dranir, he, too, had been born out of wedlock. He was a cousin to Cael and Judah. All his life, he had been loyal to the clan and, since Judah had been crowned their leader, loyal to Judah. But in the past year, he, like several of the young warriors, had grown tired of waiting, tired of being told the time was not right, that the Ansara were not ready to do battle with the Raintree.

Cael whispered in their ears, promising them a new order, one in which they would become members of his council. He also implied that Judah was afraid to face the Raintree, whereas he, Cael, was not. Although Pax believed in Cael and would stand at his side in any battle, he knew Judah Ansara was not afraid of anything or anyone.

That thought would have unnerved Greynell if he hadn't been protected by a magic spell cast upon him by Cael. He would be invincible for the next forty-eight hours. No one could harm him. Only Cael or another Ansara of his equal could penetrate the invisible forcefield surrounding him. Twenty-four hours would be more than enough time for him to accomplish his mission and escape without being captured. Afterward, he would wait for word from Cael, and then he would join his master and the others for the final battle.

Greynell adjusted his binoculars and watched while Mercy Raintree rose from the ground with the fluid grace of a ballet dancer, her long blond hair shimmering in the morning sunlight. She was beautiful. And if she were a mere mortal woman, he would rape her before he killed her. But she was not mortal, no more than he was. He dared not risk compromising his mission for a taste of her, no matter how great the temptation.

He kept the binoculars trained on her as she stood there alone, so close, yet beyond his reach. Cael had warned him not to try to enter the Raintree sanctuary, had instructed him to find a way to lure Mercy outside, away from the protection of the home place.

Smiling at his own cleverness, he drank in the sight of this delectable Raintree princess and fantasized about ravaging her before he ended her life. She, like her brothers and her cousin Echo, had been marked for death. Destroy the royal family first, eliminate the most powerful, and the rest would follow.

Sunday, 3:15 p.m.

The Ansara private jet had landed in Asheville, North Carolina, half an hour ago. A prearranged rental car had awaited Judah, so he'd been able to get on the road almost immediately. He didn't know how much time he had before Greynell struck, wasn't sure he could save Mercy Raintree. He had known his foolish young cousin was a loose cannon and, like several of the other young warriors, was eager for battle. But he had not realized the extent of Cael's power over the boy and just how unbalanced Greynell had become.

Judah knew that Cael would try to contact Greynell and warn him. But by now, Cael must have realized that his telepathic powers had been imprisoned, that he had been temporarily put out of commission. Had he also figured out that he had underestimated Judah's powers? Like the egotistical bastard he was, Cael believed himself superior to Judah, actually thought he was more powerful. Idiot. Perhaps realizing that Judah had temporarily frozen his telepathic powers would prove to Cael just who the superior brother actually was.

The only reason Judah had not called Cael out and challenged him to a Death Duel was because they were brothers. But once he had taken care of Greynell—either before or after the young warrior killed the Raintree's most revered empath—Judah would have to face his half brother in combat, once and for all ending Cael's quest to dethrone him. There was little doubt in Judah's mind as to who had been behind the assassination attempt on his life this morning, although he could not prove his suspicions.

Judah stayed on Highway 74, heading southwest, toward the eastern foothills of the Great Smoky Mountains. The Raintree sanctuary bordered the Eastern Cherokee Indian Reservation. Several members of the Raintree clan had intermarried with the Cherokee before the Trail of Tears over a hundred and seventy years ago, and the family had provided assistance to the Cherokee who had escaped from the soldiers and taken refuge in the mountains.

From childhood, Judah had made a study of the Ansara's powerful enemy, knowing that it was his destiny to one day seek revenge for the Ansara defeat in *The Battle* two centuries ago and wipe every single member of the Raintree clan from the face of the earth. But the time was not right. Not yet. Cael was overeager, he and his followers. If they went up against the Raintree too soon, they would be doomed to failure. But he could not make his brother understand the importance of patience. Wait. Soon. But not now.

It was a pity that Mercy Raintree would have to die, along with her brothers and others of their kind. But despite the pleasure he might derive in keeping her alive, in making her his slave, he could not allow one single member of the Raintree clan to live. Not even Mercy.

But Greynell had no right to the kill. Every member of the Ansara clan knew that Mercy Raintree belonged to Judah. She was his kill, as was Dante Raintree. The powers she and her elder brother possessed were Judah's to absorb upon their deaths. And the other brother, Gideon, belonged to Claude. Cael had been furious when Judah had given Claude the right to kill the third Raintree royal.

Cael had been a thorn in Judah's side for far too long. He had indulged his brother, forgiven him his sins again and again, but no longer. Cael had become extremely dangerous, not only to Judah but to the Ansara. He could no longer put off dealing with his power-hungry sibling.

The call came in at seven-forty-two Sunday evening, while Mercy, Eve and Sidonia were sitting on the expansive back porch, Sidonia in her rocking chair, Eve resting her head in Mercy's lap in the swing. An orange slice of twilight sun nestled low on the western horizon, multicolored clouds feathering out on either side like pink and lavender cottony down. Summertime insects chirped, and tree frogs croaked contentedly, as nighttime approached, here in the foothills.

Serenity. Peace.

Mercy had sensed something was wrong, had felt uneasy the entire day. And now that she had received the call, she understood why she'd been concerned. She seldom left the Sanctuary for extended periods of time. Not any longer. As the years passed and her empathic abilities grew stronger, she found it difficult to be in a crowd. Simply walking down the street in Waynesville proved difficult. Other people's thoughts and emotions bombarded her if she so much as made eye contact with them. And heaven help her if someone accidentally brushed against her. She heard their thoughts, sensed their pain, experienced their joy. And any protective spell she used had its limits and its drawbacks, so she used one only when necessary.

As a teenager, after her parents were murdered, she had longed to become a doctor, to save people as the doctors in Asheville had tried so valiantly to save her parents. She had foolishly believed that her inherited, innate empathic abilities would actually help make her a better doctor. She'd been wrong. Dr. Huxley, the oldest physician in the area and a friend of Mercy's father, had tutored Mercy and even arranged for her to accompany him on emergency calls where her empathic abilities often meant the difference between life and death for his patients. Dr. Howell had grown up near the sanctuary and understood what a special people the Raintree were and how remarkable Mercey's talent was, even among her tribe. The Raintree trusted Dr. Howell as they did few other humans, instinctively knowing he would never betray them. But then, after being homeschooled, she had left the mountains at eighteen to attend college. The University of Tennessee had been exciting, but also frightening, because of the dense population. With the help of her family—Dante had arranged for several Raintree clansmen to attend the same college—Mercy had managed to graduate. But living away from the sanctuary had shown her that she could never pursue her dream of becoming a doctor. Her empathic skills were as much a curse as a blessing.

Now, only on rare occasions did Dr. Huxley contact her for assistance. Tonight was one of those occasions. There had been a wreck on the back roads, not far from the home place, and Dr. Huxley knew she would be able to reach the scene before anyone else because of the location—within a mile of the Raintree boundaries.

"You be careful," Sidonia said as she stood beside Mercy's white Escalade, Eve at her hip. "Are you sure you don't want me to call Brenna and have her stay with Eve so I can go with you?"

Mercy caressed Sidonia's wrinkled cheek. "You worry too much. I'll be fine. Dr. Huxley is on his way with the police, and the county rescue squad should reach the accident site very soon. I won't be there alone for long."

"Don't overdo. You know how weak—"

"If anything goes wrong, Dr. Huxley will take care of me and see that I get home safe and sound."

Mercy slipped behind the wheel of her new SUV, a present from Dante. As she backed out of the driveway, she glanced in the rearview mirror and saw Sidonia and Eve waving goodbye. Focusing on the road ahead, she pressed her foot against the accelerator, knowing that the accident victims' lives might well be in her hands.

Less than five minutes away from the sanctuary's boundaries, she came upon two mutilated vehicles that had apparently crashed headlong into each other. How could that have happened, on a clear evening, with no fog, no rain and on a relatively straight stretch of highway? Had one of the drivers been drinking or taking drugs? Mercy pulled off to the side of the road, opened the door and got out, her heart racing maddeningly as she hurried toward the nearest vehicle, a red sports car that had been crushed almost beyond recognition. Without even touching the driver's bloody body, she knew he was dead.

She wished his soul a safe journey into the afterlife. That was all she could do for him. But she sensed life inside the other vehicle, a silver truck. As she approached the smoking Ford, she heard moans and cries coming from within. She had to work quickly and do her best to free this couple. The driver, a middle-aged man, was trapped by the steering wheel, which had crushed his chest. The woman beside him was the one whimpering and groaning, her pale face streaked with blood—her own and the man's.

Using both hands, Mercy reached inside through the shattered passenger window and touched the female. The frightened woman screamed, then suddenly grew very still as Mercy connected with her and began drawing the pain from her mangled body. Without saying a word, Mercy communicated with the woman, doing her best to reassure her as well as comfort her.

"My name is Mercy, and I'm here to help you."

The woman finally managed to speak. "I'm Darlene and—oh, God, my husband. Keary…"

Lifting one hand away from Darlene, Mercy reached farther into the truck cab and ran her fingertips over Keary's right shoulder. She sensed no life. The man had died.

Returning to the task of healing Darlene, of keeping her

from going into shock and from bleeding to death, Mercy concentrated completely on sustaining life, on taking the pain and suffering into her own body.

Mercy trembled as sheer agony surged through her, pain almost beyond bearing. No matter what, she must manage to remain conscious. Drawing on her inner personal strength and the powerful Raintree gifts with which she'd been blessed, she worked her magic.

Judah had picked up on Greynell's scent twenty miles away, but he had known his whereabouts from the moment he got off the Ansara jet in Asheville. He could have pinpointed the warrior's exact location sooner if he had chosen to use his clairvoyant powers, but being gifted himself, Greynell would have known someone was intruding into his thoughts. The last thing Judah wanted to do was give his opponent any advance warning. He had no doubt that he could easily defeat his cousin if they did battle. But he had already fought to the death once today and preferred to dispose of Greynell more easily.

After parking his rental car some distance from where Greynell waited and watched, Judah crept into the forest. He let his prey's scent guide him into a wooded area adjacent to the back road only a few miles from Raintree land.

Suddenly, without any warning, Judah felt a forceful jolt of awareness, a recognition so strong that it momentarily halted him mid-step. Had Cael managed to break free from the spell Judah had cast over him, and was he now trying to get his attention? No, that wasn't it at all. The compelling connection was not with Cael but with a female. One nearby. And not an Ansara. No, that all-powerful magic came from his sworn enemy, Mercy Raintree.

He felt her deep inside him, as if she were a part of him. She was close, as close as Greynell. And she was in the throes of a potent healing. Mercy was not your average empath. She possessed the rare gift of *namapathy*. True psychic healing. And for whatever reason, she was now using all her power to save a human life.

Why she would bother with a mere mortal was beyond him. She was draining her strength and depleting her power, unknowingly making herself vulnerable to Greynell. But that was what the young warrior had wanted, why he had created the accident that had called Mercy from the safety of the Raintree sanctuary.

Unable to shake off the incredible energy Mercy emitted, Judah simply absorbed it. Flashes of her gentleness, her kindness and her tender touch bombarded him. She was far more powerful now than she had been seven years ago. At twenty-three she had been no match for him. Today, she was possibly the only woman on earth who came anywhere close to being his equal.

Cloaking himself with a spell of invisibility, blocking both his physical and psychic presence, Judah proceeded deeper into the forest. The trained warrior within him took over completely as he neared his destination. He paused as Pax Greynell crept up behind Mercy and wrapped a dark cord around her slender neck. She had been too deep into an empathic trance to sense her attacker's presence. Grasping the cord, she struggled to loosen it, but to no avail.

Judah ran with lightning speed, removing his dagger from the jewel-crested sheath inside his jacket as he raced to save the life of a woman who belonged to him in a way no other woman ever had or ever would. She was his and his alone. Only he, Dranir Judah Ansara, had the right to kill her.

Just as Mercy had been taken by surprise by her attacker, so was Greynell. Judah shoved the dagger deep into his back, puncturing a kidney, killing him without a second thought. Mercy gasped for air when the cord around her neck loosened.

Her assailant's body dropped onto the pavement at her feet, crumpling into a dead heap.

Hurriedly, Judah blasted Greynell's body with an energy bolt, crushing it to dust.

Judah had accomplished his mission. It was time for him to leave. But he hesitated. For only a split second, but it was long enough to sense that Mercy was in trouble. Weakened by the healing miracle she had performed on the accident victim, Mercy was not only dangerously weak, but because of fighting Greynell with what little strength she'd had left, she was quickly fading into an unconscious state from which she might not recover.

Acting purely on possessive instinct, Judah grabbed Mercy before she fainted. The woman in the truck was still alive, healed by Mercy's magic. She slept peacefully at her dead husband's side.

The shrill cries of multiple sirens warned Judah to escape. But he could not leave Mercy. If he did, she might die. He, and he alone, could revive her.

Sidonia decided that if Mercy had not returned by midnight, she would call Dante. Dr. Huxley had phoned two hours ago to ask if Mercy had gotten home all right.

"I know she'd been to the site of the accident, because the only survivor told me that Mercy saved her life," Dr. Huxley had said. "I don't understand why she didn't wait for me. She knows I would have made sure someone saw her safely home if she was too weak to drive herself."

"You're worried about my mother, aren't you?" Eve said.

Sidonia gasped, then turned and faced the six-year-old, who was standing in the doorway between the foyer and the front parlor. "I thought I put you to bed hours ago. Did something wake you?"

"I haven't been asleep."

Intending to take Eve back to her bedroom, Sidonia marched toward her. "It's past eleven, and time for all good little girls to be fast asleep."

"I'm not a good little girl. I am Raintree." Eve narrowed her expressive green eyes. "I am more than Raintree."

A foreboding chill rippled up Sidonia's spine. "So you have said, and I have agreed. So let's not talk about it again. Not at this late hour." She grasped Eve's hand. "Now come along. Your mother will be upset with both of us if, when she comes home, you aren't in bed."

"She will come home," Eve said. "Soon. Before midnight."

Sidonia lifted an inquisitive eyebrow. "Is that right? And you'd know that because…?"

"Because I can see her. She's asleep. But she will wake up soon."

Was Mercy out there somewhere, alone and weak to the point of unconsciousness? Was that what Eve saw? "Do you know where she is? Can you tell me exactly where I can find her?"

"She's in her car, the one Uncle Dante gave her," Eve said. "It's parked somewhere dark. But she's all right. He's with her. Touching her. Taking care of her. Giving her some of his strength."

"Who…?" Sidonia's voice quivered. "Who is with your mother? Who is giving her some of his strength?"

Eve smiled, the gesture equally sweet and impish. "Why, my daddy, of course."

Chapter 2

Mercy Raintree was even more beautiful than she'd been in her early twenties and far more dangerous. Despite her present weak state, Judah sensed the tremendous power within her. She was, as he had suspected, a woman who was now his equal. Odd that he, her rightful destroyer, had saved her from one of his own clan, that at this very moment he was restoring her strength when he could easily break her neck or drain the very life from her with a mere thought. And he *would* kill her—when the time was right. When the Ansara attacked the Raintree and annihilated their entire tribe. Unlike the Raintree, the Ansara would leave no one alive, not a single man, woman or child. But he would be merciful to his beautiful Mercy and take her life quickly, with as little pain as possible.

While she lay in his arms unconscious, he probed her mind but found it impossible to gain entrance. She had placed a block between her and the outside world, a shield to prevent anyone from listening to her private thoughts. If he tried harder, he could possibly destroy the barrier, but why should he bother? It wasn't as if he needed information from her. If not for Greynell's foolish actions, he would never have been here with her. Hell, he wouldn't be within a thousand miles of her. For the past seven years, he had made certain their paths never crossed, that he stayed far away from the North Carolina mountains and the Raintree home place.

Her eyelids flickered, consciousness fighting for dominance, her mind trying to come out of the shadows. But Judah knew she would not awaken fully for many hours. After the combination of such an arduous healing and her struggle for her life, her mind and body could not recover without rest, not even with the surge of strength with which he had infused her. She lay in his arms, helpless, completely vulnerable. But she was not without her weapons, protection far more potent than the psychic barrier that safeguarded her private thoughts.

If Greynell had succeeded in killing her, all hell would have broken loose. Literally. The death of a Raintree princess would have played havoc with the senses of all who were Raintree, especially Dante and Gideon. A host of her clansmen would have swarmed home, to the sanctuary. What if the Raintree Dranir and his younger brother suspected the fatal blow had come from an Ansara? He dared not risk even the slightest possibility that Mercy's premature death could warn the Raintree of the Ansaras' resurgence.

Judah looked down at her. She was resting peacefully against him as he sat with her in his lap on the passenger side of her vehicle. Her head nestled on his shoulder, her slender arms limp at her sides, her full, round breasts rising and falling with each breath she took.

He skimmed her cheek with the back of his hand.

Memories he had forced from his mind by sheer willpower years ago broke free and reminded him of another time, another place, when he had held this woman in his arms. When he had touched her, had tutored her, had taught her...

He had known who she was when they first met, and the very fact that she was a Raintree princess had whetted his appetite for her. She'd had no idea of his true identity, and the fact that she'd succumbed to his charms so easily had amused him. She had been practically an open book to him, unable to completely shield herself, her abilities still immature and only partly tamed. He, on the other hand, had protected himself, deliberately keeping his true identity and nature from her. They had spent less than twenty-four hours together, but in that short period of time she had become like a fever in his blood. No matter how many times he'd taken her, he had still wanted her.

"You were a bewitching little virgin," Judah told the sleeping Mercy. "Sweet. Luscious. Ripe for the picking."

Caressing her long, slender neck, he allowed his fingertips to linger on her pulse.

Judah...Judah...

Hearing Mercy telepathically whispering his name stunned him. He tightened his hold about her neck, then suddenly realized what he was doing and eased his hand away from her.

On some level, she sensed his presence. That was not good. How could he explain what he was doing here, why he had just happened to be on a back road in the North Carolina mountains at the exact moment some madman tried to kill her?

He had to take her home and leave her in safe hands before she awakened. If she recalled anything about him, perhaps she would believe she had simply dreamed of him.

Did she ever dream of him? Or was he nothing more than a vague memory?

Why should I care? This woman means nothing to me. She didn't then. She doesn't now. She was only a fleeting amusement for me.

An amusement that had haunted him for far too long after their one day and night together. He had been unable to forget awakening from a deep sleep and finding her gone, his bed empty. He'd been angry that she had run away and curious as to why. But common sense had cautioned him not to follow her. And for many months afterward, he had wondered if she had somehow realized who he was—her deadly enemy—and had fled to warn her brothers of a mighty Ansara Dranir's existence. But neither Dante nor Gideon had hunted him down and sought revenge for taking their sister's innocence.

She did not know who I was.

Judah gently maneuvered Mercy so that she sat in the SUV's passenger seat. He lowered the back of the seat until she was half reclining; then he fastened her seat belt. She whimpered. His stomach muscles knotted painfully. He hated the fact that after seven years, he could still remember the sound of her sweet, feminine whimpers when he had taken her the first time. And the second time. And the third…

After starting the Cadillac's engine, Judah shifted gears, turned the vehicle around and headed back up the country road. He would take Mercy home, leave her there and return to Asheville. He had no desire to stay in the United States any longer than necessary. His place was at Terrebonne, the home of the Ansara for the past two hundred years. Once the jet had landed on the island, he would call a special council meeting. Cael and his followers had to be stopped before their foolish actions endangered the Ansara and destroyed Judah's future plans to annihilate the Raintree.

Cael wanted to be the Dranir. Everyone knew that his older

half brother believed he had been cheated out of the title by a mere chance of birth. Cael was first in line to the throne, a fact that greatly concerned Judah, who by now should have married and fathered a child. But while he could easily protect himself from Cael's evil machinations, he hesitated to put an innocent child's life in peril. Once Cael had been dealt with and the Raintree eliminated, Judah would choose an appropriate Dranira and procreate.

Within five minutes of following his instincts and driving toward his destination, the high iron gates protecting the entrance to the Raintree sanctuary came into view. Judah slowed the SUV, then hit the button inside the vehicle that opened the massive gates. Before driving through, he spoke quietly, reciting ancient words, conjuring up a potent magic. With Mercy asleep at his side, he drove onto the private road that wound around and around up the foothills, all the way to the top of the highest hill, where the royal family's house presided over the valley below, like a king on his high throne.

Lights from the veranda welcomed them, informing Judah that someone inside was waiting for Mercy, possibly concerned for her well-being. A husband? Had she married another from the Raintree clan, or had she chosen a mere human as her mate?

What did it matter? Whoever was now a part of her life— lover or husband or even children—they would all become Ansara targets and would die with Mercy on that fateful day. Judah parked the SUV, got out and rounded the hood. After opening the passenger door, he lifted Mercy up and into his arms. She nestled against him, her actions seeming to be instinctive, as if she believed herself safe and protected.

Judah hardened his heart. He would not allow this beguiling creature to tempt him. She was only a woman, one like

so many others. He had bedded her, as he had bedded countless women. She was no better. No different.

Liar, an unwelcome inner voice taunted him.

Cael cursed violently as he tore apart his living room in
the seaside villa in Beauport, a place he had called home
since Dranir Hadar had acknowledged him as his son. His
unwanted, illegitimate son. He was the bastard from an affair
the Dranir had had before he'd wed the beloved Dranira
Seana. Judah's sainted mother had died in childbirth, after
suffering several miscarriages. Miscarriages caused by a curse
put upon Seana by Cael's mother, Nusi, an enchanting sorceress. Upon learning of her wicked little spells, Hadar had
ordered his former mistress's death—a public execution.

Cael clenched his teeth, anger from his childhood and
from the present situation consuming him, his rage threatening to explode from within. How was it possible that Judah
had frozen his telepathic abilities? How dare he do such a
thing! His brother was far more dangerous than Cael had suspected, his powers far greater. If Judah could control Cael's
inherited talents, then he had to find a way to protect himself
from his younger brother's machinations.

Growling like a wounded bear, Cael shoved his fist
through the wall, tearing apart plaster that shredded as if it
were tissue paper.

"Temper, temper," Alexandria said, her voice mocking.

Cael whipped around and glared at her as she stood in the
open double doors leading to the patio. "You're like a snake,
Cousin, slithering silently about, sneaking up on unsuspect-
ing victims."

Alexandria laughed, the sound even deeper and more
throaty than her gruff voice. "You're not my victim, but from
the way you're acting, I believe you must be the victim of

some vile magic the Dranir has conjured up to prevent you from warning Greynell."

Cael stormed across the room toward his cousin. "What do you know?"

"Oh, dear, dear. Judah really did freeze your powers, didn't he?"

"He did not!"

"Perhaps only your psychic powers were affected, especially the telepathic ones. You weren't able to warn Greynell, were you?"

"Have you spoken to Judah?"

"No, I haven't spoken to him," Alexandria said. "And there is no official word from him. But Claude received a telepathic message from our revered Dranir, and I just happened to be with him at the time."

Cael paused, a good three feet separating him from his uninvited guest. "You never just happen to be anywhere."

Her lips curved in a closed-mouth smile. "I made a point of staying near Claude because I knew that if Judah contacted any one of us, it would be our dear cousin."

"If you expect me to beg you for the information—"

"Don't fret. I expect nothing from you now. But when you are Dranir, I expect to rule at your side."

"As you will." He closed the gap between them, reached out, circled her neck with one hand and drew her close. Close enough that his lips brushed hers. "You will be my Dranira."

Sighing contentedly, Alexandria wrapped her arms around Cael's neck. "Greynell is dead. Judah killed him to prevent him from disposing of Mercy Raintree."

"Fool. Son of a bitch fool. He destroyed one of his own to save a Raintree. The council will—"

"The council will be called into a special meeting once Judah returns."

Cael sucked in a hard, agitated breath. "For what purpose? To investigate the assassination attempt on his life? He will learn nothing. There is no trail leading back to me."

"Claude told me that we, the council members, must band together with Judah to stop the renegade factions within the Ansara clan. Judah truly believes we are not ready to fight the Raintree." She looked directly into Cael's eyes. "Are you sure we *are* ready, that we can win if we go to war on the day of this year's summer solstice?"

Snarling, Cael tightened his hold at the back of her neck. "There is nothing Judah can do to stop us. Not now. There are warriors in place, ready to strike. Even if Judah managed to stop Greynell, he cannot stop the others. Even he cannot be in two places at once."

"Just what do you have up your sleeve?" Alexandria's heartbeat accelerated. Cael sensed her excitement.

"Tabby is in Wilmington taking care of Echo Raintree. And then, on my command, she will eliminate Gideon."

"Tabby is a wild card. What if you can't control her? She takes perverse pleasure in killing. She could easily draw attention to herself."

"Tabby knows what I will do to her if she fails me."

"Our success might well depend upon removing the Raintree royal siblings before the great battle, yet all three are still alive and well."

"But not for long." Cael grinned. "Dante is in for quite a surprise tonight. And once Judah returns to Terrebonne and is consumed with other matters, I will send another warrior to take care of Mercy."

Sidonia heard the car drive up and park. She had taken Eve back to her room and tucked her in for a second time, warning the little imp to stay put, but she doubted the child was asleep. Eve was concerned about Mercy, just as she herself was.

Pausing at the front door, Sidonia, peered through the left sidelight and gasped when she saw a large, dark man walking toward the veranda, an unconscious Mercy in his arms. The only vehicle in sight was Mercy's Escalade, so who was this stranger and why was he with Mercy?

Closing her eyes, Sidonia called for her animal helpers to awaken and come to her. Within minutes, by the time the stranger set foot on the veranda, Magnus and Rufus, her fiercely faithful Rottweilers, appeared in the yard, one on the right, the other on the left, flanking the veranda.

Sidonia opened the front door, took one step over the threshold and faced the stranger. He paused as if he'd been expecting her, and his gaze connected with hers. He was not Raintree. His eyes were steel gray. Hard and cold, with no sign of emotion.

"I've brought your mistress home, old woman," the man told her, his voice a deep, commanding baritone.

No, he was not Raintree, but neither was he a mere mortal.

A tremor of unease jangled Sidonia's nerves. If he was not Raintree and he was not human, that meant…

"You assume correctly," he said. "I am Ansara."

Sensing Sidonia's fear, Magnus and Rufus growled.

The man—the Ansara man—stared first at Rufus and then at Magnus. They quieted instantly. Sidonia hazarded quick glances to her right and left. Both large animals stood frozen like marble statues.

"What have you done to—"

"They're unharmed. In an hour, they will be as they were and return to their sleep."

"What are you doing with Mercy? Did you harm her? If you have, the wrath of the Raintree will—"

"Be quiet, old woman, and show me where to place your mistress so she can rest and recover from her ordeal. She healed a dying woman tonight."

Confused by this Ansara's concern for Mercy, Sidonia hesitated, then backed up to allow him entrance. He was a handsome devil. Wide shouldered, at least six-two, with flowing black hair that hung in a single braid down his back, and chiseled features that made him look as if he'd been cut from stone.

"Her room is upstairs, but I think it best if you—"

Ignoring Sidonia, the man headed for the staircase.

"Wait!"

He did not wait; instead, he took the stairs two at a time, Sidonia following as quickly as her old legs would carry her. By the time she reached the second floor, he already had the door to Mercy's bedroom open, apparently being guided by his instinct.

Scurrying down the hall, Sidonia came up behind the Ansara just as he laid Mercy on her bed. From the doorway, she watched him as he stared at Mercy for a full minute, then turned and walked toward the door.

"Who are you? What is your name?" Sidonia demanded. *He couldn't be* that *Ansara, could he? Surely not.*

"I am Judah Ansara."

Sidonia gasped.

He smiled wickedly. "I once wondered if Mercy might have suspected I was an Ansara, and if that was the reason she fled from me so quickly that long ago morning."

"Stop reading my mind!" Heaven help her, she had to do something to prevent this Ansara demon from listening to her thoughts. He mustn't find out—shut up, you old fool, she told herself. Then she closed her eyes and recited an ancient spell, one that should protect her from this wicked Ansara's mental probing.

"Don't trouble yourself, Sidonia," Judah told her. "I will leave your thoughts private. But when I leave, I'm afraid I must erase from your mind all memory of my visit here tonight."

"Don't you touch my mind again, you evil beast."

Judah laughed.

"You find me amusing, do you? Don't think because I am well past eighty that my skills are not as sharp as they ever were."

"I would never insult you by underestimating your powers."

"Why are you with Mercy?" Sidonia demanded. "What are you doing here on Raintree land? How did you—"

"Why I'm here doesn't matter. I found Mercy in an unconscious state and brought her home. You should be grateful to me."

"Grateful to Ansara scum like you? Never!"

"Does Mercy feel about me the way you do? Does she hate me?"

"Of course she hates you. She is Raintree. You are Ansara."

He glanced at the bed where Mercy rested. Tempted to probe the old woman's mind for answers, Judah snorted, disgusted with himself for allowing his curiosity about Mercy's feelings to concern him.

"You can't stay here," Sidonia said. "You must leave. Immediately."

"I have no plans to remain here," Judah told her. "I leave your mistress in your capable hands."

"Yes, yes. Leave now, and go quickly."

When Judah turned to leave, his mind centered on a spell that would erase Sidonia's memories of his visit, he spotted a small shadow behind and to the side of the old woman. He paused and waited, suspecting the Raintree nanny might have conjured up some deadly little spirit to escort him out of the house. But suddenly the shadow moved from behind Sidonia and came into the room, the light from the hallway backlighting the figure, making it appear a golden white, like the glow of moonlight. The shadow was a child, a girl child, he realized.

Judah stared at the little one and saw that her eyes were a true Raintree green, and her pale blond hair flowed in long, shimmering curls to her waist. If his eyesight had not told him that Mercy was the child's mother, his inner vision would have.

So Mercy had married and had children. At least one child. This remarkably lovely little girl was so like her mother, and yet…

What was it about the child that puzzled him? She was a Raintree child, no doubt of that. But she was different.

Sidonia grabbed the girl and tried to shove the little beauty behind her, but the child wiggled free of the old nanny's hold and walked fearlessly toward Judah.

"No, child, don't!" Sidonia cried. "Stay away from him. He is evil."

The child stopped several feet away from Judah, then looked up and stared right at him, her gaze connecting boldly with his.

"I'm not afraid of him," the child said. "He won't hurt me."

Judah smiled, impressed with her bravery.

Seasoned warriors had trembled at the very sight of Judah Ansara.

When Sidonia came forward, intending to grab the child, the little girl lifted her arm and held her tiny hand in front of the old woman, who went deadly still, immobilized by magic.

Amazing. The child's abilities were greatly advanced for one so young.

"You're very powerful, little one," Judah said. He had never known an Ansara or a Raintree to possess so much power at such a young age. "I don't know of any five-year-olds capable of—"

"I'm six," she told him, her shoulders straight, her head held high. A true princess.

"Hmm… But even at six, you are far more advanced than other Raintree children, aren't you?"

She nodded. "Yes. Because I am more than Raintree."

"Are you indeed?" He glanced at the stricken expression on Sidonia's partially frozen face and realized that not only had the girl immobilized the old woman's limbs, she had rendered her temporarily mute.

"You don't know who I am, do you?" the little girl asked. When she smiled at him, Judah's gut tightened. There was something strikingly familiar about her smile.

"I believe you're Mercy Raintree's child, aren't you?"

She nodded.

"Do you know who I am?" he asked, his curiosity piqued by the child's precocious nature. He sensed an unnatural strength in her…and a kinship that wasn't possible.

She nodded again, her smile widening. "Yes, I know."

This child could not possibly know who he was. He kept his true identity protected from all who were not Ansara. "If you know who I am, what is my name?"

"I don't know your name," she admitted.

Judah sighed inwardly, relieved that he had overestimated the child's abilities and had been mistaken about the momentary sense of a familial bond. Oddly drawn to the little girl, he approached her, knelt on his haunches so that they were face-to-face and said, "My name is Judah."

She held out her little hand.

He looked at her offered hand. Oddly enough, the thought of killing this child—Mercy's child—saddened him. He would make sure her death was as quick and painless as Mercy's.

He took her hand. An electrical current shot through Judah, unlike anything he had ever experienced. A raw, untamed power of recognition and possession.

"Hello, Daddy. I'm your daughter, Eve."

An earsplitting scream shook the semi-dark bedroom as Mercy Raintree woke from her healing sleep.

Chapter 3

The sound of her own scream resounded inside Mercy's head, and for a split second she thought she was dreaming that her worst nightmare had come true. As the echoes of her terrified scream shivered all around her, remnants of a fear beyond bearing, she awoke to the reality of her nightmare. Her eyes opened and quickly adjusted to the semidarkness around her.

"Mommy!" Eve's concerned cry prompted Mercy into immediate action. Telepathically, she called her child to her, and within seconds she rose from the bed and took her daughter into her protective embrace.

"What's wrong, Mother?" Eve asked. "You mustn't be afraid."

The moment Mercy had prayed would never come was here, descending upon them like an evil plague from the depths of hell. Judah Ansara, a true prince of darkness, stood hovering over her and Eve, his icy gray eyes staring at her, questioning her, demanding answers.

"Sidonia?" Mercy said, fearing that Judah had disposed of her beloved nanny.

"Oh!" Eve gasped, then eased out of Mercy's arms, turned and waved her hand.

Mercy followed her child's line of vision to where Sidonia's body came to life, having been released from its immobile state. "Eve, did you…?"

"I'm sorry, Mother, but Sidonia didn't want me to meet my daddy. She tried to stop me from talking to him."

Mercy's gaze reconnected with Judah's. Those cold eyes shimmered with hot anger.

She is mine! Judah's three unspoken words filled the room, expanding, exploding, shaking the walls and windows.

"Stop!" Mercy cried, shoving Eve behind her. "Your rage accomplishes nothing."

Judah grabbed Mercy by the shoulders, his fingers biting into her flesh. When Mercy whimpered in pain, Eve reached up and placed her hand on Judah's arm.

"You must be gentle with my mother. I know you don't want to hurt her."

Judah's tenacious hold loosened as he glanced from Mercy's face to Eve's, and then back to Mercy. "I won't harm your mother." He glanced over at Sidonia, who glared at him with bitter hatred. "Go with your nanny, child. I need to speak to your mother alone."

"But I don't want to—" Eve whined.

Do as I tell you to do. Mercy heard the silent message Judah issued to Eve and realized that he instinctively knew Eve would hear his thoughts.

Eve looked to her mother. Mercy nodded. "Go with Sidonia. Let her put you to bed. You and I will talk in the morning."

Eve kissed Mercy on the cheek. "Good night, Mother." Then she tugged on Judah's arm and motioned for him to bend over, which he did after releasing his hold on Mercy. Eve kissed his cheek, too. "Good night, Daddy."

Neither Mercy nor Judah spoke until Sidonia took Eve away and closed the bedroom door behind them.

The moment they were alone, Judah turned on Mercy. "The child is mine?"

Mercy stood and faced her greatest fear—her child's father. "Eve is mine. She is Raintree."

"Yes, she is Raintree," Judah replied. "But she is more. She told me so herself."

"Eve has great power that she is far too young to understand. Telling herself that she is more than Raintree helps explain these things to her so that her child's mind can accept them."

"Do you deny that she is mine?"

"I neither deny nor confirm—"

"She knew me instantly," Judah said.

Was there any way she could lie to this man and convince him that Eve was not his? For nearly seven years, since the moment she conceived Judah Ansara's child, she had kept that knowledge hidden from him and from the entire world, even from her own brothers. Only Sidonia knew the truth of Eve's paternity. Until now.

"What are you doing here on Raintree land?" Mercy asked.

He eyed her speculatively. "You don't remember?"

Unsure about what he meant, she didn't respond as she sorted through her last coherent thoughts before blacking out. It was not unusual for her to faint or to simply fall asleep after a healing, but in this instance, her restorative sleep had been far deeper than normal.

She recalled the car accident and saving the sole survivor

by removing her terrible pain, then transposing enough of her own strength and healing power to keep the woman alive.

Suddenly she felt the memory of a forceful grip around her neck, cutting off her air, choking her. Mercy gasped, her gaze shooting to Judah. Taking several calming breaths, she captured those frightening moments buried deep in her subconscious and realized that someone had tried to erase those memories.

"You didn't want me to remember that someone tried to kill me."

Judah simply glared at her.

"Do you want me to think it was you who tried to strangle me?" she said. "I know it wasn't."

He said nothing.

"You won't allow me to remember my attacker. Why? And what were you doing so close to the Raintree home place at the very time it happened?"

"Coincidence." His deep baritone rumbled the one word.

"No, I don't believe you. You knew someone was going to… You came here to save me, didn't you? But I don't understand." How would Judah have known her life was in danger? And why would he bother to come to the hills of North Carolina to save her, a Raintree princess?

"Why would I not save the mother of my child?"

"You didn't know Eve existed. Not until you came here. Not until she introduced herself to you."

"Why I came here is not important," Judah said. "Not now. All that matters is the fact that you gave birth to my child and have kept her from me for six years. How could you have done that?"

Mercy laughed, the sound false and nervous. "Eve is my child. It doesn't matter who her father is." Oh, God, if only that were true. If only…

Judah growled, the sound as bestial as the man himself. No matter what, she could never allow herself to see him as anything other than what he was—an Ansara demon. It did not matter that even now, knowing him for who and what he was, she found herself drawn to him on a purely sexual level. He possessed a power over her that she could not deny. But she could—and would—resist.

Judah scanned Mercy from head to toe, his gaze appreciative and sensual.

"The protective spell you cast over Eve must be very powerful, one that takes a great deal of your strength to keep in place."

Mercy shivered. "There is nothing I wouldn't do for Eve. She is—"

"She is an Ansara."

"Eve is a Raintree princess, the granddaughter of Dranir Michael, the daughter of Princess Mercy."

"A rare and highly unique child," Judah said. "There has been no mixing of the bloodlines for thousands of years, not since the first great battle when all Ansara and Raintree became sworn enemies. Any mixed-breed offspring have been disposed of before birth or as infants."

"If there is one drop of decency in you, you will not claim her," Mercy said. "If she is forced to choose between two heritages, it could destroy her. And you know, as well as I do, that your people would never accept her. They would try to kill her."

Judah's smile sent waves of terror through Mercy. "Then you admit that she is mine."

"I admit nothing."

Judah reached out and grabbed her by the back of her neck, his large hand clasping forcefully, his thick fingers threading through her hair. If she chose to do so, she could battle him here and now, both physically and mentally. But she had learned at a young age to choose her battles, to save her strength for the moments of greatest need. Standing her ground, neither resisting nor accepting his hold on her, Mercy faced her deadly enemy.

"When did you realize I was Ansara?" Judah asked.

"The moment I conceived your child," she admitted.

His hold tightened as he brought her closer, then lowered his head until only a hairsbreadth separated his lips from hers. "That must have been the last time we had sex. If it had been before, any of the other times, you would have left me sooner."

I didn't leave you even then, the last time, when your seed took root within me and I knew that I would give birth to an Ansara. I stayed with you until you fell asleep, assisted by an ancient sleep spell that Sidonia had taught me. And when I knew you would not awaken for hours, I searched and found the mark of the Ansara on your neck, hidden by your long hair.

Judah brushed her lips with his. She sucked in a deep gulp of air.

"I knew you were Raintree from the moment I saw you," he said. "I disregarded my better judgment, which told me to avoid you, that you were trouble. But I couldn't resist you. You were the most beautiful creature I'd ever seen."

And I couldn't resist you. I wanted you the way I'd never wanted another man. You were a stranger, and yet I gave myself to you.

I loved you.

Even now, Mercy found it difficult to admit the complete truth, because it was so heinous. The very thought that she had fallen in love with an Ansara was an abomination, a betrayal of her people, an unforgivable treachery.

And if Dante and Gideon ever learned that their beloved niece was half Ansara...

"You were a delightful amusement," Judah told her, his breath hot against her lips. "But don't think that I've given you a second thought in the past seven years. You were nothing to me then, and are nothing to me now. But Eve…"

Fear boiled fiercely within Mercy, a mother's protective fear for her child. "The only way you can claim Eve is to kill me."

"I could kill you as easily as I squash an insect beneath my feet."

His words proclaimed indifference, but his actions spoke a different language. Judah took Mercy's mouth in a possessive, conquering kiss that startled her and yet stirred to life the hunger she had known only for this man. She tried to resist him but found herself powerless. Not against his strength, but against her own need.

How could she want him, knowing who he was?

When they were both breathless and aroused, Judah ended the kiss and lifted his head. "You're still mine, aren't you?" He sneered. "I could lay you down here and now and take you, and you wouldn't protest."

Mercy jerked away from him, humiliated by her own actions.

"I am Raintree. Eve is Raintree," Mercy said. "You cannot claim either of us."

Judah ran his index finger over Mercy's lips, down her chin and throat, pausing in the center of her chest, between her breasts. "You are of no importance. You were nothing more than a vessel to carry my child. But Eve is very important to me. She is Ansara, and when the time is right, I *will* claim her."

Mercy sensed a frightening truth when she caught a momentary glimpse into Judah's mind. The instant he realized she had invaded his thoughts, he cloaked them entirely, shutting her out. But not before she saw her own death. Death at the hands of her child's father.

"If you kill me, Dante and Gideon—"

"Dante and Gideon are the least of my worries at the moment."

Puzzled by his statement, she glowered at him. "If you harm me, if you try to take Eve, my brothers will fight you to the death."

"The time is not right for others to know of Eve's existence." He grasped Mercy's shoulders and shook her none too gently. "I have an enemy who would kill Eve if he knew she was my child. And many others who would take her life simply because she is a mixed-breed."

With his hands on Mercy's body, he passed currents from within him into her, a physical and mental awareness that he could not prevent.

"The protective cloak I've kept around Eve since before she was born has been penetrated," Mercy said. "This was your doing. If you truly wish to keep her safe, you have to help me form a stronger barrier around her. Now that she is aware of you and you of her, it will take both of us to protect her. Will you help me?"

Do you actually trust me to protect her?" Judah ran his hands up and down Mercy's arms, then released her. "After all, she is half Raintree and the Ansara have sworn an oath to destroy such children."

"She is also half Ansara, and yet I love her with all my heart and would protect her with my own life."

"What makes you think that I would do the same?"

Mercy saw past the exterior steel crust to the center of Judah's soul. Not a soft or pliable soul, not one easily touched by the pain and suffering of others, but a male soul. Strong, fierce, loyal, protective and possessive. He had been unable to hide that truth from her seven years ago, and he still could not.

"Blood calls to blood," Mercy said. "It is true of mankind, but even truer of the Raintree and the Ansara."

"If you knew I wouldn't harm Eve, why keep her a secret from me all these years?"

Mercy hesitated. She felt Judah probing, trying to invade her thoughts again.

"I was afraid that you would try to take her from me," she said. "I couldn't allow that. If you had tried—if you try now—Dante and Gideon will join forces with me and stop you from taking her."

"They might try, but…"

Mercy realized that Judah had seen beyond the obvious.

Judah's lips curved downward into a speculative frown. "Dante and Gideon don't know that Eve is Ansara, do they? You were afraid of how they would react, perhaps afraid that they would kill her."

"No! My brothers would never harm Eve. The Raintree do not murder innocent children."

"Then who were you protecting by hiding the truth from them?"

"I had hoped to protect Eve from the truth," Mercy said. "I should have known that she would soon realize she was more than Raintree, and that eventually she would have sought you out and found you."

"Blood calls to blood," Judah repeated her words.

"Then we are in agreement—we will protect Eve."

"We will never be in agreement," he said. "But for the time being, yes, I will help you keep your secret. It will be difficult, now that Eve knows I am her father. Because she is so young, she doesn't have complete command of her powers, and that alone puts her in danger. Since she is unable to control her powers, we must do it for her. For her own protection."

"You are welcome to try. I've managed to subdue her powers from time to time, to keep them partially under control, but…" She hesitated to admit the truth to this man, this Ansara who could try to use their daughter's unparalleled gifts against the Raintree.

"Is her power that great?" he asked.

Mercy kept silent, afraid she had already said too much.

"Eve has equal measures of Ansara and Raintree power," Judah said in astonishment. "She inherited your powers and mine, didn't she? My God, do you realize…? Our child possesses more power than anyone in either clan."

"More than you or I." Mercy bowed her head and silently uttered an ancient incantation.

Judah grabbed her. She gasped, startled by his actions, not realizing that he had somehow figured out what she was doing.

"It won't work," he told her. "You cannot use your magic on me. Surely you know I won't allow you to—"

Mercy focused, sending a sharp mental blow to Judah's body, hitting him square in the stomach. He groaned as the shock wave hit him, then narrowed his gaze, burning through the shield around Mercy, retaliating with a searing pain that radiated from her belly. She cried out, then vanquished the fire inside her.

"Do you truly believe you are as strong as I am, that you are capable of defeating me?" he asked.

"Yes."

He stared at her, apparently skeptical, unable to believe that her power not only equaled his but might surpass it. As they stood there glaring at each other, neither backing down nor escalating the battle, Judah studied her intently.

"You're different," he told her. "And it's more than that you've matured into the premiere empath that you are today. That was always your destiny."

She held her breath, realizing that he was on the verge of understanding a truth that even she herself had not wanted to accept.

"Having my child changed you," Judah said. "Giving birth to Eve increased your powers. You, too, are more than Raintree, aren't you?"

"No, I am not—"

"Quiet!" Judah issued the order in a commanding manner. "Control your tongue and your thoughts."

"Why? Tell me—what are you so afraid of? Is this enemy of yours powerful enough to threaten your very life?"

Judah ruled the Ansara, his power unequaled by any other, not even his half brother. He, not Cael, was the superior, the mightiest of all Ansara, but he could control his brother only to a certain extent and only for brief periods of time. Cael was at this very moment fighting the spell that had quieted his telepathic abilities. His fiendish curses were bombarding Judah, who knew he could not deal with Mercy Raintree and Cael Ansara at the same time. Both were powerful creatures, each his enemy.

Cael's thoughts converged into a jumbled mass of hysteria and rage, but as he fought Judah's spell, he revealed more of his inner self than he realized. Cael was determined to escalate the impending war, the final Ansara and Raintree battle, and he had set events into motion that could not be stopped.

Judah's head pounded with the knowledge of his brother's treachery—not only against himself but against the entire tribe. The Ansara were not ready for the final battle. Not yet. If Cael forced them to fight now, they could be defeated. And this time, they could not count on the Raintrees' benevolence. Two hundred years ago the Raintree had allowed a handful of Ansara to live, one the youngest daughter of the old Dranir. It was through her—Dranira Melisande—that the royal bloodline had survived.

"Judah?" Mercy called his name again.

"Silence!"

Do not issue me orders, she told him telepathically.

If you wish to keep your child safe, protect not only your spoken words but your thoughts, Judah warned her.

She stared at him but said nothing. Then he felt a shield lift between them. Even if Mercy knew nothing of Cael, she understood that someone—other than Judah—posed a threat to Eve.

Chapter 4

"That beast is not staying the night here at the sanctuary," Sidonia said vehemently. "You cannot allow it."

"He is staying," Mercy replied. "Until we can decide how best to protect Eve."

Sidonia grabbed Mercy's arm. "He's the one you need to protect her from. He is an Ansara, the vilest creature on earth. Pure evil."

"Hush up," Mercy warned.

"I don't care if he hears me." Scrunching her wrinkled face into a frown, Sidonia spat on the floor.

"I don't want Eve to hear you. She knows Judah is her father."

"Poor little lamb." Sidonia adored Eve, would do anything for her, but she feared for the child because of her father's blood. She vigilantly watched for signs of the struggle between good and evil within Eve.

Mercy sighed heavily. "Judah will not go away meekly,

and I'm afraid that I can't force him to leave, not as long as Eve wishes him to stay. You understand what I'm saying?"

"Yes, I understand only too well—the father's and daughter's combined powers are greater than yours. And because Eve's powers are untrained, she could be dangerous without meaning to be."

Mercy nodded, then lowered her voice to a whisper. "Judah is concerned about a man who's his enemy, someone who isn't a Raintree, a man who would kill Eve if he knew of her existence. I don't know who this man is, but I'm certain he is another Ansara."

"We should have wiped their kind from the face of the earth two hundred years ago when we had the chance. Old Dranir Dante made a deadly mistake in allowing even a handful of Ansara to live."

"All that is ancient history."

"Humph." Sidonia glared at Mercy. "Why did Judah Ansara come here? And why were you with him tonight?"

"I don't know why he came to North Carolina. And as for my being with him—I don't remember everything, only that someone tried to kill me, and Judah saved me."

"Why would an Ansara save a Raintree's life?" Sidonia eyed her suspiciously. "You haven't had any contact with him since you conceived Eve, have you?"

"Of course not!"

"Hmm… There is more to this than meets the eye. I think you should contact Dante and tell him that an Ansara has shown up here at the sanctuary, that he was able to cross the boundaries of protection."

"Dante will want to know how that was possible."

"I'm sure he will."

"I can't tell him that it might have been because of Eve…. because she's half Ansara."

"You have to do what is necessary," Sidonia told Mercy.

"It's for me to decide what that is."

"That Ansara poses a threat to all of us, all who are Raintree."

"Judah poses a threat to no one but Eve," Mercy said. "He's a single Ansara, one man. What could he possibly do to harm our entire clan?"

"Call Dante."

"No."

"It's past time that you told your brothers the truth about Eve."

"No. And you won't call Dante. Do you hear me?

Sidonia nodded. "This man tricked you once, took you to his bed and gave you his child. Don't let him fool you again."

"I didn't know he was Ansara then. Now I do."

"Seven years ago, he wanted your virginity. Now he wants something far more precious. He wants *your* child."

"She's *his* child, too, as much as I wish she were not."

"I believe he knew about Eve before he came here," Sidonia said. "It's the only explanation for him coming to you after all these years. Is it possible that somehow subconsciously you…?"

"No! I've shielded myself from Judah, just as I have shielded Eve."

"You did not shield either of you when you were giving birth to Eve. You wanted him there with you. You kept calling for him."

Mercy glanced away, then turned her back on Sidonia.

Sidonia walked up beside Mercy and draped her thin arm around Mercy's shoulders. "I did my best to protect you and your child that night, because you couldn't. And if for any reason you cannot protect the two of you from him now, you must allow me to contact Dante."

"Please, go to bed and get some sleep. I need to be alone. I need time to think."

Sidonia patted Mercy on the back with tender affection. She had no children of her own and loved the royal siblings as if they were her grandchildren. As much as she loved Dante and Gideon, Mercy had always been her favorite. She had been a beautiful child. with the disposition of an angel. Even as a little girl, she had possessed a heart filled with goodness and kindness. And by the age of six—the age Eve was now—Mercy's abilities as an empath had been evident.

"I'll do as you ask," Sidonia said. "But be careful. You can't allow your heart to rule your head."

She left Mercy alone. But she didn't go to her room. Instead, she checked on Eve. The little princess lay in her antique canopy bed, her golden curls shimmering against the white embroidered pillowcase, highlighted by moonbeams streaming through the windows. Asleep, Eve was all innocence. Awake, she was a delightful little imp.

Mischievousness is not evil, Sidonia reminded herself.

My precious darling. You must be protected. Your mother would die to keep you safe. And so would I. We have safeguarded the secret of your paternity since you were born, praying that neither you nor your father would ever learn the truth. But now that both of you know, now that Judah Ansara has come to claim you, I fear not only for your safety, but for the safety of our people. And your mother seems to have a peculiar weakness for this Ansara man that makes her vulnerable to him.

Sidonia touched the sleeping child's cheek as she recalled the night Eve was born. Mercy had requested that no one other than Sidonia be present, acquiring a pledge of complete secrecy from Sidonia before she went into labor.

Eve had come into the world howling, as if proclaiming loud and clear, "I'm here!" Round and fat and pink, with puffs of white-blonde hair and the hereditary green eyes, Eve was a perfect little Raintree. Except for the birthmark on her head, just above the uppermost tip of her spine. An indigo blue crescent moon. The mark of the Ansara.

Mercy had grasped Sidonia's hand that night and looked at her pleadingly. "You must never tell anyone. No one can know that my baby's father is Ansara."

"How is this possible? You wouldn't knowingly give yourself to one of those demons."

"I didn't know Judah was Ansara until…not until I had conceived."

"You called for him when you were in labor. Even knowing what he is, you still long for him."

Mercy had glanced away, tears in her eyes.

It was then that Sidonia knew Mercy loved her child's father. God help her.

Mercy sensed Judah's presence. Not near her, but close. Outside.

She crossed the room, drew back the lace curtain on her window and stared down at the courtyard below. Judah stood there on the stone terrace, in the moonlight, rigid as a statue, his face and body in shadowed silhouette. He had released his hair, letting it fall about his shoulders, as free and wild as the man himself. He was savagely handsome, and exuded an aura of strength and masculinity that no woman could resist.

Once *she* had been unable to resist. And for the brief span of a day and a night, she had believed his lies, had surrendered to his charm, had given herself freely and completely.

For Eve's sake, she had hoped she would never see Judah again. And for her own sake, also. As much as she despised him, she didn't hate him. Hating him would be like hating a part of Eve.

Even though she realized that he still possessed some kind

of sexual hold over her, she knew Judah was her enemy. And even though he was Eve's father, he was Eve's enemy, too. Hadn't the Ansara been the ones to issue a decree that any child born of a Raintree/Ansara union would be put to death? No half-breeds allowed.

Had Judah actually come here to kill Eve?

No, that wasn't possible, was it? He had been genuinely shocked to learn of Eve's existence.

But now that he knew…

It didn't matter what he knew. He was only one Ansara, albeit a seemingly powerful wizard. But Mercy possessed equal power, didn't she? And Sidonia was not without powers, as were several Raintree now visiting the home place and staying in the surrounding cottages. There was no need to call in Dante or Gideon. If necessary, she could enlist Sidonia and the others to help her vanquish Judah…if he truly posed a threat to Eve.

If?

Was there really any doubt that Judah was a major problem? He would either claim Eve or kill her. Neither was acceptable.

As she stared outside at Judah's dark back, at his wide shoulders and flowing black hair, Mercy asked herself aloud, "How could I ever have loved you?"

It hadn't been love, she told herself. It had been infatuation. She'd been young, a novice in the ways of the world and, in the matter of sexual attraction, a true virgin. She now knew that Judah had deliberately seduced her because he had recognized her as Raintree, and not just any Raintree, but a Raintree princess. His ability to have shielded himself from her empathic probing—something that was as natural to her as breathing—meant that either he was extremely powerful or he had been gifted with a potent spell by a mighty wizard. Instinct told her it was the former. And that led her to ask other questions.

Just who are you, Judah Ansara? Why did you come to the sanctuary? Why did you save my life? And just how many Ansara are out there in the world now?

The Raintree had given the Ansara clan little thought for the past two hundred years. Occasionally a Raintree would encounter a lone Ansara, but it was a rare event, leading them to believe that the Ansara had not flourished since *The Battle,* that the Ansara would never again pose a threat to the Raintree.

And there was no reason for Mercy to think otherwise. Despite Judah's tremendous power, only he posed a threat to Mercy and Eve. Whatever his reasons for coming to North Carolina, he had come alone. If he helped her protect Eve and did not betray the secret of their child's paternity…

Suddenly Judah turned around and looked up at her window—at her. Mercy gasped but did not shrink, did not turn away from his intense stare.

Mercy.

She heard him speak her name. Telepathically.

Shut him out, she told herself. *Don't listen.*

And then she heard his laughter. Deep, throaty. He was amused at her reaction.

Damn you, Judah Ansara!

Without warning, a sensation of fingertips caressing her skin enveloped Mercy. For a moment the seductive touch mesmerized her.

Remember.

Hearing him utter that one word broke the spell, allowing her to put up a protective barrier against temptation.

Judah turned around so that he couldn't see Mercy and walked away, farther into the backyard behind the home of the Raintree royal family. It wasn't as if the Ansara hadn't known for at least a hundred years where the Raintree sanctuary was or that it was the home of the royal family; but until Judah's generation came into power, the Ansara had not dared provoke their arch rivals. As a boy, his father had told Judah that when he became the Dranir, it was his destiny to lead his people into battle against the Raintree.

His destiny, not Cael's.

But the time was not right. It would be at least another five years before the Ansara were ready to go up against their enemy and win. If they did as Cael wanted and rushed into battle too soon, the odds were against them. And if the Ansara were defeated again, the Raintree would not be merciful. He knew this because he knew who their Dranir was— Dante Raintree, a man not unlike Judah in many ways. A fitting opponent, one who could be as savagely brutal as Judah could.

And he was Mercy's elder brother.

Judah had claimed them both as his kill. Dante because it was his right as the Ansara Dranir to do battle with the Raintree Dranir. And he had claimed Mercy because...

Because she was his, and no one else had the right to take her life.

And what of Eve?

How could he have impregnated Mercy that night? Since they had reached puberty, he and Claude had periodically gifted each other with protection. Sexual protection. If his own father had used such protection, Cael would not exist. And think how much easier life would be for all the Ansara without Cael.

Judah knew the gift of sexual protection worked with Ansara women and with human women, so why would it have failed with a Raintree woman?

Did it really matter? Eve existed. She was six years old. And she was his daughter.

She might be a tiny replica of Mercy, with the hereditary green Raintree eyes, but she was half Ansara. It was there in her spirit, in her very soul. And in her powers. Powers that would one day exceed those belonging to any Raintree or Ansara.

In days past, the Ansara had issued a decree that any child born of a tainted union would be put to death. But there had been no such child born in centuries, and as Dranir, he possessed the power to rescind the decree.

But did he want to?

Would it not simplify everything if he killed Eve now, before she came into her full powers?

But how can I kill her? She's my child.

If it were for the good of the Ansara clan for him to destroy his own daughter, would he? *Could* he?

Eve was a complication he had not anticipated.

A sharp pain, excruciating in its intensity, pierced Judah's mind.

Pressing his fingers against his temples, he closed his eyes and fought the pain. Cael's rage bombarded him. Curses. Threats. Dire warnings.

How dare you freeze my telepathic powers? Cael bellowed. *You had no right!*

No, brother, how dare you try to usurp my authority and send Greynell to kill Mercy Raintree?

Greynell was like so many of our young warriors—he grew tired of waiting to confront the Raintree. If you do not strike soon, they will think you a weak leader, an old woman.

You have incited the young warriors, knowing we are not ready to do battle with the Raintree, Judah said. *Your actions border on treason. Be careful that you don't force me to kill you.*

Silence.

Judah felt his brother probing, trying to lock on to Judah's thoughts. Instantly he shut Cael out. He allowed no one inside his mind, least of all a man intent upon stealing his birthright. Cael would never be satisfied until he was crowned Dranir. And Judah would never allow such an atrocity to happen. His brother would lead their people to sure and certain annihilation.

We have much to discuss, many decisions to be made. When will you return home? Cael asked, breaking the silence.

In my own good time, Judah replied, then blocked Cael, shutting him off completely, ending their telepathic conversation.

This trip to North Carolina to stop Greynell from killing Mercy and thwart Cael's machinations had not turned out as Judah had planned. He had intended to slip in and out unnoticed, leaving Mercy without any memory of his visit. But Eve's existence complicated matters.

At present, he had enough trouble without having to concern himself with a child. Keeping Cael in line had become a full-time job. And the recent attempt on his own life had cemented his brother's fate as far as Judah was concerned. He had no doubt that Cael had been behind the botched assassination. As the Ansara Dranir, it was not only his right but his duty to protect the monarchy from a toxic force such as Cael.

He should return to Terrebonne first thing in the morning. The longer he stayed away, the more chaos Cael would create.

But what about Eve?

Mercy had protected her for six years, and she would continue to protect her. No one other than the two of them—and the old nanny—knew that Eve was as much Ansara as she was Raintree.

Eve knew.

Who would protect Eve from herself?

It was only a matter of time before she would be able to

override her mother's protective spells, if she so chose. And if Eve were to try to contact him, what would happen? If she were to send out vibes into the universe, there was no way to know who might intercept them.

If Cael knew of Eve's existence…he would use her against Judah.

It was at that moment Judah realized he did not want any harm to come to his daughter. Having a child made him vulnerable.

The very thought of having any weakness enraged him. But he could not turn back the clock. He could not prevent Eve's conception.

The possessive elements in his nature claimed Eve as a part of him, an Ansara, to be cared for, nurtured, trained properly, and protected at all costs. His daughter was not simply Ansara and Raintree—she was the heir to two royal bloodlines, a fact he must keep hidden. If Mercy had any idea that the Ansara had grown in strength and numbers, that they were ruled by a Dranir as powerful as her brother Dante, she would realize the danger his clan posed to hers.

When the time was right and the Raintree were vanquished, Eve would take her rightful place as an Ansara princess. In the meantime, he would leave her with Mercy. But before he left them, he had to make sure they were safe.

Yes, *they,* both mother and daughter.

Until he dealt with Cael and could be assured Eve would be safe with his people, he needed Mercy to protect their child. Once he had eliminated his brother and overturned the ancient decree to kill all half-breed children, he would take what was his.

But how could he take Eve from Mercy without killing Mercy and bringing down the wrath of hell from Dante and Gideon?

A question not easily answered, if there was an answer.

Whenever he was restless, whenever trouble weighed

heavily on his shoulders, Judah would walk. Sometimes for miles. He needed the cool night air more than ever now, to clear his head and help him devise a plan before morning.

Cael threw open the doors that led outside to the deck of his beachfront home, the rage he had felt at his brother reduced to bitterness. Judah was proud and arrogant, secure in his position as Dranir. The beloved son. The chosen one.

Anger simmered a few degrees below boiling inside Cael, just enough to create rumbles of distant thunder, but not strong enough to bring lightning down or spark blazing fires.

Judah's days were numbered. Cael had spent the past few years gradually injecting the seeds of anarchy into the bloodstream of the Ansara clan. At least half the young warriors were ready for battle, eager to prove themselves. But only a handful were loyal to Cael. Judah possessed a mighty hold over the tribe.

Stripping off his robe, Cael walked down from the deck and onto the beach, then straight into the ocean. He and the water became one. Powerful beyond measure. Primeval. A force to be reckoned with. With each stroke he went farther and farther out into the sea. Fearless. Reckless.

And then he paused and willed his body to float, gliding along with the current, as much a part of the ocean as the creatures who called the earth's waters their home. Using only his mind and the more-than-human abilities he had inherited from his parents, he concentrated on transporting himself back to dry land without moving a muscle. He silently whispered ancient words his mother had taught him, adding strong magic to his supernatural skills.

His body trembled externally and internally as a current of pure energy shot through him. He felt himself lifting above the water. Even though all previous attempts to teleport himself had failed, he knew this time he would achieve his goal.

As suddenly as he had risen from the water, he fell, making a loud splash as his body shot a good ten feet down into the ocean. Forced to concentrate on making his way to the surface again, Cael focused all his energy on saving his life. After he managed to regain his composure, he swam upward and then back across the sea to the sandy beach.

He dragged himself out of the ocean, stood at the edge of water as the waves washed over his feet, and cursed the heavens. Cursed his own inabilities. How could he hope to defeat Judah unless he could surpass his brother in power and strength? The day would come—and soon—when he and Judah would face their destiny. One destiny. Winning and losing, flip sides of the same coin. Judah's defeat. Cael's triumph.

Why are you still in America, brother, still in North Carolina, near the Raintree sanctuary? What keeps you there one moment longer than necessary?

When he had conversed with Judah, Cael had picked up on a momentary flicker, just a flash of something, before Judah shut him out and protected his thoughts.

No, not a flash of something, a flash of some*one*.

A whiff of vision, there one minute, gone the next.

Green Raintree eyes.

I have to find out what Judah is hiding from me. There is something he doesn't want me to know. A secret. A secret with green Raintree eyes.

Chapter 5

Monday Morning, 5:00 a.m.

Judah stood atop a low hill less than half a mile from the Raintree home, darkness surrounding him, a man alone with many decision to make. Suddenly the small phone in the inside pocket of his jacket vibrated. He retrieved the phone and checked the lighted screen for the identity of the caller. Claude. He and his cousin occasionally communicated telepathically, but since telepathic exchanges used up precious energy, they usually simply telephoned each other. And since using telepathy also made one's thoughts susceptible to being sensed by others with the same capabilities, a secure phone was safer. The last thing he needed right now was Cael trying to listen to his private conversations.

"You're up awfully early," Judah said to his cousin.

"Where are you?" Claude asked.

"What's wrong?"

"I'm not sure. It could be nothing."

"You wouldn't contact me if you thought it was nothing. Is there a business problem or—"

"Bartholomew sent for me a short time ago," Claude said. "Sidra had a vision."

The two elderly council members had been married for over fifty years. Bartholomew possessed many powers in varying degrees, but his wife's abilities were limited to a few, one quite powerful. She was a psychic of unparalleled talent.

Judah's gut tightened. "Tell me."

"She saw fire and blood. In the center of the fire was a Dranir's crown. A Raintree Dranir. And within the pool of blood rested a gun that shot lighting."

"We know that Dante Raintree possesses many of the same skills that I do, including dominion over fire."

"Yes. That's why we assumed her vision was about him and…" Claude hesitated for a moment. "Prince Gideon works as a police detective, doesn't he? And we believe his greatest gift is connected to electrical energy and the elements, such as lightning."

"You've surmised that Sidra had a vision about the royal Raintree brothers, but you haven't told me why this is of importance to us…to the Ansara."

"The fire consuming the crown and the blood surrounding the gun both came from Cael. Sidra saw this. Before she fell into a deep sleep, she told Bartholomew that this was not a prophecy, that these events had already occurred. She believes that Cael has already struck against the Raintree Dranir and his brother."

The ground beneath Judah's feet trembled. Rage shot through him swiftly, igniting fire on each of his fingertips. Clenching his hands, he extinguished the blazes. Puffs of smoke rose from inside his closed fists.

"Cael has to be stopped," Judah said.

"He has a small but loyal following. We will have to deal with them, as well."

"We need to move quickly," Judah said. "Speak only to those you trust. Gather information. I'll be home by this evening."

"Why the delay? Sidra believes action should be taken immediately to counteract whatever Cael has done."

"There are complications here."

"Where is here?"

"I am at the Raintree sanctuary."

"*Inside* the sanctuary?"

"Yes."

"Isn't the place surrounded by a force field? How did you use your powers to get inside without alerting—"

"I'll explain more when I see you this evening."

"Do these complications involve Mercy Raintree?" Claude asked.

"What?"

"You flew to North Carolina to save her from Greynell, didn't you?"

"She was not his kill. She's mine. I thought you and everyone on the council understood my reasons for coming here to save her life."

"No one questions your right to kill her and her brother Dante in *The Battle* that is to come, but… I know you, Judah. I know you better than anyone else knows you. I have seen inside your mind."

"And I into yours, but I don't understand what you're getting at."

"I've seen Mercy Raintree in your mind on several occasions, before you were able to shut out thoughts of her."

Judah could deny Claude's accusation, but his cousin would know he was lying.

"You know that I had sex with her years ago," Judah said. "I took the Raintree princess's virginity."

"So is she what keeps you there?" Claude grunted. "No doubt she's never forgotten *you*, either."

"She is of no importance. I simply have something to settle with her before I return to Terrebonne."

"Very well," Claude replied. "I'll speak to Benedict and Bartholomew. We will call a private meeting for tonight, and make plans to stop Cael before he moves prematurely against the Raintree and brings their wrath down on all of us."

"Stay safe," Judah warned. "Don't turn your back on Cael. Not for a single moment. If he's bold enough to send an assassin to kill me, you aren't safe, either. No one who is loyal to me is safe from him."

Monday Morning, 5:35 a.m.

When the telephone rang, Mercy grabbed the receiver from the nightstand, sat up and kicked back the covers. She hadn't slept more than a few minutes at a time and still had her clothes on from yesterday. When she glanced down at the phone, she noted Gideon's number on the caller I.D.

"What's wrong?"

"Don't get upset," her brother said. "I'm fine. Dante's fine."

"But?"

"But there was a fire at Dante's casino."

"How bad?"

"He said it could be worse, but that it was bad enough."

"You're sure he's all right?"

"Yeah, he's okay. He phoned me a couple of hours ago and told me to call you. He didn't want either of us to read it in the newspaper or for you to see it on TV."

"The fire must have been really bad if Dante thinks it'll make the national news."

"Yeah, it probably was."

"I wish you two wouldn't shut me out all the time. If you'd—"

Gideon grumbled under his breath. "You're our little sister. We don't want you messing around inside our heads and getting involved in our private lives."

Ignoring his explanation just as she had numerous times in the past, Mercy asked, "Are you going to Reno to make sure he's all right and see what you can do to help him?" If she didn't have her hands full here at the Sanctuary, she could be on the next plane out of Asheville. But dealing with Judah Ansara was just about all she could handle right now.

"Dante said for us to stay put, that he can handle things without help from either us. But he's going to be pretty busy for the next few days, so don't worry if he's not in touch with us for a while."

"If you talk to him again, give him my love. Tell him… Gideon?"

"What's the matter?"

"Nothing," she lied. "It's just…I worry about you and Dante."

"We're big boys. We can take care of ourselves. You just keep the home fires burning and take care of Eve."

"I can do that."

"I've got to go."

"I love you," Mercy said.

"Yeah, me too."

Mercy replaced the receiver, then sighed heavily. Could she really take care of Eve now that she had to protect her from her own father? She hadn't seen Judah since late last night and had no idea where he was this morning. He wasn't in the house, that she knew for certain. She would have sensed his presence. For the time being Eve was safe from him. But where was he, and what was he doing? *Plotting against me,* Mercy thought. *He's probably making plans to take Eve.*

Or worse.

The Ansara were not like the Raintree, but they weren't like mere mortals, either. Given the right provocation, they could and would kill their own offspring. The evil that had taken root inside them centuries ago had altered the entire clan, making a once kindred tribe of the Raintree their sworn enemies. Judah was Ansara. He was evil. She couldn't allow herself to believe otherwise, no matter how much she wished she could.

During the past seven years, she had tried countless ways to erase her memories of the night she had spent in his arms, a willing pupil, giving herself to him completely, yearning to learn all that he could teach her. Thoughts of his lips on hers, of his large, strong hands tenderly caressing her body, his heated words of passion, tormented her, reminding her what a reckless young fool she had been. And far too trusting.

But she would not make that mistake again.

7:00 a.m.

"What do you mean, you don't know where he is?" Sidonia glared at Mercy. "Didn't he stay here last night?"

Mercy set the table for four, instinctively knowing Judah would join them. Wherever he was, he hadn't left the sanctuary. If he had, she would know. She felt the presence of every living creature within the boundaries of their nine hundred and ninety-nine acres. Her domain. Her responsibility.

"He didn't stay inside the house," Mercy replied. "But he is still here."

"Humph." Sidonia busied herself with meal preparations but kept glancing toward Mercy, checking on her. As Sidonia took ingredients from the cupboards, her back to Mercy, she said, "I heard the phone ring quite early this morning…"

"Gideon called. There was a fire at Dante's casino. He's fine, but apparently there was extensive damage, enough so that the fire will probably be reported on the national news."

Mercy sensed Judah's presence the moment he entered the room, only seconds after she had spoken.

"I'm surprised that one of your Raintree psychics wasn't able to predict the fire," he said.

Mercy didn't respond as she crossed the room to the pantry, removed paper napkins and laid one at each place setting. Sidonia glowered at him but also said nothing.

"We need to talk," Judah told Mercy. "Privately."

"Sidonia is preparing breakfast. Will you join us? Eve will be down soon, and I assume you would like to see her before you leave."

Judah's lips curved slightly, as if he were amused with Mercy. "Interesting. A Raintree being hospitable to an Ansara."

"Not just any Ansara. You are, after all, Eve's father."

"A fact you would prefer to forget, one that you kept secret from me and your brothers for six years."

"I can be reasonable if you can," Mercy said, finally looking directly at Judah. She wished she hadn't. He was not a man she could ignore on any level. Physical, mental…sexual…

"And being reasonable would entail…?" he asked.

"I am willing for you to visit Eve. We can arrange a—"

"No."

"If you prefer not to see her, that's—"

"I prefer to take her with me."

"I won't allow you to do that."

"I didn't say I *would* take her with me, only that it's what I'd prefer to do."

The kitchen door swung open. Wearing pink footed

pajamas and carrying a seen-better-days stuffed lion in one hand, Eve bounded into the room. She rushed first to Mercy, who scooped her into her arms and gave her a good morning hug and kiss. With Eve on her hip, Mercy eyed Judah. "We will finish our discussion in private after breakfast."

"Is Daddy going to eat breakfast with us?" Eve asked.

"Yes, he is," Mercy replied.

Eve squirmed until Mercy set her on her feet, at which point she walked over to Judah and looked up at him. "Good morning."

"Good morning." Judah studied his daughter.

Eve waited. Mercy knew her child expected Judah to respond to her in some fatherly way, to ruffle her hair or kiss her or begin a conversation with her. When he didn't, Eve took matters into her own hands. She held her stuffed lion up in front of her, showing him to Judah.

"I have lots of animals and dolls," Eve said. "This one is my favorite. I picked him out myself when I was little, didn't I, Mother?" She glanced at Eve, who nodded agreement. "His name is Jasper."

Judah's expression hardened as if Eve had said something that upset him.

"Are you mad at me, Daddy?" Eve asked.

"No."

"What are you thinking?" Eve stared questioningly at Judah. "I can't read your thoughts at all, but that's okay. Mommy won't let me read hers, either."

"When I was a boy, I had a pet lion—a real one," Judah said.

"And his name was Jasper, wasn't it?" Eve beamed with delight, as if she had solved some important puzzle.

"Yes" was all Judah said.

Eve lifted her arm, reached out and grasped Judah's hand. For an instant her eyes flickered, turning from green to gold and then back to green. Mercy's heart stopped for a millisecond.

I imagined it, Mercy tried to tell herself. But she knew better. Something powerful had occurred between Judah and Eve, even if neither of them was aware of it.

Mercy knew. She felt it down to her bones.

All during breakfast, Eve chatted away like a little magpie, filling Judah in on her likes, her dislikes, her daily routine. Basically, she told him the story of her life. Mercy picked at her food, but Judah ate heartily.

"If you're finished, we can go into the study now," Mercy told Judah as she scooted back her chair and stood.

He glanced over his shoulder at Sidonia. "The breakfast was delicious. Thank you."

Sidonia snarled, giving him a withering glare.

He chuckled, then tossed down his napkin and stood. He waved his hand in a gentlemanly gesture and said, "After you."

Eve hopped out of her chair. "Me too."

"No," Mercy said. "You stay here with Sidonia. Judah… your father and I need—"

"You're going to talk about me." Eve planted her hands on her hips and frowned. "I should be there so I can tell you both what I think."

"No." Mercy shook her head.

"Yes." Eve stomped her foot.

"You will stay with Sidonia."

Eve looked at Judah. "I want to go, too. Please, Daddy."

Before Judah had a chance to respond, Mercy said, "Enough, young lady. You will stay with Sidonia." She glared at Judah, daring him to contradict her.

Suddenly an empty glass flew off the table and crashed against the wall, then another and another. Within a minute, every dish, glass and cup on the table flew into the air, whirling around in a frenzy, then one by one crashed to the floor and smashed into shards of glass and pottery.

Mercy narrowed her gaze and concentrated on her daughter, using her powers to counteract Eve's and put an end to the temper tantrum. With each passing year, Eve's talents grew stronger, and Mercy knew that the day would come when her child's abilities would surpass hers. She prayed that by that time Eve would be mature enough to handle such awesome power.

"You will do as your mother requested," Judah said. "You will stay with your nanny."

Knowing she had been defeated, Eve puckered her lips into a pout and managed to squeeze a single tear from one eye.

"Sidonia, be sure that Eve cleans up the mess she made," Mercy said. "And I don't want you to help her."

"Daddy!" Eve looked to Judah to save her from her punishment.

Ignoring Eve completely, Judah grasped Mercy's arm and led her out of the kitchen. As soon as they reached the hallway leading to her study, Mercy jerked away from him and paused to regain her composure.

"She's quite a handful, isn't she?" Judah said.

"You sound rather proud of that fact."

"Would you rather she be some sniveling, weak little mouse?"

"I imagine you were a handful when you were a child, weren't you?"

"I still am," he said, his tone teasing.

This was the Judah she remembered, a charming man with a sense of humor. If only she had known all those years ago that beneath the charm lay a wild beast, one capable of ripping out her heart. She walked away from him, down the hall to the open study door. Without looking back, she knew he had followed her. Once they entered the study, she closed the door behind them.

"Please, sit down." With the sweep of her hand, she indicated a specific chair.

He sat, lifted one leg and crossed his ankle over the opposite knee, then leaned back in the chair and looked up at her.

She sat across from him, on the sofa, and folded her hands demurely in her lap.

"Eve is my child. She is Raintree. I will not allow you to harm her, and I will never allow you to take her."

"You aren't leaving us any room for compromise."

"You're right, I'm not."

"Then let's say that—for the time being—I agree with you. I will leave Eve here with you, knowing you will continue to safeguard my child as you have done since before she was born."

Mercy didn't trust Judah. And with good reason. He had said, "for the time being." Did that mean he intended to eventually claim Eve as his?

"Eve will stay here with me until she is an adult." Mercy wanted to make sure Judah understood.

"We won't argue over details of when and what. Not now," Judah said. "I'm leaving this afternoon, and Eve will remain here with you."

"But you plan to return."

"Someday."

"Don't."

"Don't leave?" he asked, his tone light.

"Don't ever come back."

"I'd forgotten how spirited you are." His gaze raked over her. "Actually, I'd forgotten many delightful things about you."

Mercy willed herself not to react to his taunts, to show no sign of emotion. She stood slowly. "I don't see any need for you to stay a minute longer. If you'd like, I can arrange transportation for you immediately."

Judah burrowed deeper into the chair, relaxing even

more. "I'll leave this afternoon. And I'll arrange my own transportation."

"Why stay?"

"I want to spend a few hours with my daughter."

"No."

"Don't make this a test of power." Judah rose to his feet and faced Mercy. "We don't want things to get nasty, do we? Not in front of our daughter."

"If I allow you time with Eve, do you promise not to harm her in any way? And that includes any kind of mental or emotional indoctrination. And will you leave here without her and never come back?"

"I promise to leave without her. And there is no need for me to try to undermine the Raintree side of Eve's nature. The Ansara part of her may, for the most part, be lying dormant inside her, but one day it will become dominant and Eve will be a true Ansara."

Mercy hated Judah for painting such a frightening picture of Eve's future, but he hadn't said anything that she hadn't thought about a thousand times since her child was born.

"You may spend a few hours with Eve, but not alone," Mercy said. "Sidonia will stay with her."

"No, not Sidonia," Judah replied. "If you don't want her to be alone with me, then *you* can stay with her. With *us*."

Terrebonne, Monday, 10:30 a.m.

Cael enjoyed breakfast on the terrace. Alone. Although he and Alexandria had consummated their relationship and she believed she would one day be his Dranira, he had no intention of being faithful to her now or in the future. He preferred sex with human women, because they were so easily controlled. He kept a small harem of bewitched females in a secret brothel, solely for his physical pleasure. Often he shared his whores with the young warriors he wanted to woo into his service.

As Cael drank a glass of freshly squeezed orange juice, he glanced through the open doors and into the house, his gaze locking onto the television. The all-news channel was once again showing film of the raging fire that had swept through a Reno casino. Dante Raintree's casino.

Cael smiled.

He had sent several of his most talented warriors to Reno, with one objective—Raintree destruction. Dante was still alive, but they had hit him hard. Mission at least partially accomplished. And Cael had sent a very special Ansara to Wilmington, North Carolina, to kill a very special Raintree. Tabby was such a vicious little bitch, which made her perfect for the job he had sent her to do. Before *The Battle* with the Raintree, which was now less than a week away, Cael wanted the royal siblings and a few key members of the Raintree family disposed of, by whatever means necessary. Unfortunately, the siblings were still alive—but only for the time being. At least Echo, the premiere Raintree seer, was now dead, thanks to Tabby.

Cael had cast a spell that clouded the vision of the other Raintree seers and psychics, but Echo had been too powerful for his spell to be fully effective, and so she'd had to be eliminated. Although Cael believed that the Ansara were more than ready to battle the Raintree and win, he wanted to maintain the advantage of a surprise attack. That would be more easily accomplished with Echo Raintree dead and unable to foresee the future annihilation of her people.

Revenge against the Raintree. What a sweet victory it would be.

Cael's plans were coming together nicely, although he had only a handful of faithful followers. Already it was too late to turn back, too late for Judah to stop the inevitable. With the strikes that had already been made against the Raintree, it would be only a matter of time before they realized the Ansara were responsible. The high council would see that the time to strike was before the Raintree suspected the Ansara were once again a strong and powerful clan. And Judah's pleas to wait another five years would fall on deaf ears. Even he, the seemingly invincible Dranir, would have no choice but to go into battle at Cael's side.

Judah would die in battle, of course. Cael would make certain of it. And the people would mourn Judah. But on the wings of sweet victory, Cael would be swept up into his rightful position as the new Dranir.

He couldn't allow anything to interfere with his plans. He was so close to getting what he wanted that he shouldn't allow any doubts to enter his mind and make him second-guess himself.

But he could not forget that momentary glimpse into Judah's mind last night. If only he had seen more before Judah had shut him out, but he had seen just enough to worry him. Why had Judah not returned home? What was keeping him in America?

No, not what, but who? Whoever it was, they had green Raintree eyes.

Mercy Raintree, perhaps.

Had Judah done more than save the princess's life?

Whatever Judah's secret was, Cael intended to find it out. He picked up his tiny digital phone from where it rested on the glass table and hurriedly placed a call. The moment Horace, one of his faithful minions, answered, Cael said, "I need to find out as much as possible about Mercy Raintree and anyone else living at the Raintree sanctuary. Your inquiries must be discreet. We can't risk Judah finding out. Do you understand?"

"Yes, my lord, I understand."

"I need the information immediately."

Cael laid the phone back on the table, picked up his fork and devoured the eggs Benedict his cook had prepared for him. Perfect. To his exact specifications. Once he was Dranir, everything would be done to his specifications by every person on earth. Not only every Ansara but every human, would worship him as the god he was destined to become.

Chapter 6

Judah had always known that, as the Ansara Dranir, he would one day be expected to provide the clan with an heir to the throne. But he hadn't actually given fatherhood a thought, and if he had, he would have seen himself as the father to a male heir. Females were different, be they human, Ansara or Raintree. A daughter needed a type of protection that a son didn't. Protection from men such as he had always been.

As he watched Eve picking wildflowers in the meadow, he thought about what she represented, not only to him, but to the Raintree. A mixed-breed child had not been born in many centuries, and none had been allowed to live beyond infancy in thousands of years. During his studies as a youth, he had thought the ancient tales of such children were little more than fabrications by the venerable Ansara scribes. Supposedly such a child possessed not only the unique abilities of each parent, making him or her more powerful than either parent alone, but if the parents were royals, the child would possess the ability to create a new and unique clan that was neither Ansara nor Raintree.

Is that what you are, my little Eve? The mother of a new clan?

Nonsense! The day would come when Eve would be completely Ansara, and even if he fathered other children in the future, she could still become the Ansara Dranira. It would be his choice to make.

But would Eve want to rule the clan that had wiped her mother's people from the face of the earth? Would she willingly join forces with the man who had killed her mother?

"Daddy, watch!" Eve called, as she dropped her hand-picked bouquet on the ground. "I can do a somersault."

"Be careful," Mercy cautioned. "Don't show off."

Ignoring her mother, Eve bounded up on her hands and flipped over, again and again, until she moved so quickly that her little body became a whirling blur.

Judah smiled. She was most definitely showing off. For him.

"Eve! Stop that before you hurt yourself."

"Leave her alone," Judah said. "She's having fun. I used to do all sorts of things to make my parents pay attention to me."

Suddenly Eve slowed, and the force she had used to create such rapid speed came to a screeching halt, projecting her small body a good twenty feet through the air.

"Oh, my God!" Mercy cried.

Before Eve's body hit the ground, she wavered several inches above the grassy earth where she would have fallen if not for her parents' intervention. Mercy glanced at Judah and he at her, and he realized that both of them had used their powers to protect Eve.

Judah walked across the meadow while his thoughts kept Eve suspended in thin air. She turned her head sideways and smiled at him as he approached. He reached out and pulled Eve into his arms.

"Mother's angry," Eve said.

"Leave your mother to me."

Mercy came up alongside Judah and glowered at Eve. "I've warned you about doing that. You can't control your powers, and until you can, you must curtail your—"

"She has to practice, doesn't she?" Judah said as he set Eve on her feet.

Eve looked up at Judah with absolute adoration. Mercy winced.

"There are safer ways to practice," Mercy said.

Eve clutched Judah's hand, as if she knew he would protect her from her mother's displeasure. "Daddy can help me with my lessons."

"No!" Mercy all but screamed the one word response.

"Why not?" Eve whined.

"Because your father is leaving today." Mercy shot Judah a warning glare, daring him to contradict her.

"No, Daddy, please don't leave." Eve tugged on Judah's arm. "I want you to stay."

"I have to go," he told her. "I can't stay."

"You're making him go away!" Eve shouted at Mercy. "I hate you! I hate you!"

Eve clenched her teeth tightly and narrowed her gaze, concentrating on her mother. Without warning, a high wind came up and the sky turned gray. Streaks of lightning shot out of the clouds and hit in several spots surrounding Mercy.

Stop! Judah ordered his daughter. *I know you're angry, but you might hurt your mother. You don't want to do that, do you?*

Immediately the wind died down, though the thunder continued to rumble repeatedly. Within moments the sky cleared and the sun reappeared.

Judah began to understand his daughter's true powers. He had never known a child of six who was capable of half of what he'd seen from Eve. And he also understood Mercy's concern for their child. Untutored power such as Eve possessed most certainly could be dangerous, not only to others but to Eve herself.

With tears caught in her long, honey-gold lashes, Eve ran straight to Mercy and threw her arms around her mother's unsteady knees. "I'm sorry, Mommy. I didn't mean it. I'd never hurt you. I love you. I don't hate you."

Mercy lifted Eve into her arms and hugged her fiercely to her breast. Judah exchanged a glance with Mercy and noted the sheen of tears in her eyes.

"I know. I know." Mercy soothed her remorseful child. "You must promise me that you will try harder to control your temper and not use your powers when you're angry."

"I—I promise…I'll try." Eve clung to her mother.

Judah turned and walked away.

"Daddy!"

He paused and glanced over his shoulder. Eve was resting on her mother's hip, her bright Raintree eyes shimmering with tears. "Will you come back to see me very soon?"

"I'll come back to see you when the time is right," Judah replied.

2:00 p.m.

The house was unusually quiet, with Sidonia working in the herb garden and Eve taking an afternoon nap. Mercy sat alone in her study, the blinds drawn, the lights out, and thought about her predicament. Judah was gone. But for how long? He had left with nothing settled between them. In less than twenty-four hours he had saved her life, discovered he had a daughter and turned their world upside down.

Who had tried to kill her last night, and why? How could Judah have known? And why would he bother to save her life? Was it possible that like her, he had never been able to forget their brief time together?

Stop thinking romantic nonsense!

Judah Ansara is no mortal man, nor is he Raintree. He doesn't love, he conquers. And that's all you were to him—a very special conquest. Never forget that he knew you were a Raintree princess before he took you to his bed.

For all these years, she had been certain that if she ever saw Judah again, she would feel nothing except fear for her child. She was afraid, deathly afraid, of what Judah might yet do. But she wouldn't lie to herself. There was more to her feelings for him than fear.

Sexual attraction is a powerful thing.

She suspected that Judah was not as indifferent to her as he had proclaimed. And perhaps, if that was true, she could use it to her advantage. Just how far would she be willing to go to protect Eve? As far as was necessary, even if it meant seducing Judah and using her feminine wiles on him.

Be totally honest with yourself. You know what has to be done.

Yes, she knew. There was only one sure way to protect Eve from her father. Even if Eve never forgave her, Mercy had no choice but to kill Judah.

The thought of killing the man she had once loved, or at least had believed she loved, created a tightening in her chest. She had been born to heal, not destroy. But she had also been born a Raintree princess. The blood of warriors, both male and female, flowed in her veins.

Mercy looked above the mantle over the fireplace and

visually inspected the golden sword hanging on the wall. Dranira Ancelin's sword, the one she had used in *The Battle* against the Ansara. Her ancestress had also been an empath, a healer who had used her powers for good. But when called upon to defend her clan, she had fought alongside her husband. When they came to the mountains of North Carolina and built a refuge for themselves and their people, Ancelin had placed her sword above the fireplace in what had then been the living room of her home. The jewel-encrusted, golden sword had not been removed from that spot in two centuries.

"That sword has great power," her father had once told her. "It can be used for no other purpose than to defend the Raintree, and only a female descendant of Ancelin can remove it from the wall."

She had always known the sword was hers and sensed that someday she would be called upon to use it. But she had never thought that she would use it to kill her child's father.

"Judah. Oh, Judah…"

Mercy?

She heard Judah's voice as clearly as if he were standing at her side.

Had he heard her thoughts? Did he know that she…?

Judah?

Why have you contacted me? he asked telepathically.

I didn't contact you. You contacted me.

Silence.

Hurriedly, Mercy protected her thoughts, although she had believed she was already safe from anyone's mental probing.

She heard Judah's laughter.

I don't want to talk to you, she told him. *Go away.*

I would if I could.

What do you mean by that?

*Have a talk with our daughter. Tell her that she mustn't
connect us again.*

Eve did this? Mercy asked. *That mischievous little… Eve,
you're listening, aren't you? Cut the connection now. Your
father and I do not want to—*

Sooner or later you'll have to talk to each other again, Eve
said.

Silence. Eve had severed the connection to Judah. And
to herself.

Mercy sighed, then walked across the room and stopped in
front of the fireplace. She lifted her hand to Ancelin's sword
and caressed the jewels glimmering in an intricate design on
the hilt.

When Judah returned—and she knew that someday he
would come back for Eve—she would do what any mother
would do to protect her child from certain damnation. She
would fight the devil for her daughter's soul.

Beauport, on the island of Terrebonne
Monday Evening, 8:15

When Judah arrived at Claude's home, half a mile from his
own palatial estate, Claude's wife, Nadine, met him at the
door. After bowing to him and then welcoming him with a kiss
on the cheek, she escorted him into the large, open grand room
of their elegant home. As instructed, Claude had assembled
members of the high council whom he trusted without
question. When Judah entered the room, everyone stood and
bowed. Claude and Nadine were as dear to Judah as any
beloved brother and sister could be. And he respected few as
he did Councilman Bartholomew and Councilwoman Sidra.
He quickly studied the others congregated, including Galen,
Tymon, Felicia and Esther. His cousin Alexandria was con-

spicuously absent. Undoubtedly Claude shared Judah's suspicions, believing that Alexandria had aligned herself with Cael.

Judah looked directly at Claude. "What have you been able to find out?"

"As you know, we have several spies in Cael's camp," Claude said. "Each one reports to a different council member under the guise of trying to persuade the council member to be sympathetic to Cael's cause."

"Yes, yes," Judah said impatiently.

Claude looked to Galen, who bowed to Judah again before he spoke. "I have learned that Cael has promised Alexandria that she will be his Dranira when he becomes Dranir. There can be no doubt that she is working with Cael against you, my lord."

Judah nodded, not at all surprised to have his suspicions confirmed.

Claude turned to Tymon, who bowed before speaking to Judah. "Although we have no actual proof, we know that Cael sent Stein to kill you." Tymon glanced around the room. "We are in agreement that this crime cannot go unpunished."

"It won't," Judah assured them.

"Taking Cael down will involve others," Claude said. "A group of young warriors, as well as Alexandria and two other council members."

"They will all be dealt with," Judah told his cousin.

"When?" Galen asked.

"Soon," Judah replied.

Galen bowed his head in a show of respect.

Claude then looked to Felicia, who walked forward, bowed, then locked her gaze with Judah's. "My lord, your brother not only sent Greynell to kill the great Raintree empath, Princess Mercy, but he ordered strikes on both of the royal brothers."

Felicia waited for a response from Judah, but when he didn't respond, she continued. "Along with hits on Dante and

Gideon, Cael ordered the murder of Echo Raintree. These attempts failed. The Raintree casino in Reno was all but destroyed by fire, but Dante is alive. Tabby was sent to kill Echo and then Gideon. Unfortunately, she killed Echo's look-alike roommate instead, and now Echo has gone into hiding."

"Damn the fool." Judah's voice boomed like thunder. "Cael's actions have all but announced to the Raintree that the Ansara have regrouped after two hundred years and are now on the warpath. It can be only a matter of time before they figure out who made these strikes against them, if they have not already."

Claude placed his hand on Judah's shoulder. "I'm afraid it's far worse than we anticipated. We believe that Cael plans to strike the Raintree sanctuary very soon."

"We're not ready," Judah said. "We can't win a war against them now."

"Cael believes we *are* ready," Bartholomew said. "He doesn't plan to wait until you decide we are strong enough to defeat the Raintree. He is going to strike when *he* decides."

"And when will that be?" Judah asked.

"We don't know, but we believe it won't be long, possibly in a few months or even sooner," Bartholomew replied.

"He intends to force my hand." Judah clenched his jaw, barely managing to contain his anger. "My brother is insane if he believes we are ready to face the Raintree in battle, and unfortunately, he has infected others with his insanity."

"What are we going to do?" Sidra asked, speaking for the first time. "If you arrest Cael, his followers will rise up against us and an Ansara civil war will erupt. If you choose that path, we cannot keep our existence a secret from the Raintree. But if you choose to go into battle against the Raintree when Cael plans his attack, I see the end of our clan."

Judah walked across the room to the elderly Sidra, took both her hands in his and spoke to her as reverently as a son would speak to his aged mother. "You are our wise woman. Your visions have served us well all your life. The only two choices open to me seem to predict that the Ansara are doomed."

Tightening her hold on Judah's hands, Sidra closed her eyes and trembled from head to toe. Judah tried to pull away, but she held on to him fiercely. "The day of the Ansara is coming to an end."

Judah jerked free. Sidra opened her eyes. "You have difficult choices to make, my lord. Whatever you decide, we, your loyal subjects, will obey your commands."

Judah couldn't be sure, but he sensed that Sidra knew about Eve.

"The Dranir is tired after his trip," Claude told the others. "As Sidra said, he has difficult choices to make, decisions that require time and thought."

Within ten minutes the council members were gone and Nadine had slipped away to her private quarters, leaving Judah alone with Claude.

"I think you need a drink," Claude said as he approached the bar area.

"No, nothing for me."

Claude paused and turned around to face Judah. "Sidra could be wrong, or she could be interpreting her visions incorrectly. She's not infallible."

"Choosing between battling Cael or going up against the Raintree on Cael's timetable is not the only decision I have to make." Judah looked deep into Claude's consciousness, needing to know if he dared share his secret with his cousin.

"Does this decision have something to do with why you were able to enter the Raintree sanctuary so easily and why you stayed there after you stopped Greynell from killing Mercy Raintree?"

"Mercy Raintree has a child, a six-year-old daughter."

Claude stared questioningly at Judah.

"My…affair with Mercy was seven years ago."

Realization dawned. "This child is yours!" Claude gasped. "She is a mixed-breed, half Ansara and half Raintree?"

"Yes, she is." Judah riveted his gaze to his cousin's. "My daughter possesses unparalleled power. She could become our secret weapon against the Raintree."

"Or she could be our downfall," Claude said.

Cael showed Horace into his home and poured his loyal subject a drink. Although he was eager to learn what this brilliant Ansara detective had unearthed about Mercy Raintree, he would play dutiful host in order to keep Horace allied with him and against Judah. He was counting on good news, a revelation of some sort that he could use against his brother. Up to this point, the first two days of this all-important week had been terribly disappointing. Stein had failed in the assassination attempt against Judah. And not only were Dante and Gideon Raintree still alive, but so was Echo. It turned out that Tabby had killed the wrong woman. Nothing had gone as he had planned.

"Sit, relax," Cael said.

"Thank you, my lord." Horace's hand trembled as he lifted the hundred-proof to his lips. After taking a sip of whiskey and gasping as the liquor slid down his throat, Horace sat, as Cael had instructed.

Hoping to put the man at ease, Cael sat across from him, doing his best not to seem overeager. "I'm pleased that you have worked so quickly to compile a report on Mercy Raintree."

Horace took a second sip of whiskey, then set the glass aside. "In the outside world, little is known of her. She seldom leaves the sanctuary, except in local emergencies and occasionally to visit her brothers."

"That is what I expected. After all, she is the Keeper of the Raintree home place."

Horace nodded. "A position she acquired when the old guardian, Gillian, died six and a half years ago. Before that time—"

"I'm really not interested in what was happening in the princess's life before then," Cael said, growing impatient.

"Very well. Where shall I start, my lord?"

"With the present," Cael said. "With this year."

Apparently perplexed, Horace stared at Cael. "As I said, little is known of her. Our psychics have tried to study her, but she has a powerful protective cloak around her, as do her brothers. We know only that she is the Keeper, the Guardian, and the greatest Raintree empath."

"She is the greatest empath alive, Raintree or Ansara," Cael corrected.

"Yes, my lord."

"Has she ventured from the sanctuary this year, other than to help in local emergencies?"

"No, my lord. She has not. Dranir Dante and Prince Gideon visited her in late March, as they do every year, but she has not visited either of them since last year. Her last trip was when she and her daughter went to Wilmington to visit Prince Gideon."

Her daughter? "Did you say her daughter?"

"Yes, my lord."

"Mercy Raintree has a child?"

"Yes, my lord. A six-year-old."

"And her husband?"

"I've found no evidence of a husband," Horace said.

"Are you telling me that the Raintree princess gave birth to a bastard child?"

"It would seem so."

"Who is the father?"

"I don't know."

"Hmm…"

"If you'd like, I can e-mail you the complete report." Horace fidgeted nervously.

"Before the child was born, where was Mercy living? Who were her friends? And in what hospital was the child born?"

"There is no record of the child's birth at any hospital. We assume she was born at home, at the sanctuary." Horace swallowed hard. "Princess Mercy grew up at the home place, as did her brothers. She was homeschooled. When she went away to college, several Raintree were sent with her, to protect her."

"Protect her from what? From whom? The Raintree have not considered the Ansara a threat in two hundred years."

"It is tradition that an underage princess has escorts. And just as with our empaths, any young Raintree empath must be protected from the outside world by others of her clan who can absorb the thoughts and feelings of humans before they reach the empath and flood her senses."

"Yes, of course." Cael's mind went into overdrive, processing various tidbits of information. "Do you know of any time when the princess was out in the world on her own, say seven years ago, before she became the Guardian?"

"No, my lord, but if you wish, I can dig deeper and see if I can find out for you."

"Dig deeper."

Horace nodded.

"Are there any photographs of the child?"

"No, my lord."

"What about a description?"

"No, but I can try to get that information, too, if you'd like."

"Yes, do it." When Horace started to get up, Cael motioned for him to sit. "Finish your drink before you leave, then let yourself out."

Cael stood, crossed the room and opened the doors to the patio. Until only a few moments ago, he had believed there was no Raintree heir, that if all three royal siblings were killed before the great battle, there would be a fight among the royal cousins, each possibly claiming the throne. But now he knew that Princess Mercy had a daughter, a successor.

The child is a bastard.

No matter. She would not be the first bastard child to become a ruler. He, too, was a bastard, and one day he would be the Dranir.

Cael was uncertain why the news of Princess Mercy's daughter concerned him so greatly. After all, the child would be killed along with her mother and uncles in *The Battle* that was to come. And once the Ansara took the sanctuary, they would prepare to go throughout the world and eliminate all Raintree everywhere.

Suddenly Cael heard a voice, as clearly as if someone were speaking nearby.

The child...the child. She could be our downfall.

Where had those thoughts come from? Not from him. Whose thoughts had he picked up on? Was it possible another Ansara knew about Mercy Raintree's child and was thinking about her? If so, why would anyone believe the Raintree child was a threat to the Ansara?

Chapter 7

Monday Night, 10:30 p.m.

Mercy looked down from her bedroom window at the patio where only last night Judah Ansara had stood. In her mind's eye she could see him glancing up at her, and she remembered the way his heated gaze raking over her body had made her feel. Desired. Ravaged. Ashamed. How could she still have feelings for such a man? Why did her traitorous body still yearn for his touch?

Until only a few moments ago, when Eve had finally fallen asleep and Sidonia had decided to rest in the adjoining room, Mercy had been too busy to think about her feelings for Judah. After he left today, she'd had to deal with Eve's tears. Her mother's heart understood her daughter's dismay over losing the father she had only just met. And there was no way Mercy could make Eve understand what sort of man Judah was.

How could she tell her child that her father was an Ansara, a member of an evil clan, a deadly enemy of the Raintree?

By the time she had pacified Eve by allowing her to try out several of her powers to a limited degree—something Eve loved to do— Mercy had been faced with a Raintree crisis. Sisters Lili and Lynette had arrived at the sanctuary, both overwrought and greatly concerned because suddenly and without warning each had lost her most powerful ability: her psychic ability to look into the future. Lili and Lynette, distant cousins to the royal family, were in their late twenties and had mastered their gifts, but neither possessed the psychic power that Echo did. Once Echo matured and learned to harness her great power, she would be the premiere Raintree seer.

After working with Lili and Lynette, Mercy's first impression had been that someone had cast a spell to blind the sisters' sight. But who would have done such an unkind thing, and for what reason? She had assigned the sisters a cabin and promised to work with them again tomorrow to help them regain their lost talent. If she couldn't heal them, then she would have no choice but to contact Dante and inform him that someone in their clan was playing wicked tricks. But she wouldn't bother her brother this week. He had enough problems of his own, dealing with the aftermath of the casino fire.

As if having to pacify Eve and begin the healing process with Lili and Lynette hadn't been enough for one afternoon, she had been called upon to deal with a human who had tried to enter the sanctuary. He had been rendered unconscious by the force field protecting the acreage, so Mercy had restored him and sent him on his way after convincing him that he had received a severe shock from an electrified fence. It had been easy enough to plant the false memory in his mind. He wasn't the first human who had tried to trespass, and he probably wouldn't be the last.

Mercy was mentally and emotionally weary, as well as

physically tired. She doubted she would sleep much tonight. She needed to devise a plan to deal with Judah.

You mean a plan to kill him, an inner voice said.

But she didn't have to figure out a way to eliminate Judah tonight, did she? After all, it wasn't as if he would return for Eve tomorrow. It could be months, even years, before he came for her. *But what if it's not? What if...?*

The telephone rang. Startled, Mercy shivered and glanced at the bedside clock. A call this late in the evening was no doubt more bad news. Rushing to the telephone on the night-stand, she caught her bare toe on the wool rug and barely managed to right herself. Clumsy. She reached the phone before the fifth ring and didn't bother checking the Caller I.D.

"Hello," Mercy said.

"Hi, yourself. Are you okay? You sound out of breath."

"Echo?"

"Yeah, it's me."

"I'm fine. But you're not all right, are you?" Mercy said, sensing her young cousin's uneasiness. "Tell me what's wrong."

"Look, before you get all bent out of shape, I'm all in one piece and I'm safe."

"Safe from what?"

"Gideon didn't call you, did he?"

"He phoned early this morning to tell me about the fire at Dante's casino, but he didn't mention you."

"He didn't know about it then."

Mercy closed her eyes and concentrated, bringing her clair-empathy powers into play. She made a habit of using her lesser powers, such as her ability to sense the emotional and physical condition of others from a distance, only when necessary.

Echo was an emotional wreck but was putting up a brave front. And she was scared.

"Who are you afraid of?" Mercy asked.

"Jeez, I wish you wouldn't do that without telling me. You're probing around inside me, and I didn't give you permission to."

"You called me. I didn't call you," Mercy reminded her.

"You're right. Sorry. I'm in Charlotte, staying with a friend. Dewey. I've told you about him."

"The saxophone player?"

"Yeah, that's him. Anyway, Gideon knows where I am. As a matter of fact he sort of sent me here. You see…well…somebody killed my roommate, Sherry, last night and…well…you know how Gideon can talk to spirits and all—"

"Do you need to come to the sanctuary?" Mercy asked.

"God, no! I'm fine right here. Honest. It's just there's a possibility that whoever killed Sherry killed her by mistake. You see, she'd dyed her hair blond and pink, just like mine, and—"

"Have you had any visions recently about being in danger?"

Echo laughed nervously. "Gideon asked me the same question."

"Well?"

"Heck, I don't know. You know what it's like with me. I'm always getting these weird visions."

"Come home," Mercy said.

"Nah, I'll stay here for a few days, then we'll see."

"Echo, be careful. Just in case."

"Sure thing."

Lost in thought, Mercy held the phone for a bit too long after Echo hung up, long enough so that she heard the recorded message asking her to hang up and dial again. She placed the receiver on the base and sat on the edge of the bed. Echo was such a free spirit, so independent. Mercy worried about her because her parents didn't. They were too busy jet setting around the world.

Who would want to kill a sweet girl like Echo? Okay, so she had some really flaky friends, like Dewey the saxophone player, and she did play in a band. Musicians were notorious for taking drugs. Was it possible that Echo had heard or seen something she shouldn't have? Or could it be even more ominous? Maybe she'd had a vision that threatened someone.

Mercy didn't like the idea that three Raintree psychics—

"Mommy!"

Mercy's heart stopped when she heard Eve's terrified scream. She jumped up, yanked open her bedroom door and raced across the hall to her daughter's room. When she flung open the door and rushed into the semidarkness, she saw Sidonia trying to calm Eve, but Eve was fighting Sidonia not only with all her physical strength but with a little magical power kicking in, too. Books and dolls and stuffed animals flew around the room, whirling and spinning as if hanging from invisible wires and being propelled by a storm-force wind.

"Mommy!"

Mercy concentrated on breaking the energy that kept the objects levitated. Eve didn't fight her, so within seconds all the objects dropped to the floor, a book hitting Mercy on the arm and two stuffed animals grazing Sidonia's head. Sidonia moved aside as Mercy sat down on the side of the bed and took Eve into her arms.

"It's all right, sweetheart. Mommy's here. Mommy's here."

Eve clung to Mercy, her small body trembling uncontrollably.

"Did you have a nightmare?" Mercy asked.

"It wasn't a nightmare." Eve's voice quivered.

When Mercy smoothed Eve's long, blond curls out of her face, she realized her daughter was sweating profusely, her hair and face damp with perspiration.

"My daddy's in trouble," Eve said. "We have to help him."

Mercy exchanged a quick, concerned glance with Sidonia, then concentrated fully on her child. "It must have been a nightmare. I'm sure your father is all right."

"He wants to kill my daddy."

"Who wants to kill your father?"

"That evil man. He hates my daddy and wants to kill him."

"What?"

"I won't let him hurt my daddy." Eve grabbed Mercy's hand. "We have to help Daddy."

"All right," Mercy said. "In the morning we'll contact your father, and you can warn him that someone evil wants to harm him."

"Why can't I talk to Daddy tonight?"

Knowing how stubborn Eve was, Mercy realized that there was only one way to reassure her daughter. "If you need to contact Judah right now, then go ahead."

"No!" Sidonia cried. "What are you thinking, letting her use such powers without testing her first? And to contact that man…"

Mercy glanced over her shoulder at Sidonia. "Eve has already spoken to her father. As a matter of fact, she connected my mind and Judah's and listened in. Didn't you, my little minx?"

"Heaven help us," Sidonia mumbled.

"Go to bed in your own room," Mercy said. "I'll stay the night with Eve."

Grumbling all kinds of dire warnings, Sidonia shook her head sadly, then left mother and daughter alone.

Eve looked up at Mercy and asked, "May I talk to my daddy now?"

"Yes, you may."

Mercy didn't doubt that there was someone out there, besides herself, who wanted Judah Ansara dead. Although she knew very little about him, she did know that he was probably enormously wealthy. When they'd first met, his lifestyle had indicated he was a man with a vast fortune. He had told her that he was an international banker. Being an Ansara, he was hardly a legitimate businessman. There was no telling how many illegal deals he had bartered and how many enemies he had made over the years.

Eve closed her eyes and concentrated. While she was deep in thought, Mercy held Eve's hand and connected to her daughter's mind, sharing her consciousness.

Daddy.

No response.

Daddy, can you hear me?

Silence.

Eve opened her eyes and looked at Mercy. "He's not answering me. He won't let me in."

Mercy sensed that her child was on the verge of another psychic hissy-fit. She squeezed Eve's hand. "We'll try together."

Eve's precious smile melted her mother's heart. *Judah's smile.*

Mercy was grateful that Eve resembled her so much, with her slender frame and blond hair; and thankfully, she had been born with the Raintree eyes. Unfortunately, she also bore the Ansara blue crescent moon birthmark, which lay hidden beneath her hair. And from the first moment Eve had smiled, Mercy had known that she had inherited her father's mouth.

After Eve closed her eyes, Mercy did, too, and together they called out to the same man.

Daddy.

Judah.

Beauport, Terrebonne, the royal palace, 11:00 p.m.

Judah sat alone in his bedroom, unable to rest, his mind filled with thoughts of the secret council meeting earlier that evening. There had to be a way to stop Cael without plunging the Ansara into a bloody civil war. It had taken them two hundred years to regroup and rebuild after *The Battle* with the Raintree. Hiding away on this island in the Caribbean, slowly growing in size and strength until they were once again a mighty clan, the Ansara now ruled a vast economic empire, fueled by both legal and illegal activities worldwide. As far as the world of mankind knew, Judah Ansara was a banker.

Daddy.

Judah.

What the hell?

He heard Eve's voice. And Mercy's.

Daddy, please answer me. I have to warn you.

Stop this now! Judah sent the mental message with harsh force, enough to startle Mercy without harming Eve. *If you must contact me, call me on my cell phone.* He recited the number. Once. Then, using all his power, he blocked his daughter and her mother completely.

By the time Judah reached out and picked up his cell phone lying on the round table near the French doors that led outside to a second story balcony, the phone was already vibrating.

He answered immediately. "Yes?"

"Judah, Eve insists on speaking to you," Mercy said.

"You must never allow her to contact me telepathically again. Do you understand?"

"No, I don't understand," Mercy said. "Explain it to me."

Judah huffed. He was the Ansara Dranir. He explained himself to no one.

"I have enemies."

"Enemies with the ability to intercept telepathic messages?"

How did he respond? Half-truths were always best. Neither a lie nor the complete truth. "Yes. I have a half brother. We were once business partners. Now we're bitter enemies."

"Then he must be the evil man Eve believes intends to harm you."

Judah heard Eve say, "Let me tell him, Mother."

"Eve wants to talk to you."

The next voice he heard belonged to his daughter. "Daddy?"

"Yes, Eve."

"He hates you, Daddy. He wants to kill you. But I won't let him. Mother and I will help you."

Despite being slightly in awe of the child his one night of passion with Mercy Raintree had created, Judah couldn't help smiling at the thought of how Mercy must hate the fact that Eve had allied herself with him. With her father, the Ansara Dranir.

But Mercy didn't know he was the Dranir, that the Ansara had once again become a mighty clan that would soon be as powerful and plentiful as the Raintree.

"Eve, I don't want you to worry about me. I know who this man is, and I can fight him on my own. I don't need you to help me."

"You will, Daddy. You will."

"Put your mother back on the phone," Judah said.

"Be very careful," Eve cautioned.

"Judah?" Was that a hint of concern he heard in Mercy's voice? Surely not. She hated him, didn't she?

"Don't allow Eve to contact me again."

"And if I can't stop her?"

"Persuade her," Judah said.

"Maybe if you called her occasionally…"

"I thought you wanted me out of her life. Have you changed your mind?"

"No, I haven't changed my mind," Mercy told him in no uncertain terms. "But Eve is not willing to let you go and I don't want her constantly upset."

What sort of game was Mercy playing, blowing hot and cold? Go away. Come back. Never see Eve again. Call her occasionally.

"Tell Eve that I'll call her soon."

"I'll tell her. And Judah…"

"Yes?"

"You know how I feel about you."

Judah smiled. "I know. I'm Ansara and you're Raintree. We're mortal enemies."

"That's right. I just wanted to make sure we understood each other."

"Sleep well, Mercy. And dream of me."

Tuesday, 1:45 p.m.

Cael had been informed that Judah had returned to Terrebonne late yesterday and had spent this morning in his office, was in fact still there. Unfortunately Cael didn't have any spies among his brother's office staff, so other than relying on minions who watched the royal palace from afar, he had no knowledge of what was going on behind closed doors.

He had wasted the entire morning in fruitless efforts to discover the identity of the person whose thoughts he had overheard last night. *The child…the child. She could be our downfall.* The voice had been male and slightly familiar, yet contemplatively soft and not quite recognizable.

Frustrated by his failure, Cael had gone to the brothel an hour ago and vented his anger by beating one of his whores, then taking her savagely. Refreshed by these amusements, he was now prepared to try a different tactic in his search. If he couldn't discover who had been voicing concern about a certain child and how she could be "our" downfall, perhaps he could find the child herself.

"Who are you? Where are you?" Cael asked aloud.

The doorbell rang, but Cael ignored it. One of the servants

would see to it. He didn't concern himself with mundane
matters.

Was the child a threat to the Ansara? *Our downfall.* What
child could possess the power to threaten the mighty Ansara?

My child? Cael thought.

But he had no children. He had made certain of that.

Judah's child?

Why would the Dranir's child pose a threat to the Ansara,
especially a female child?

Are you out there, little one?

Do I have a niece being kept hidden away so that I cannot
find her? Had Judah secretly married and fathered a child?
He couldn't imagine his brother producing a bastard child.

Bastard child. The child...the child. She—

Mercy Raintree had a bastard child!

Could it be that this Raintree child was somehow a threat
to the Ansara?

*Little Raintree princess, open your mind to me, allow me
entrance.*

Nothing.

Mercy Raintree's daughter, I wish to speak to you.

Dead silence.

If only he knew the child's name.

*If you wish to know the names of your greatest enemies,
repeat these words nine times, and nine names will appear
in your mind, the last name the one you must fear the most.*
Even now, after all these years, he could hear his mother's
voice.

"Thank you, Mother," Cael said, then spoke the ancient
words of a potent spell she had taught him when he was only
a small boy.

He waited for the names to appear, until slowly as if im-
printed on a puff of gray smoke, the first name appeared,

and then the second, the third and the fourth. All were names of council members loyal to Judah. The fifth appeared. Nadine. Then the sixth. Claude. The seventh was Sidra. No surprises.

But the eighth name puzzled Cael.

Judah.

He believed his brother to be his greatest enemy. How could there be someone of more danger to him than the Dranir?

And then the ninth name appeared, a name Cael did not recognize.

Eve.

Who was Eve?

The spell-induced vision ended, and Cael's mind cleared. *Eve, who are you? If you can hear me, open your mind to me.*

A vigorous surge of mental energy shot through him, bringing him to his knees. As the pain radiated through him and then quickly dispersed, he cursed loudly, damning whatever force had attacked him.

Someone did not want him contacting Eve. Could that someone be Eve herself?

You caught me off guard, Cael said. *I am more powerful than any Ansara. You cannot win in a fight against me. Do you hear me, Eve?*

Another blow zapped Cael, sending him flying halfway across the room and landing him in a heap against the far wall.

Damn you! I warn you. Don't make an enemy of me. You will regret it.

I'm not afraid of you, a child's voice replied. *I will not let you hurt my daddy.*

Cael's heartbeat accelerated. *Who is your father?*

I am Eve, and I hate you!

Tapping into the child's anger, Cael returned a psychic blow and laughed when he heard the little girl's screams.

* * *

Screaming, Eve doubled over in pain, then dropped to the ground as if she'd been hit by a giant fist. Sidonia, who had been sitting in the swing watching Eve as she raced around in the yard, playing with Magnus and Rufus, rushed to the child as quickly as her old legs would carry her. Mercy, who had been picking peaches from the lower branches of one of the many trees in the fruit orchard, saw in her mind's eye what happened to her child the instant it occurred. Someone had attacked Eve! Running as fast as possible from the orchard, Mercy sent several powerful bursts of retaliation energy, disrupting the flow attacking her child and reversing the blows so that they would strike their sender.

When Mercy reached Eve, she found her wrapped in Sidonia's comforting arms.

Her old nanny looked right at her and said, "This is Ansara evil."

"Mommy…" Eve's voice was a mere whisper.

"I'm here, baby. Mommy's here." She took Eve from Sidonia and held her close.

"He's a very evil man."

"Who is, baby? Who attacked you?"

"The man who wants to kill my daddy."

Mercy's heart sank. No! Please, God, no. How had Judah's half brother, his former business partner and now his enemy, found out about Eve? Did it really matter? Apparently this man, whatever his name was, thought he could somehow get to Judah through his daughter.

Half an hour later, when Eve had calmed somewhat, Mercy questioned her about what had happened. There was only one way anyone could have gotten past the protective barrier that Mercy kept around Eve.

Eve must have let him in.

"Why did you let him in?" Mercy asked.

"I didn't. Honest, I didn't. I just heard him call my name. He said Eve. And I knew who he was. I blasted him to make him go away, but he didn't."

No, it wasn't possible. Only someone as powerful as she, as Dante and Gideon, could have broken through such a powerful protective barrier.

"I knew who he was—my daddy's enemy—so I socked him again and again."

"Oh, Eve, you didn't."

"I did, and I warned him that I wouldn't let him hurt my daddy."

"Oh, God, Eve, what am I going to do with you?"

"He thinks he's more powerful than my daddy, but he isn't. I'll show him."

Mercy shook Eve gently. "No more communicating with this man. Do you hear me?"

"Yes, Mother." Eve hung her head.

"Now you run into the kitchen and have Sidonia get you some milk and tea cakes."

Eve grasped Mercy's hand. "You come, too, Mother. We'll have a tea party."

"You go ahead. I'll be there in a few minutes."

"All right."

As soon as Eve disappeared down the hall, Mercy headed straight for her study. After closing the door behind her, she used her cell phone to make a call.

A gruff male voice said, "Why the hell are you—"

"Your brother knows about Eve," Mercy told Judah. "Less than an hour ago, our daughter exchanged psychic blows with him."

Chapter 8

Tuesday, 3:00 p.m.

There were only two Ansara psychics loyal to Cael: Natalie, a girl of twenty, who had predicted that in the upcoming battle with the Raintree, many Ansara lives would be lost but they would not lose the battle; and Risa, older, wiser, more cautious, one of Judah's discarded lovers who now often warmed Cael's bed. Neither woman possessed half the ability that Sidra did. The old councilwoman, fiercely loyal to Judah, was the most gifted Ansara psychic. To his knowledge, the only Raintree psychic who had the potential to reach Sidra's level was Echo. But that little bitch would be dead long before she could harness and control her gifts.

At his request, Natalie and Risa, who intensely disliked each other, arrived at his home together. Cael greeted the two women cordially, then personally escorted them into the living room and offered them refreshments. After they declined his offer, they obeyed his command and took seats on the sleek leather sofa.

He stood over them, glancing back and forth from one to the other. "I need information that I cannot gain by normal methods. You understand?"

"Yes, my lord," they replied simultaneously, then glowered at each other.

"What I'm going to share with you is not to go beyond this room. If it does, there will be severe consequences."

Natalie's facial muscles tightened. "I swear my loyalty to you. I'll take an oath in blood if your require it, Dranir Cael."

Smiling, Cael reached down and caressed the blond girl's tanned cheek. She returned his smile. He slapped her. Stunned by his actions, she reeled backward and gazed at him in shock.

"I displeased you?" her voice quivered.

"Not at all," he said. "The slap was merely a test to judge your reaction."

"Yes, my lord," Natalie replied.

"I'd prefer not to be tested," Risa told him when he turned to her. "I'm your loyal servant, but I am not your doormat. You'd do well to remember that."

Cael focused directly on Risa, tall, elegantly slender, with black hair and dark blue eyes. When he was Dranir, he would prove to her that she was whatever he wanted her to be. The thought of forcing her to lie prostrate before him while he walked across her prone body brought a wide smile to his face. "I will remember," he told her.

"Why did you summon us?" Risa asked, giving Natalie another displeased sidelong glance.

"I want you to work together to find the answer to a question. I need you to seek a child named Eve. I believe she's

Mercy Raintree's daughter." Then Cael added, "The little girl has powers, so be forewarned."

"How old is the child?" Risa asked.

"Six."

Natalie laughed. "A six-year-old with powers that we should fear?"

Cael nodded. "Unusual, but not unheard of. Remember, she is a Raintree princess."

"What do you want to know about this child?" Natalie asked.

"I want to know who her father is."

"What possible interest could the paternity of a Raintree child be to you, my lord?" Risa asked.

Cael barely managed to control his anger. How dare Risa question him? But for now, he would allow her disrespect to go unpunished. He realized she was jealous that he had shown an interest in Natalie, and by summoning them to his home together, he had placed the younger psychic on an equal level with the older. For the present, he needed Risa. Once she had served her purpose…

"Why I am interested in this child is not your concern," he said. "Not at this time."

Apparently finally realizing that she had stepped over the line, Risa acquiesced without further comment. She bowed her head, then turned to Natalie. "Prepare to link your mind to my mind."

The two women sat facing each other. Risa took both Natalie's hands in hers and stared into the younger woman's eyes. "Go deep and let yourself travel across the ocean to the Raintree sanctuary, but do not project your thoughts into the future. Concentrate solely on the child named Eve."

Natalie nodded agreement.

"I will clear the path for you, so that you can reach the child's mind," Cael said, certain that if he had made contact with Eve once, he could break through the barrier surrounding her once again. He found the anticipation exhilarating.

Judah walked along the beach, Claude at his side, as he so often was. His cousin had been at his side, literally and figuratively, since they were boys. They had shared many things over the years—their first taste of liquor, their first woman, their first kill. They had left the island and gone to America to college together, and had joined the business world together as young men.

"Could it be a trick of some kind?" Claude asked.

"For what purpose? If it's not the truth, why would Mercy want me to believe that Cael knows about Eve? Why tell me that he actually exchanged psychic blows with my daughter?

"To lure you back to North Carolina?"

"For what reason? The woman despises me and has made it perfectly clear that she doesn't want me anywhere near Eve."

"Forgive me for asking, but are you sure Eve is your daughter? Isn't it possible that—"

"She's mine." Judah was as certain of that fact as he was that the sun would rise in the East tomorrow morning.

"If Cael even suspects that this child is yours, he will try to kill her," Claude said. "And no one would stop him or judge him for his actions, because he would be obeying the ancient decree to kill any mixed-breed child."

"I'm going to call a council meeting tonight. Only those loyal to me. And I will announce that I have revoked the ancient decree. With nothing more than my signature, witnessed by two council members, I have the power to revoke any decree."

"The council will want to know why—"

"I am the Dranir. I am not obligated to answer to anyone, not even the high council."

Claude paused, laid his hand on Judah's shoulder and

made direct eye contact. "Is now the time to alienate even one council member? Cael is preparing for a premature war with the Raintree. The more high council members he can turn against you, the easier it will be for him to follow through with his plans." Claude squeezed Judah's shoulder. "Your brother won't stop until he kills you or you kill him."

Judah pulled away from his cousin. "Are you saying that I shouldn't protect my daughter?"

"I'm saying that your priority should be keeping Cael in check. Only you can prevent him from destroying us."

"And you think I should be willing to sacrifice my daughter's life? Don't you believe I can protect Eve and also safeguard my people from my insane brother?"

"Why is the child so important to you? You didn't choose to father her. You didn't even know she existed until two days ago. And you can't forget that she is Raintree."

Judah seethed. "Eve is Ansara!"

"No, she isn't," Claude said. "She is only half Ansara. The other half is Raintree. And she has been reared for the past six years within the Raintree sanctuary by Princess Mercy. If your daughter had to choose between you and her mother, between the Ansara and the Raintree, who do you think she'd choose?"

Whirlwinds of sand swirled upward from the beach, shooting high into the air. Fire shot from Judah's fingertips, and the ground beneath their feet trembled.

"Enough already. I get it," Claude said. "You're pissed at me for speaking the truth."

Claude understood Judah as no one else did and accepted him without question. Instead of being irritated by Judah's hair-trigger temper, his cousin usually seemed amused. There were times when Judah envied Claude's innate calmness, an inner peace that he himself didn't possess.

As Judah's anger subsided, the whirlwinds died down one

by one. He flung red-hot flashes out toward the ocean, where they sizzled and died in the salty surf. Then, when he continued walking up the beach, Claude followed, neither of them saying a word. The tropical June sun warmed them, while at the same time the breeze off the water cooled them. The Ansara lived in paradise.

"I can't claim Eve until after *The Battle,* when the Raintree are defeated," Judah said. "If I try to take her before then…"

"What will you do about Princess Mercy now that you know she gave birth to your child?"

"Nothing has changed. Mercy is still my kill on the day of *The Battle.*" Judah paused and looked out over the ocean toward the far horizon. Now that she had come into her full powers, Mercy would be a worthy adversary. She would fight him with all her strength. "As long as the Raintree exist, they will be a threat to us."

"It won't be easy to kill your child's mother."

"My father had Cael's mother put to death. He never regretted it."

"Uncle Hadar hated Nusi for what she did to your mother. Nusi was an evil sorceress, and crazy, just as her son is."

"And Mercy is Raintree. That alone is reason enough to kill her."

Before Claude could respond, they noticed one of the servants from the palace, a youth named Bru, running down the stairway that led from the palace grounds to the private beach. He waved his hands and called out for the Dranir.

When Bru reached them, he bowed hurriedly before gasping several deep breaths and saying, "Councilwoman Sidra is waiting for you, my lord. She said to tell you that you must come to her immediately. She has dire news."

Judah broke into a run, flying up the rock stairs, Claude and Bru following. Undoubtedly Sidra had experienced another vision. If she said the news was dire, it was. She never panicked, and never exaggerated the importance of her revelations.

When they reached the palace grounds, they found the old seer sitting calmly on a lower level patio, her wrinkled hands folded and resting in her lap. Her husband, Bartholomew, stood behind her, as always, her fierce guardian.

Judah went to Sidra, and when she tried to stand on unsteady legs, he helped her back into the chair and knelt at her feet. As the Dranir, he didn't bow to anyone, but Sidra was not just anyone. Not only was she their greatest soothsayer, she had been one of his mother's ladies-in-waiting and her dearest friend.

Sidra squeezed Judah's hands. "I have seen the mother of a new clan. She is a child of light. Golden hair. Golden eyes."

Judah's gut tightened. He would never forget the moment when he had seen his daughter's eyes flash golden, just for a millisecond. "The child's existence—what does it mean for the Ansara?"

"Transformation," Sidra said.

Judah looked up at Bartholomew and then over at Claude. *Transformation? Not annihilation? Not their downfall? And not their salvation.*

Sidra clasped his hands tightly once again. Judah focused on her. "If you are to save your people, you must protect the child from…" Sidra's voice grew weak, her eyelids fluttering wearily. "Guard yourself against Cael, against his evil. You must reverse the ancient decree…today." Sidra dropped off into a sudden and deep, restorative sleep, as she usually did after a powerful vision sapped her strength.

Bartholomew lifted the cloak from his shoulders and laid it across his wife, then faced Judah. "My lord, you know which ancient decree she was talking about."

Judah rose to his feet. "Yes, I know."

"Sidra believes her vision to be a true one," Bartholomew said. "If it is…there is a mixed-breed child out there somewhere, a child who is half Ansara and half Raintree."

"Yes, there is."

"You already knew of the child's existence?" Bartholomew asked.

Judah hesitated. "Yes."

"After what Sidra has seen, I agree that you have to protect the child," Claude said. "Write a new decree and sign it, with Bartholomew and me as witnesses. Revoke the ancient decree that demands the death of any mixed-breed offspring."

"Claude is right, my lord." Bartholomew glanced down lovingly at his wife. "Sidra believes Cael will try to kill the child, and you must not allow that to happen. Without her, the Ansara are doomed."

"I swear on my father's honor that I won't let anything happen to the child," Judah said. *I'll protect you, Eve. Do you hear me? No one will harm you. Now or ever.*

Mercy sensed a triad of minds searching inside the sanctuary boundaries—powerful thoughts that had combined in order to increase their strength. Instinctively, she realized the psychic exploration originated from far away. Lying aside the book that she'd been reading—an ancient script filled with spells and incantations of protection—she concentrated fully on the hostile energy. It took only a minute for her to understand the danger.

Ansara!

One mind was leading the other two, guiding them as it struggled to contact Eve.

I won't allow it. Closing her eyes and taking a deep, strengthening breath, she concentrated on surrounding Eve, adding extra protection to the magical boundary that already guarded her.

It's all right, Mother. I'm not afraid of him. He can't hurt me.

Oh, God, Eve. Don't! Whatever you're thinking about doing, don't do it.

Silly Mommy.

You'd better listen to me, Eve Raintree!

No, I'm Eve Ansara.

Striving to maintain the second level of protection around Eve, Mercy opened her eyes and ran from her study, seeking her daughter. She found Eve sitting on a cushion on the floor in the living room, surrounded by an array of stuffed animals, all marching around Eve, their little stuffed appendages bounding up and down against the wooden floor.

"Eve!"

Eve gasped. Her eyes widened as she faced Mercy and abruptly aborted the spell she had used to animate her stuffed animals.

"I was just practicing." Eve's beguiling smile pleaded for understanding.

"That man—your father's enemy—did you say or do anything—"

"Don't worry." Eve stood, shoulders straight and head held high. Self-assured in a way few six-year-olds were. A true princess.

"I sent him and the other two away," Eve said. "They wanted to know who my father was and—"

"You didn't tell them, did you?"

"Of course not." Eve stepped over a tiger and a bear as she approached Mercy. "I shut them out. It made him mad." She gazed up at Mercy, a deceptive innocence in her green Raintree eyes.

Eve had been headstrong, stubborn and not easy to control before Judah entered her life, but she was always Mercy's sweet little girl who might resist her mother's wishes but would obey in the end. Without being able to pinpoint exactly the moment it had happened, Mercy recognized that Eve was no longer under her control. Perhaps it would have happened eventually, when Eve was older, whether or not she ever met her father, but somehow meeting Judah had changed Eve. And it had forever altered Mercy's relationship with her daughter.

"I love you just as much as ever." Eve wrapped her arms around Mercy's waist, laid her head on Mercy's tummy, and hugged her.

Mercy caressed Eve's head. "I love you, too."

Eve eased away from Mercy and looked up at her. "I'm sorry you're sad because I'm an Ansara."

Mercy bit down on her bottom lip in an effort to neither cry nor scream. Sighing heavily, she looked right at Eve. "I am Raintree. You're my daughter. You are Raintree."

"Mother, Mother." Eve shook her head. "I was born into the Raintree clan, but I was born for the Ansara. For my father."

A shiver of realization chilled Mercy, sending the cold, hard truth shooting to her brain. The fear that she had kept buried deep inside her since Eve's conception came out of hiding, bursting from her in a psychic energy storm that shook the entire house.

Mercy seldom if ever lost control of her powers, but this reaction had been entirely involuntary, a knee-jerk response to suspecting that her daughter's destiny was to save the Raintree's mortal enemies.

Eve grabbed Mercy's hand, instantly calming her. For one brief instant, as mother's and daughter's powers linked, Mercy felt the immense power Eve possessed.

Once again in control of herself, Mercy said, "Your father's people, the Ansara, and my people, the Raintree, have been enemies since time immemorial. Sidonia has told you the stories of our people, how long ago we defeated the Ansara in a terrible battle and only a handful of their kind survived."

"I love it when Sidonia tells me those stories," Eve said. "She always tells me how mean and bad the Ansara are, and how good and kind the Raintree are. Does that mean *I'm* both good and bad?"

How was it possible that one minute Eve was wise and powerful beyond her years, and then the next minute she seemed to be only an adorable six-year-old?

"We are all good and bad," Mercy said.

"Even my daddy?"

"Yes, perhaps." Mercy could not bring herself to tell Eve that Judah was as wicked and evil as all his kind. *But how do you know that to be true?* a taunting inner voice asked. *Judah is the only Ansara you've ever know, the only one you've ever met.*

The Raintrees' knowledge of the Ansara came from historical accounts two hundred years old.

And from an inborn psychic instinct that Mercy could not deny.

Tuesday, 8:45 p.m.

Three whores from his private brothel stroked and petted and pleasured Cael as he lay on black satin sheets. Risa and Natalie had disappointed him bitterly earlier today. He had sent both women out of his sight, placing all the blame for his failure to penetrate Eve Raintree's mind squarely on the psychics' shoulders. He had spent hours fuming, the anger inside him building to an explosive point.

Needing to release his rage and find temporary ease and forgetfulness, he had sent for a diversion. Each of his whores had taken her turn under his whip, screaming and begging as his blows brought blood to their backs and buttocks. Their pain aroused Cael unbearably, adding heightened sensation to the sex act. As the redhead with the talented tongue brought him to yet another climax, Cael clutched her by the hair of her head, making her scream in pain as he shuddered with fulfillment.

As he rested there, sated and sleepy, the double doors to his bedroom suite swung open as if a gale-force wind had ripped them from the hinges. Cael laughed when he saw Alexandria storming into his private quarters. No doubt she would throw a jealous tantrum.

"Send your whores away," she said, her voice oddly calm. "I need to speak to you without an audience."

Naked and reeking of sex, Cael shoved the women aside as he eased to the side of the bed and stood to face Alexandria. When he looked her in the eye, he saw neither anger nor jealousy.

With a wave of his hand, he dismissed the whores. "Go. Leave me. Return to the brothel."

The women obeyed instantly, hurrying to put on their robes as they exited the room. Once they were gone, Cael walked over to Alexandria and smiled at her.

"You disappoint me, my love. I had expected a jealous tantrum."

"You flatter yourself if you think I care who else you screw, now or in the future. As long as I rule at your side as the Dranira, you're welcome to keep as many whores as it takes to satisfy your sexual appetites."

Cael's smile widened. "We make a perfect couple."

"Only if you can defeat the Raintree and kill Judah."

Cael lifted his black silk robe from the floor and slipped into it. "I intend to do both very soon." He reached out and stroked Alexandria's cheek. "What brings you here tonight? You said you needed to speak with me privately."

"I have learned about a secret meeting of the Dranir and three council members."

"When?"

"This afternoon."

"Who met with Judah, and why?"

"Claude was there, along with Bartholomew and Sidra."

"Sidra?"

"I don't know who arranged the meeting, but Sidra and Bartholomew showed up at the palace and stayed for several hours."

"That old witch probably had a vision of some kind. I've been careful to protect my plans from others. That is why only I know the exact moment when we will strike the Raintree. I cannot risk Sidra seeing—"

"We have more to concern us than Sidra foreseeing your plans," Alexandria said. "Judah has done the unthinkable."

Pure fear gripped Cael. He hated the fact that his brother could evoke such terror in him. "What has he done?"

"He has revoked an ancient decree. Judah signed the nullification proclamation. Claude and Bartholomew acted as witnesses."

"Which decree was overturned?"

"The one declaring that any mixed-breed child would be put to death."

"Why would Judah...?" *The child, the child. She could be our downfall.*

"What it is?" Alexandria asked. "What do you know?"

Cael grasped Alexandria's arm and yanked her to him. Eye to eye with her, he growled. "Such a child undoubtedly exists. And for Judah to revoke a decree issued thousands of years ago, this child must be very special to him."

"Are you implying that Judah has fathered a Raintree woman's child?"

Cael snarled. "Not just any Raintree woman, but a Raintree princess. Mercy Raintree has a daughter named Eve, a little girl with extraordinary power."

Wednesday Morning, 1:49 a.m.

Mercy debated her options. Try to handle the situation alone. Contact Dante and tell him the truth about Eve's paternity. Trust Judah to protect Eve.

If only she had another choice.

But whatever decision she made, it needed to be made soon. No later than tomorrow morning.

Sidonia knocked before entering the study. She paused several feet away from where Mercy stood in front of the fireplace, staring up at Ancelin's sword.

"Eve is finally asleep," Sidonia said. "It's time you were in bed, too. You need rest."

"I can't rest until I decide what to do."

"Call Dante."

"As much as I dread the thought of confessing my sins to my big brother, I may have no other choice."

"He'll be angry. No doubt about that. He'll want to hunt down Judah Ansara and kill him," Sidonia said. "Is that what's stopping you? You don't want Dante to kill Judah?"

Mercy snapped around and glared at Sidonia. "It's possible that Judah could kill Dante."

"That's hardly likely. You know as well as I do that Dante has not only his own unique individual powers, but he possesses the abilities inherent in all Dranirs. Judah would be no match for him."

"We don't know what powers Judah possesses, but they must be very great for Eve to be endowed with such incredible abilities."

Sidonia walked over to the desk and picked up the telephone. "Call Dante. Do it now."

Mercy stared at the phone, a war of uncertainty being waged inside her.

The study door burst open. Wearing her pink footed pajamas, Eve bounded into the room, wide-awake and all smiles. She ran to Mercy, grabbed her hand and said, "Come on. Let's go."

"Go where?" Mercy asked.

"To the front door to meet him. My daddy's coming. I let him in."

Chapter 9

"Judah is…?"

"Come on. He's almost here." Eve tugged on Mercy's hand.

"Bar that black devil from this house," Sidonia said.

Ignoring Sidonia's warning, Mercy went with Eve out into the hallway that led to the foyer. Sidonia followed, grumbling her fears aloud.

Just as they reached the foyer, Eve waved her little hand and the front door whooshed open. Judah Ansara, hand raised to knock, was standing on the front porch. Surrounded by darkness, with only moonlight illuminating his silhouette, he did indeed look like the black devil Sidonia had professed him to be.

"Daddy!" Eve cried as she released Mercy's hand and ran straight to her father.

Judah stepped over the threshold, the night wind entering with him, his long hair slightly disheveled, his gaze riveted to his daughter. Without hesitation, he dropped the suitcase he held, swept Eve up into his arms and kicked the door closed behind him.

Eve wrapped her arms around his neck and planted a kiss on his cheek. "I knew you'd come back. I knew you would."

Mercy watched in awed fascination at the exchange between father and daughter. Even without her empathic abilities, she would have been able to see the bond that had already begun forming between them. And knowing she was powerless to stop what was happening frightened her.

Eve's words echoed inside Mercy's head. *I was born for the Ansara.*

Unable to completely ignore Sidonia's constant mumbling, Mercy turned, gave the old nanny a withering glare and telepathically told her to hush. Sidonia glowered at Mercy and shook her head, but she reluctantly quieted before shuffling off and making her way slowly up the stairs.

Mercy took several tentative steps toward Judah. As if only then aware of Mercy's presence, he adjusted Eve so that she rested on his hip and looked at Mercy.

She couldn't explain her feelings, not even to herself. She despised Judah, and resented his presence here at the sanctuary and in her daughter's life. But at the same time, the very fact that he was here reassured her that he cared about Eve, that he was ready to help her protect their child. Their gazes locked for a brief instant; then Judah refocused on his daughter.

"I want you to promise me something," he said to Eve.

"What do you want me to promise?"

"Promise me that until I tell you it's all right, you won't use your mind to speak with anyone except your mother and me."

With her arms clinging about Judah's neck, Eve pulled back, cocked her head to one side and looked directly into her father's eyes. "He's a bad man, isn't he, Daddy? He wants to hurt us."

"Yes, he's a bad man." Judah frowned. "Now, give me your promise that—"

"I promise," Eve said.

As easily as that, she had agreed to do as Judah requested. Mercy sighed inwardly, fearing that Eve would never question her father's orders.

Judah set Eve on her feet. She grabbed his hand. He glanced down at her and smiled. "It's late. You should be in bed asleep."

"I was," Eve said. "But when I heard you calling to me, I woke up and let you in. That's what you wanted, wasn't it?"

Judah grunted. "Yes, it's what I wanted. But now I want you to go upstairs and hop back into bed." He glanced at Mercy. "Your mother and I have things we need to talk about."

"I want a promise, too. I want you to promise me that you won't fuss." Eve looked from one parent to the other. "Be nice, okay?."

"I'll be as nice to Mercy as she is to me," Judah said.

Eve smiled triumphantly, then eyed Judah's suitcase. "You'll be here in the morning when I get up, won't you?"

"I'll be here."

Eve bounced up the stairs, a bundle of happy energy.

Once Mercy and Judah were alone, she said, "I'll arrange for you to stay in one of the cabins."

"No, I'll stay here in the house." He approached her so quickly that she had no time to react until he grasped her upper arm. "I need to be close to Eve...and to you."

Mercy's heartbeat accelerated. *He's a master charmer,* she reminded herself. He would say whatever he thought she wanted to hear in order to get what he wanted. And she could never let herself forget for one moment that what he wanted was Eve.

"You can't stay here for very long." She forced herself to maintain eye contact, to prove to him that she wasn't afraid of him, that he had no emotional hold on her simply because she had given birth to his child. "Keeping your presence here a secret will be impossible for more than a day or two. There are other Raintree visiting the sanctuary. More than half the cottages are filled. Whatever you need to do to protect Eve from your brother, do it quickly and then leave."

"I'm afraid things are more complicated than that."

Mercy eyed him suspiciously.

Tightening his hold on her arm, he said, "You have every right to be afraid."

Mercy gazed into Judah's cold gray eyes and felt the hypnotic draw of his masculine power. The only way to free herself of this man and keep him from taking their daughter was to kill him. But not yet. Not until she knew that Eve would be safe from Judah's enemies.

He raked his gaze over her as if stripping her bare, then slowly released her. Mercy shivered.

"All you have to do is ask," Judah said, "and I'll give you what you want."

Tightening her hands into fists, Mercy willed herself not to strike out and wipe that cocky smirk off his face. "I want you dead," she told him.

"That wasn't a very nice thing to say to me."

"No it wasn't, but it's the truth."

"Only half the truth." His gaze caressed her roughly, creating an ache deep inside her. But he didn't physically touch her again. "Before you kill me, you want me to pleasure you first, to lay you beneath me and—"

"You're an egotistical bastard."

"And you're a woman hungry for what only I can give you."

"You mean no more to me than I do to you," Mercy told him. "If you weren't Eve's father—"

"But I am." He focused on her lips. "And you can never forget how it was between us the night you conceived my child. The excitement. The passion." He moved closer, until their bodies almost touched, never once removing his gaze from her lips. "I remember the way you whimpered and pleaded. The way you clung to me, shivering and moaning."

Involuntarily, as if manipulated by a force she couldn't control, Mercy reached out and laid her hand on Judah's chest, placing her palm over his heart.

"I taught you what true pleasure is," he said. "And you loved it." He glanced down at her hand. "You loved me."

Mercy jerked her hand away. "No, I never loved you," she lied—to herself and to him. She *had* loved him, if only for those few brief hours before she had learned who he really was. An Ansara.

Straightening his shoulders, Judah stood tall and aloof. "Your destiny was to give me a child. You've done that. You've served your purpose."

Mercy stared at him, suddenly realizing that she had somehow wounded him. He had switched from seductive charm to cruel indifference in a matter of seconds. Had she discovered the chink in Judah's protective armor? Male pride? Or was it something far more personal?

Storing that insight away for later use, she asked, "Will he try to harm Eve?"

"What?"

"Your brother. Will he come here to the sanctuary and try to get to Eve? That's why you're here, isn't it, to make sure he doesn't harm her?"

"My brother's days are numbered. It was inevitable that I'd be forced to kill him."

"I can't imagine hating my own brother enough to kill him."

"It's Cael's hatred that will force me to kill him. He's left me no choice."

"What about your parents? Can't they—"

"Our father is dead. And Cael's mother murdered mine."

"Oh."

Judah picked up his suitcase. "Show me to a room near Eve."

"The closest room to Eve's, other than the nanny's connecting room, is mine."

"Is that an invitation?" Judah's lips curved into a suggestive smile.

"Perhaps it is." Mercy's lips mimicked his, a smile without warmth or sincerity. "But if you come to my bed, you'll have to sleep with one eye open to prevent me from murdering you in your sleep."

"As tempting as the offer is…"

"There's a guest room at the end of the hall. You can stay there tonight."

"And tomorrow night?"

"You'll be gone," Mercy told him. "You and I will settle this matter tomorrow, and then you'll leave the sanctuary and never return."

As Judah studied her, she felt him probing her thoughts.

Don't even try, she warned him.

If I show you a little bit of mine, will you show me a little bit of yours?

No!

Aren't you the least bit curious? he asked.

No!

Liar.

"Come upstairs with me. I'll take you to your room," Mercy said aloud. "And when you wake later this morning, be sure to stay close to the house. If you venture too far away during the day, someone might see you and question who you are."

"Don't you think I could pass myself off as a Raintree?"

"Not with those ice-cold gray eyes of yours."

"Point well made," Judah said.

Mercy led him up the stairs to the second floor. He paused as they passed Eve's room, pushed open the door halfway and looked inside at his sleeping daughter.

"Why do you suppose her eyes are Raintree green?"

"Because she *is* Raintree," Mercy replied.

When Judah entered Eve's bedroom, Mercy followed but didn't try to stop him.

He halted beside the mattress, where Eve rested on her tummy, her arms thrown out on her pillow on either side of her head. He reached down and touched her long, pale hair.

Mercy held her breath. He lifted Eve's hair, then parted it with his fingers to reveal the distinct blue crescent moon birthmark that proclaimed her heritage. The brand of the Ansara.

Judah allowed Eve's hair to fall back into place. He caressed her little head, then turned, looked at Mercy and smiled. And for that one moment Mercy saw love in Judah's eyes. Love for his daughter.

Wednesday Morning, 8:45 a.m.

Judah's cell phone woke him from a sound sleep.

Damn! Whoever was calling had better have a good reason.

He grabbed the ringing phone from the nightstand, checked the caller I.D. and answered. "Claude?"

"Cael left Terrebonne this morning."

Judah sat straight up. "When?"

"An hour ago."

"Was he alone?"

"No."

"How many?"

"We're not sure, but Sidra says only three went with him."

"Who?" Judah asked.

"We believe he took Risa, Aron and Travis."

"They could be here in North Carolina by this afternoon."

"They can't enter the sanctuary, can they?" Claude asked.

"No, I don't think so. Not unless…"

"Unless what?"

"Unless they can somehow use Eve."

"Is that possible?"

"I have no way of knowing for sure. It's possible that her presence here has somehow compromised the shield that protects the sanctuary from the outside world."

"As you well know, that shield also protects the sanctuary from those of us who do not possess power equal to Mercy Raintree," Claude said. "If that shield has been weakened, then think how much easier it would be for us to take control of the sanctuary. With access to the Raintree home place, we could—"

"No." Judah lowered his voice. "Even with that advantage, we're still not ready to battle the Raintree."

"Not yet, but surely sooner than we had thought."

"Before we alter our plans for the timing of the next great battle, I have to make sure Eve is safe."

"That will mean killing Cael before he can harm her or find a way to use her against you."

"Yes, I know. But it's either face a possible civil war when his followers rebel or go to war with the Raintree before we're ready. Moving against Cael now is the lesser of two evils."

"Do you want me to send someone after Cael and the others?" Claude asked. "Or I can—"

"No, stay there. I need you in Terrebonne. I don't think Cael will show up here himself. He'll send Aron and Travis. When they arrive, I'll be waiting for them, and if they try to enter the sanctuary, I'll send what's left of them back to Cael in a gift box."

"Perhaps you should have waited before revoking the ancient decree," Claude said. "Once Cael heard what you'd done, he must have known there was no doubt that there was a mixed-blood child out there. A child of yours."

"I had no choice. If I hadn't revoked the ancient decree, countless Ansara would have demanded my daughter's death."

"I'm sorry I questioned your decision. If Sidra says the child must be protected, then we must protect her."

"Use whatever means necessary to keep Cael under surveillance. And it doesn't matter if knows he's being watched. In fact, all the better if does."

The door to Judah's bedroom swung open, and Eve sailed in, like a little morning sunbeam, bright and cheerful.

"Good morning, Daddy."

Crap! Judah slept in the nude; so here he was sitting on the side of the bed stark naked. Holding the cell phone to his ear with one hand, he grabbed the top sheet with his other and yanked it up and over, covering himself properly from waist to knees.

"Who are you talking to on the phone?" Eve bounced up on the bed and smiled at him.

He clutched the top sheet, holding it in place as she scooted closer. "Let me call you back," he told Claude.

"Don't hang up," Eve said. "I want to say hello to your friend."

Judah shook his head, then asked, "Where's your mother?"

Ignoring his question, Eve pulled herself up on her knees and reached for the cell phone. Judah gave her a stern look. She hesitated, then called loudly, "Hello, Claude. I'm Eve."

Claude chuckled. "Having a discipline problem?"

"She's quite the little psychic, isn't she, to have intuitively known my name," Claude said.

"I want to talk to Claude." Eve reached for the phone.

"My daughter's talents are quite impressive," Judah admitted. "Look, just say hello to her, will you?" He handed the phone to Eve.

She smiled. "Thank you, Daddy." She put the phone to her ear and said, "Hi there. You're calling from far away, aren't you?"

Judah telepathically tuned in to the conversation.

"Yes, I am," Claude replied "How did you know?"

"I know things. I have lots of powers, but my mother won't let me use most of them 'cause I can't always make them mind me." Eve lowered her voice to a whisper. "Just like I don't always mind her."

She giggled. Claude chuckled.

"I once knew a little boy like you. He possessed great power, but when he was your age, he couldn't control his powers any more than his father could control him."

Eve giggled again. "That was my daddy, wasn't it?" She looked at Judah with pure adoration in her eyes.

Damn those green Raintree eyes!

So like Mercy's.

"Say goodbye to Cousin Claude," Judah said.

"Goodbye, Cousin Claude. I'll see you very soon."

She handed Judah the phone, then snuggled up against him as he held the sheet in place over his lower body and put in a telepathic SOS to Mercy.

"Your little Eve is quite a charmer," Claude said to Judah. "Like father, like daughter, huh?"

"Could be."

"Why does she think she'll see me very soon?" Claude asked. "Have you told her that you're bringing her to Terrebonne?"

"No. The subject hasn't come up."

Eve tapped Judah on the shoulder. Turning his head to face her, he asked, "What?"

"Tell Cousin Claude I said that I'd see him very soon because he's coming here to the sanctuary."

Judah stared at his daughter.

"Why does she think—" Claude began.

"Eve Raintree, come here right this minute!" Mercy stood in the doorway, hands on hips, a parental scowl on her face.

Eve popped off the bed and raced over to her mother. "I got to talk to Cousin Claude. He's coming to the sanctuary very soon, and we'll get to meet him."

Mercy's gaze met Judah's, the concern and puzzlement in her eyes matching his.

"We'll talk later," Judah told Claude. "Keep me posted on that matter we discussed."

He didn't wait for a reply before ending the conversation and tossing his cell phone onto the nightstand. "Eve, why don't you go with your mother while I grab a shower and get dressed?"

Mercy's glance skimmed over Judah's naked chest and shoulders, appreciating his lean body, although she wasn't consciously aware of what she was doing. He returned the admiring glance. Mercy was certainly easy on the eye. The first moment he'd seen her seven years ago, he'd been struck by how beautiful she was. Even before he looked into her striking green eyes and realized she was Raintree, he had wanted her.

Clearing her throat, Mercy clasped Eve's hand. "It isn't polite to barge into someone's room without being invited." She looked at Judah. "I'm sorry she bothered you. It won't happen again." When she pulled on Eve's hand, Eve balked.

Judah grinned.

Eve yanked on Mercy's hand and motioned for her to bend down, which Mercy did. Eve whispered loudly, "I'll go to my room and play for a while. You and Daddy need to talk about me some more."

Mercy didn't have a chance to respond before Eve scurried out of the room, lightning fast, and closed the door behind her.

"She's quite a little bossy-butt, isn't she?" Judah said.

"She's a Raintree princess. Giving orders comes naturally to her, as it should. Unfortunately, she hasn't learned the art of diplomacy yet."

"Diplomacy is an overrated art. I prefer action to talk, and I expect my daughter is the same."

"Eve does like to have her own way. But she's young, and she'll learn that she can't always have everything she wants."

Judah whipped back the sheet that covered his naked body and rose from the bed. Mercy gasped. He grinned.

"If you see anything you like, you can have it. Right now."

Mercy stared at him, drinking him in, her gaze lingering over his erection. Then she looked him square in the eyes. "Sometimes what we want is very bad for us, and we learn from experience to avoid danger."

Judah moved toward her, one slow, provocative step at a time. She stood her ground, not backing away, keeping her eyes glued to his face.

When he reached out and caressed her cheek with the back of his hand, she closed her eyes. "You still want me."

She said nothing.

From that one brief touch, he sensed her desire. "I want you, too." He slipped his hand around her neck and lowered his head. She sighed. His breath mingled with hers. She opened her eyes, and for just an instant, unaware of her vulnerability, she let the barrier protecting her thoughts weaken.

My God!

He yanked her to him, pressing his sex intimately against her. If she were as naked as he was... "There hasn't been anyone else, has there? You're as much mine now as you were that night."

When he kissed her hungrily, she stood there rigid and unresponsive. But when he gentled the kiss, she whimpered. As he ravaged her mouth with tender passion, she pressed both hands against his chest and tried to shove him away.

Judah grabbed her and pulled her with him as he backed up against the bed. Taking her now would be almost like taking her for the first time. She was untouched by any other man, untutored, practically a virgin.

He toppled her into the bed and came down over her, holding her lifted arms out to either side as she struggled against his superior strength. Straddling her, his knees holding her hips in place, he stared down at her flushed face, and saw both desire and anger in her expression.

"Do you think I'll let you rape me?" she spat the words at him.

"It wouldn't be rape, and we both know it. You want me."

Breathing hard, Mercy narrowed her gaze and focused on him.

He bellowed in pain, and rolled off her and onto his side. Damn her! She'd sent a psychic punch straight to the most vulnerable area of his anatomy, the equivalent of kneeing him in the groin. While he caught his breath and mumbled curses, she got out of bed and walked to the door. Pausing, she glanced over her shoulder.

"I allow you to live only because of Eve," she said.

He shot a spray of fire arrows at her, their glowing tips outlining the space around her body. She extinguished them before they singed the door behind her.

"You may wish me dead, but you won't kill me." His cold stare pinned her to the spot. "And I won't kill you. Not until I've fucked you again."

Chapter 10

Judah had spent the entire morning with Eve. Under Mercy's supervision, of course. She had tried to stay in the background, at least part of the time, but she didn't trust Judah enough to leave her daughter alone with him. Watching father and daughter together exposed her to a side of Judah that she hated to admit existed. In his fascination with and adoration of his child, Judah seemed no different than any Raintree father. He played games with Eve, read to her, ate a mid-morning snack of fruit, cheese and crackers with her, and watched as she tested several of her powers. He instructed her on how to channel her abilities and use them properly. He praised her when she succeeded, and when she failed, he told her that she simply needed more practice.

Kindness, patience and the ability to love were not traits she would ever have associated with Judah Ansara. Since she had fled from his bed that morning seven years ago, she had thought of him as a charmer, a seducer, an uncaring, unfeeling son of a bitch. She had hated him for being an Ansara, a clan she had been taught from childhood were the spawn of the devil.

"Let's go on a picnic," Eve insisted when Sidonia had inquired if "that man" would be staying for lunch.

"Eve, honey, I don't think—" Mercy tried to object.

"A picnic is a great idea." Judah winked at Eve. "Why don't you and I raid the kitchen and put our picnic lunch together while your mother changes clothes."

Mercy glanced down at her attire: neat navy gabardine trousers, a tan cotton sweater, and sensible navy loafers. What was wrong with what she was wearing?

As if reading her mind—God, had he?—Judah said, "Wouldn't you be more comfortable in jeans or shorts?"

"Yeah, Mommy. Put on shorts like I've got on."

"I'll change before we leave." Mercy recognized defeat and accepted it, at least on this one issue. "For now, I'll go with y'all to kitchen and help fix our picnic lunch." In her peripheral vision, she caught a glimpse of Sidonia shaking her head disapprovingly.

Half an hour later, Mercy, in cut-off jeans and a red T-shirt, found herself sitting on an old quilt spread out under a huge oak tree in the middle of a nearby meadow. Not a single cloud marred the crisp blue sky. The afternoon June sun filtered through the tree branches, dappling golden shards of light around and over them.

Eve chattered away as she munched on her chicken salad sandwich and potato chips. Judah got a word in edgewise occasionally and seemed amused by his magpie daughter's endless babble. Several times during the meal, Mercy noticed Judah checking his wristwatch. And when he thought she wasn't looking, he stared at her. She pretended not to notice the way he was studying her.

After gobbling up two chocolate chip cookies and washing them down with milk from her thermos, Eve bounded up off the quilt and looked from Judah to Mercy. "I want to practice some more." She ran several yards away and said, "Watch, Mother. Look at me, Daddy."

Without waiting for permission, Eve concentrated very hard, and gradually her feet lifted off the ground a few inches. Then a foot. Two feet. Three feet.

"Be careful," Mercy cautioned.

"Daddy, what's this called?" Eve asked, spreading her arms and waving them up and down, as if they were wings.

"Levitation," Judah replied as Eve rose a good ten feet off the ground.

"Oh, that's right. Mother told me. Lev-i-ta-tion."

Leaning forward, intending to intervene and catch Eve if she fell, Mercy held her breath. If only Eve weren't so head-strong and adventurous.

"You're overprotective." Judah manacled Mercy's wrist. "Let her have some fun. She just wants our attention and our approval."

Mercy glowered at him. "Eve has been the center of my existence since the day she was born. But it's my job as her mother to approve of appropriate behavior and disapprove of what's inappropriate. And more than anything else, it is my duty to protect her, even if that means protecting her from herself."

Judah grunted. "You've lived in fear that the Ansara in her would come out, haven't you? Every time she's acted up, been unruly, thrown a temper tantrum, you've wondered if it was a sign of the innate evil side of her nature—the Ansara in her."

"I'm going higher," Eve called. "Watch me. Watch me!"

When Eve levitated a good twenty feet in the air, Mercy

jumped up and motioned to her daughter. "That's high enough, sweetheart. That was great." She clapped several times. "Now come back down."

"Do I have to?" Eve asked. "This is fun."

"Come down, and you and I will play a game," Judah said.

Eve came sailing down, slowly and carefully, as if showing Mercy that she shouldn't be concerned. The minute her feet hit the ground, Eve ran to Judah.

"What sort of game are we going to play?"

He eyed Mercy, his look daring her to interfere. "Have you ever played with fire?"

Eve snapped around and looked up at Mercy. "Mother says I'm too young to play with fire the way Uncle Dante does. She said when I'm older—"

"If one of your abilities is psychopyresis, the younger you learn to master that skill, the better," Judah said directly to Eve as he laid his hand on Mercy's shoulder. "My father began my lessons when I was seven."

"Oh, please, Mommy, please," Eve said. "Let Daddy give me lessons."

Any decision she made might prove to be the wrong one. She couldn't be certain that a negative response wouldn't be based on her resentment toward Judah for intruding in their lives.

Mercy nodded. "All right. Just this once." She glared at Judah. "You'll have to stay in control at all times. When she was two—" Mercy hesitated to share this information with him but finally did "—Eve set the house on fire."

Judah's eyes widened in surprise; then he smiled. "She was capable of doing that when she was two?"

"I'm very gifted," Eve said. "Mother says it's 'cause I'm special."

Judah beamed with fatherly pride as he placed his hands on Eve's little shoulders. "Your mother's right—you *are* special."

He grasped Eve's hand. "Come on, let's go over there by the pond and set off some fireworks. What do you say?"

Jiggling up and down with excitement, Eve grinned from ear to ear.

Despite having reservations, Mercy followed them to the pond. To watch. And to censor, if Judah allowed Eve to do anything truly dangerous…

Eve had exhausted herself practicing first one talent and then another, all under Judah's supervision. He realized that what Mercy had feared was Eve revealing to him just how truly powerful she was. And there was now no doubt in his mind that his daughter possessed the potential to be the most powerful creature on earth, more powerful than any other Ansara or Raintree.

He glanced down at Eve as she lay curled in a fetal ball on the quilt, deep in a restorative sleep. A feeling like none he'd ever known welled up from deep inside him. This was his child. Beautiful, smart and talented to the extreme. And she had instantly recognized him as her father and accepted him into her life without question.

He recalled Sidra's words: *If you are to save your people, you must protect the child.*

In that moment Judah realized that he would protect Eve for the sake of the Ansara, but more importantly, he would protect her because she was his child and he loved her.

He turned and gazed out over the meadow as he struggled to come to terms with what was happening to him. In his position as Dranir, he made instant life-and-death decisions without blinking an eye. His word was law. Like his father before him, he ruled supreme over his people. As a boy, he had known he would grow up to become the premiere Ansara, the most powerful member of the clan, the Dranir. He could be ruthless when the occasion called for it, but he believed he was always fair and just. He had lived his life by the Ansara code of honor, and had sworn his allegiance to his people the day he was crowned Dranir.

And he had accepted the burden that fate had placed on his shoulders: to lead his people in another great battle against the Raintree.

For most of Judah's life, Cael had been little more than a nuisance, a brother he neither loved nor hated. But gradually, Cael had proven himself to be a vile creature controlled by the evil insanity that had doomed his mother. And now he had to be stopped once and for all.

"Judah?" Mercy called quietly as she came up behind him.

He glanced back at her.

"We haven't talked about the reason you returned to the sanctuary," she said. "I've allowed you time with Eve. But you can't stay here. You can't be a part of her life."

"Eve is in danger from my brother. Until she's safe from Cael, I'll remain a part of her life, with or without your permission." Narrowing his gaze, he issued a warning. "Don't try to force me to leave."

"Or you'll do what?" Mercy marched straight up to Judah and stood in front of him. Defiant. Fearless.

He wanted to tell her that he found her foolhardy but brave. Powerful men quaked in their boots if they displeased him. He had broken arms and legs, snapped off heads and sent traitors to a fiery death. He was Dranir Judah. But he could hardly proclaim himself to be the ruler of a mighty clan, not when the Raintree believed the handful of Ansara left alive after the great battle had scattered to the four corners of the earth and, for the most part, been absorbed into the human population. It was best if she continued believing that Ansara such as he were few and far between, only a handful who still possessed their ancient powers. A talented Ansara here and there could be dealt with easily; but a reborn clan of mighty warriors would pose a threat.

"We shouldn't argue," Judah said. "We have the same goal—to protect Eve."

"The only difference in our goals is that I want to protect her from you as well as your brother."

"You really think I'm the devil incarnate, don't you?"

"You're an Ansara."

"Yes, I am. And proud of the fact. But you seem to believe I should be ashamed to belong to a noble, ancient race."

"Noble? The Ansara? Hardly."

"The Raintree don't have a monopoly on nobility," Judah told her.

"If you believe that the Ansara are noble, then our definitions of the word must differ greatly."

"Loyalty to one's family and friends and clan. Using our abilities to provide for and protect the people for whom we are responsible. Revering the elderly ones who possess great knowledge. Defending ourselves against our enemies."

Mercy stared at him, a puzzled expression on her face. Had he said too much? Did she suspect he was more than just a single Ansara with power equal to any Raintree? Was she wondering just how many more like him were out there?

"The Ansara used their powers to take whatever they wanted—from humans and Raintree alike. Allowed to go unchecked, your people would have subjugated everyone on earth instead of living in harmony with the Ungifted as we Raintree do now and have done for thousands of years."

"You Raintree took it upon yourselves to become the guardians of the human race, and in doing so, you chose those who are mere mortals over those of your own kind. That decision locked our two clans into what seemed like an eternal war."

"The Ansara are not our kind," Mercy said emphatically. "Even your ancient Dranirs recognized that fact. That's why they issued the decree to kill any mixed-breed children."

I have revoked that decree! But Judah couldn't tell Mercy what he'd done, didn't dare reveal to her that he was the Ansara Dranir.

"Are you saying you agree with the decree?" Judah asked, deliberately baiting her. "Do you think mixed-breed children should be put to death?"

"No, of course not! How can you ask me such a question?"

"Eve is Raintree," Judah said. "She is your kind. But she is also Ansara, which means she is my kind. Her bloodline goes back over seven thousand years to those from whom both the Ansara and the Raintree came. We were once the same people."

"And for that reason, Dranir Dante and Dranira Ancelin did not annihilate all Ansara after *The Battle* two hundred years ago. The few Ansara who remained were allowed to live, in hopes that they would learn to coexist in the world with the Ungifted and find the humanity they had once shared with the Raintree thousands of years ago." She looked Judah in the eyes. "But knowing you, I see that that hope was not fulfilled. You and your brother hate each other. His mother killed your mother. And he intends to kill you. He wants to harm Eve, and you want to take her away from me. The Ansara are still violent and cruel and uncaring and—"

Judah grabbed her by the shoulders. Mercy quieted immediately, glaring at him, her rigid stance challenging him. "You judge me without knowing me," he told her. "My half brother isn't typical of our kind, nor was his mother. Cael is insane, just as she was."

When he felt Mercy relax, he eased his hold, but he didn't release her. They stood there for several minutes, looking at each other, each trying to sense what the other was thinking.

Mercy wouldn't budge, keeping her defensive barriers in place. He did the same, not daring to risk her realizing who he really was.

"Because of Eve, I'd like to believe you," Mercy said. "I'd like to know that the Ansara part of her will never turn her into someone totally alien to me. I know she's high-strung and mischievous, but—" Mercy swallowed hard. "What you did to me was cruel and uncaring. Can you deny that?"

Judah ran his hands down her arms, from shoulders to wrists; then he let her go.

"At the time, I didn't consider it cruel. I wanted you. You wanted me. We had sex several times. You gave me pleasure. I gave you pleasure. No promises were exchanged. I didn't declare my undying love."

Mercy's expression hardened; her face paled. "No, but I told you that I loved you." She bowed her head as if the sight of him caused her pain. "You must have found that amusing. Not only had you taken the Raintree princess's virginity, but she told you that she loved you."

Judah reached out and tilted her chin, forcing her to look up at him. "I knew you weren't in love with me. You were just in love with the way I'd made you feel. Really good sex can do that to a woman when it's a new experience for her."

"If I had known you were Ansara…"

"You'd have run like hell." He grunted. "Actually, that's what you *did* do when you found out, wasn't it?" He studied her briefly, then asked, "Why didn't you abort your pregnancy? Why didn't you just get rid of my baby?"

"She was my baby, too. I could never have…"

Mercy went still as a statue. Her eyes glazed over, then rolled back in her head as she shivered. Judah realized she was experiencing some kind of trance.

"Mercy?" He had seen something similar to this with

Ansara psychics, seers and empaths. He didn't touch her. He simply waited.

As quickly as she had gone under, she emerged. "Someone is testing the shield around the sanctuary. And he's not alone."

Judah hadn't thought his brother was foolish enough to actually show up at the sanctuary, knowing full well that he was here and would never let him get anywhere near Eve. But he could hear Cael calling to him. Not a challenge; simply a preliminary warning.

"It's Cael," Judah said.

"Your brother? How do you know for sure that—"

"I know."

"We have to stop him! He's trying to connect with Eve while she's sleeping."

"He's playing games," Judah told her. "He's trying to show me how vulnerable Eve is."

Mercy grabbed his forearm. "Just how vulnerable is she? How powerful is your brother?"

"Powerful enough to cause trouble." Judah removed her hand from his arm and gave it a reassuring squeeze. "You stay here and protect Eve by any method necessary. Conjure up the strongest spell you know that will guard her from Cael's attempts to enter her dreams. My brother possesses the power of oneiromancy. He can telepathically enter someone's dreams and affect their well-being."

Mercy clutched his hand. "What are you going to do?"

"I'm going to have a talk with Cael."

"I should go with you to—"

"I don't need you." Judah pulled away from her. "I can deal with my brother. You take care of Eve."

"You'll need transportation if you're going outside to meet him. There's an old truck parked in the garage. Take it," Mercy told him. "The keys are in the ignition."

They shared a moment of complete understanding, bound together in a common cause that superseded any clan rivalry or personal animosity.

Mercy reinforced the shield that protected Eve from outside forces, then placed a special guard around her dreams. Finally she cast a sleeping spell over her daughter, something mild that would keep her subdued for a short period of time without leaving any aftereffects. There was no way to know what Eve might do if she thought her parents were in danger. Then, with the utmost gentleness, Mercy lifted Eve into her arms and carried her child back to the house.

Sidonia, who was removing heavy winter quilts from the clothesline out back, looked up and saw them. She dropped the sunned quilts into the large wicker basket at her feet and scurried toward Mercy.

"What's wrong with her?" Sidonia asked. "Is she hurt? Did he—"

"She's fine. Just sleeping. I cast a mild sleeping spell over her." Mercy held out her child to Sidonia. "Here, take her, then go inside and stay there with her until I come back. I've made sure that she's well protected, but... Guard her with your life."

Sidonia took Eve into her arms, then looked squarely at Mercy. "What's happening? Where are you going?"

"To join Judah. His brother has come to the sanctuary. He's gone out to meet him, to stop him from carrying out the ancient decree."

"Dear God! That monstrous edict to kill babies." Sidonia gazed pleadingly at Mercy. "Call the others that are here at the sanctuary to help you. Don't trust Judah Ansara to save our little Eve."

"Take her inside now," Mercy said. "And don't alert anyone else. Judah and I can handle this."

"Oh, my poor girl." Sidonia tsked-tsked sadly. "You actually trust him, don't you?"

"I—I don't know, but…yes, I believe he'll protect Eve from his brother. I believe he cares for Eve as much as an Ansara is capable of caring."

Mercy rushed past Sidonia and into the house. She retrieved the keys to her Escalade from a bowl on the kitchen counter, then ran back outside and straight to the garage. She slid behind the wheel of her SUV, started the engine, backed out and headed up the road.

When she reached the entrance to the sanctuary, she saw the old truck parked just inside the iron gates, but she didn't see Judah. Her heartbeat accelerated. She pulled up behind the truck and parked, then jumped out and stopped dead in her tracks. Judah had gone outside. He was standing just beyond the closed gates, his back to her. Four strangers— three men and one woman—stood across the road, all focused on Judah. The woman, probably in her mid-thirties, stood apart from the other three. Two young men, little more than teenagers, flanked the man in the middle, the tall, lean blonde with eyes as silvery cold as Judah's.

Cael. The murderous half brother.

Suddenly the woman noticed Mercy. They exchanged heated glares, and the woman zeroed in on Mercy, sending a quick telepathic zing in her direction. Mercy intercepted the mediocre attempt, added a touch more power to it and returned it to its sender. The zing knocked the woman backward so strongly that she barely managed to keep her balance.

"I see you're not alone," Cael said to Judah, who didn't move a muscle. "Your Raintree whore seems to think you need help."

Judah stood fast, not responding in any way.

Mercy walked down the road and up to the gate. She stood slightly to Judah's left, only the closed gates and less than five feet separating her from him.

"The child isn't safe," Cael said. "I can breach the shield surrounding this place, so that means others can, too. As parents, you should be watchful. You never know when someone might try to harm Eve."

"Anyone who tries to hurt my daughter will have to face me," Judah said.

Cael smiled. Cold, calculating and sinister. And filled with a bloodlust unlike anything Mercy had ever sensed in another being. She realized that this man was as unlike Judah as he was unlike Dante or Gideon. He was what she had believed all Ansara to be: pure evil.

"I don't suppose you'd like to invite me in and introduce Eve to her uncle Cael?" Judah's brother made direct eye contact with Mercy for a moment. "I see why you screwed her, brother. She's remarkably lovely. Which did you enjoy more—taking a Raintree princess's virginity or making a fool of her?"

"Leave this place," Judah said. "If you don't—"

Cael roared like a beast, the rage inside barely controlled. Ten foot flames shot up from the paved road between him and Judah. Mercy moved to open the gates, but she heard Judah telepathically telling her to stay where she was as he drew back his fist, opened it into a claw and whirled his hand in the air. From out of nowhere rain poured down in one spot, onto the flames Cael had created. The water extinguished the fire, leaving only whiffs of gray smoke.

Apparently Judah had the ability not only to create fire but to extinguish it. Dominion over fire was a talent possessed by only a few Raintree, her brother Dante to name one.

"We can end this here and now," Judah told his brother. "Is that what you want?"

Cael smiled again. "Not yet. But soon." He looked at Mercy again. "Did he tell you that he killed one of his own to save your life?"

Then, laughing, he turned and walked away toward a black limousine parked down the road. The others followed him like obedient puppy dogs lapping at their master's feet.

Judah didn't move from the spot nor did he speak until the limousine disappeared from sight. Then he turned and faced Mercy, the closed gate still between them. "Don't ask," he said.

"How can I not ask? I know someone tried to kill me Sunday, and you stopped them. How did you know? Why would you save me?"

"I told you not to ask." Judah stared at the gate. "I could enter the sanctuary without your help, but it would expend a great deal of my energy. And I don't want to disturb Eve."

Mercy opened the gate and held out her hand. Judah took her hand in his and stepped through the protective shield that separated the Raintree sanctuary from the outside world. Once inside, he didn't release her. Instead, he pulled her up to him, his gaze boring into her, chiseling through the barriers that protected her mind from intrusions. She didn't try to stop him, knowing that as he worked so feverishly to expose her thoughts, he left his own thoughts and feelings unguarded.

She sensed great worry, a deep and true concern for those he loved. Loved? Was Judah actually capable of love?

"Does that surprise you?" he asked, apparently realizing that she had picked up on his emotions.

Once again shielding herself and ending their mental connection, Mercy jerked free and turned away from him. "I want you to leave as soon as possible. You can't stay. If the others find out you're here, you won't be safe."

"You can't protect Eve now without my help," Judah said.

She whirled back around. "Then go after your brother

and…and do whatever you need to do to protect our daughter. I don't understand why you didn't kill him just now."

"Because he wasn't alone," Judah said. "I could have easily dispensed with the three he had with him, but…" He hesitated, as if uncertain whether or not to share the information with her. "There were ten others—a tiny band of Ansara who are loyal to my brother—nearby, waiting for Cael to summon them. If I had challenged him to a death-fight, I would have been at a distinct disadvantage."

"I could have called for help," Mercy said, then gasped when the absurd reality of the situation hit her. "If I had called in the Raintree who are here at the Sanctuary, you would have been the enemy to them as well as to your brother."

"I had no desire to be a lone man against a small group of Ansara on one side and Raintree on the other."

"So, what do we do now?"

"We keep Eve safe."

Chapter 11

Cael and his small band of Ansara warriors arrived at the private compound in a rural area off Interstate 40, between Asheville and the Raintree sanctuary, well before sunset. While the others ate and drank and screwed, psyching themselves up for the battle that was only days away, Cael closed himself off in his private quarters and contemplated his next move. He had leased this property over two years ago, once he had decided on a date for the Ansara attack on the Raintree home place. Slowly, cautiously, secretly, he had combed the world in search of renegade Ansara who would be willing to do his bidding and fight at his side on the chosen day. His army now exceeded a hundred warriors, small in comparison to the number Judah commanded, but adequate for the attack Cael had planned. By Saturday, they would all have arrived here at this secluded retreat, armed and ready for battle.

The element of surprise was essential to the success of his

strategy. He would lead an army of Ansara warriors against a handful of visiting Raintree and the lone guardian, Princess Mercy, the Keeper of the Sanctuary. On the day of the summer solstice. Before other Raintree could be summoned, word would already have reached Terrebonne, and all the Ansara warriors would have no choice but to join Cael in the final great battle between the two warring clans. This time the Ansara would be the victors, and they would decimate the Raintree. He would personally kill Judah and his bastard child, Eve; then he would see to it that every Raintree on earth was put to death.

He would rule supreme. His people would hail him as the conquering hero. The Ungifted would become the Ansaras' slaves and be forced to worship at his feet.

Thoughts of the future were indeed sweet. Victory. Annihilation of the Raintree. Judah slaughtered. The subjugation of mankind.

I will be a true god.

But only when Judah is dead.

Cael cursed loudly as he rammed psychic bolts through the wall, venting his frustration over years of waiting to claim what was rightfully his.

Keeping Judah in the dark about the exact date he planned to strike the sanctuary was vital to his success. His brother might suspect him of treason and probably knew he intended to go to war with the Raintree on his own timetable, but without actual proof, Judah couldn't bring him before the council and demand his execution.

How auspicious that divine providence had provided such a perfect distraction—little Eve Raintree—to keep his brother's mind occupied. Judah was the possessive, protective type. A little too noble for Cael's taste. Like his mother, Seana, that insipid empath their father had chosen as his

Dranira, Judah was weak. He chose the old Ansara methods in dealing with others only when all else failed. He was far more businessman than warrior.

Liar! Cael's inner voice taunted. *You wish that Judah was not a true Ansara warrior, but our father trained him well in all things. A Dranir had to be a warrior, a businessman, a true leader capable of judging and executing.*

No matter. His brother might be a worthy opponent in combat, but he, Prince Cael, would prove himself superior.

Stay where you are, with your Raintree bitch, and guard little Eve day and night, dear brother. Concentrate solely on keeping her safe from me. And all the while you neglect matters on Terrebonne, I will be assembling my army and spreading anarchy among the Ansara.

We strike the sanctuary on *Alban Heruin*, when the sun is most powerful and I, too, will be filled with my ultimate strength. I will kill your child and your woman first, so I can have the pleasure of seeing you watch them die. And then I will kill *you*.

"You can't allow him to stay here!" Sidonia shouted. "No good will come of it."

"He needs to be here to protect Eve," Mercy explained.

"If he's going to kill his brother anyway, why doesn't he just go ahead and do it?"

"Lower your voice. Eve might overhear you."

Sidonia snorted. "Not likely. She's too wrapped up in spending time with her daddy to be eavesdropping."

Keeping her voice low and calm, Mercy said, "Cael has a group of friends who guard his back, so until Cael issues Judah a one-on-one challenge, which Judah believes will happen soon, the wisest course is for Judah not to hunt his brother down."

"For all you know he's playing you for a fool. Again."
Sidonia's gaze met Mercy's. "This could be some sort of ploy
to ingratiate himself with you, to show himself in a favorable
light, when all he's doing is buying time to bond with Eve so
that when he decides to take her away, she'll go with him willingly."

"Judah *is* bonding with Eve. And he does plan to take her
from me," Mercy said. "But his hatred for his brother and
Cael's threats to Eve are real. I know it."

Sidonia nodded. "You've sensed this, and you are certain?"

"Yes."

Knowing that Mercy would never lie to her about such a
vitally important matter, Sidonia reluctantly agreed. "Very
well. Keep him here, and somehow we'll pass him off as a
human visitor when the others ask. For now, you and he will
stand against his brother. Then later, when the brother is no
longer a threat, you'll have to fight Judah to save Eve."

"I know."

"When that time comes, you'll need Dante and Gideon."

"Probably, but not now. Not yet."

"When? You mustn't wait until it's too late."

"Eve will know when Judah decides to take her. She'll tell
me when it's time."

Sidonia's gaze held numerous questions.

"Eve can't leave the sanctuary without my knowing in
advance what is going to happen," Mercy said.

Sidonia gasped. "No, tell me you didn't!"

"I did. I had no choice."

"But when did you do it? You would have needed another
Raintree to help."

"Eve helped me. When she was only hours old and completely dependent on me. I had no way of knowing if Judah
would somehow realize I was carrying his child and come

after me—either to kill her or take her. I used the old binding spell because I had no other choice. I had to be able to know at all times where Eve was."

"If only you had told your brothers who your baby's father was before she was born, we wouldn't have to deal with him or his brother now. They would have hunted Judah down and killed him." Sidonia squinted as she looked soulfully at Mercy. "You poor child. I know. I know. You loved him. You didn't want him dead."

"Enough! We've had this discussion too many times."

"You *still* love him, don't you?"

"Of course not!"

Sidonia grabbed Mercy's arm. "What if he wanted you as well as Eve? Would you go with him?"

"Shut up! Stop talking nonsense." Mercy stormed out of the kitchen and through the house, stopping only when she reached the open front door and heard Eve's laughter.

She eased open the screen door and stepped out onto the porch. Twilight had settled in around the valley, a pinkish orange glow in the evening sky, a haze of translucent clouds hugging the mountains surrounding them. Out in the middle of the grassy green yard, Judah stood holding a glass jar, holes punched in the metal lid, and watched while Eve chased fireflies. Several little captives already blinked brightly inside the jar.

Eve zeroed in on another lightning bug and caught it between her cupped palms. "I got him! I got him!" She ran to Judah, who opened the jar's lid a fraction, just enough so that Eve could drop her hostage into the glass prison.

When Eve sensed Mercy's presence, she looked at her and smiled. "Daddy's never caught lightning bugs before, not even when he was a little boy. I had to explain that I wouldn't hurt them, and that after I see how many I can catch, I'll let them all go free."

"Well, I believe it's emancipation time," Mercy said. "It's after eight. You need to take a bath before you go to bed, my little princess."

"No, not yet. Please, just another hour." Whining, Eve put her hands together in a prayer-like gesture. "Daddy and I are having so much fun." She turned to Judah. "Aren't we, Daddy? Tell her. Tell her that I don't have to go to bed right now."

Judah handed Eve the jar filled with fireflies. "Let them go."

Eve tilted her head to one side and stared up at him. "I guess this means I have to do what Mother told me to do."

He playfully ruffled her hair. "I guess it does."

Once again, Judah's actions showed him to be like any other father. How was it possible that an Ansara could be so similar to a Raintree? Perhaps Sidonia was right. Judah could be playing her for a fool, showing her what she wanted to see in him. A false impression.

Reluctantly, Eve unscrewed the lid and shook the jar gently, encouraging the lightning bugs to fly free. When the last one escaped, she walked up on the porch, handed the jar to Mercy and put on her sad face, the one she used to evoke pity.

Heaving a deep sigh, Eve said dramatically, "I'm ready to go—if I have to."

Mercy barely managed not to smile. "Go inside and let Sidonia help you with your bath. I'll be up later to kiss you good-night."

"Daddy, too?"

"Yes," Judah and Mercy replied simultaneously.

As soon as Eve went into the house, letting the screen door slam loudly behind her, Mercy set the empty Mason jar on the porch and stepped down into the yard. Judah looked up at the sky and the towering hills surrounding them, then settled his gaze on her.

"Nice evening," he said. "It's certainly peaceful here in these mountains. Don't you ever get bored?"

"I stay busy," she told him.

"Healing the bodies and hearts and minds of your fellow Raintree?"

"Yes, if and when I can. It's my job as the Keeper of the Sanctuary to use my gifts as an empathic healer to help those who come to me." Her gaze met his and held. "But then, you already knew that, didn't you? You knew the day we met that I was the appointed one."

"The moment I saw your eyes, I knew you were Raintree. I managed to see into your thoughts enough to learn you were a princess and that you were slated to become some sort of guardian," Judah admitted. "I picked up only fragments of thought before I realized that, for the most part, your thoughts were shielded."

"You used a shield, too. A powerful shield. I just didn't realize it at the time," she said. "I thought it strange that I couldn't read you at all, that when I touched you, I sensed only that I could trust you. You blocked me completely and then sent me a deceptive message."

"I did what was necessary in order to get what I wanted."

"And you wanted me."

"Very much."

Why did he make his reply sound as if he were talking about the present and not the past? Even if he did want her now, he wanted only the use of her body, just as he had that night seven years ago.

No, that wasn't the complete truth. He had wanted more than her body that night. He had wanted to take a Raintree princess's innocence and make her fall in love with him. He had done both.

"Why didn't you use protection that night?" Mercy asked.

His mouth curved upward in a sarcastic smirk. "Why didn't *you?*"

"I could say that it was because I was young and stupid and got carried away with feelings I'd never experienced. But the truth is that when I knew I was going to spend the night with you, give myself to you… I tried to conjure up a temporary protection spell. Apparently it didn't work."

"Apparently."

"So what's *your* excuse?"

"I thought I was protected," he admitted.

Her eyes widened. "You used a sexual protection spell, too?"

He nodded. "Sort of. A long-term gift that my cousin Claude and I have been exchanging since we were teenagers. It worked perfectly with Ansara and human women."

"If we were both protected, then how—oh, my God! Sexual protection spells and gifts must not work when a Raintree mates with an Ansara."

"At least not in our case," Judah agreed.

"I don't understand. They should have worked. We should have been protected."

"The only explanation I can think of is that Eve was meant to be."

"Are you saying you believe that a higher power ordained Eve's conception?"

"It's possible. Perhaps she was born for a specific reason."

Judah sounded so certain, as if he knew something she didn't. But that wasn't possible, was it? He might be a talented Ansara, with many abilities, but he was not a seer who could look into the future.

"Did someone tell you that Eve was destined to—"

"No one knew about Eve's existence, except for you and Sidonia, until three days ago. How could anyone have told me anything about her?"

"Yes, of course."

"She's an amazing child, our little Eve."

When he stared at Mercy, visually stripping her bare as he so often did, she glanced away. "If by chance you encounter any other Raintree while you're here, tell them your name is Judah Blackstone, and that you're an old friend of mine from college. We've allowed visitors to come to the sanctuary before, friends of my family who needed the peace and solitude the home place offers. No one will question you further."

"And if Eve tells someone that I'm her father, how will we handle that?"

"I'll speak to her and explain that, for the present, we need to keep that fact our little secret."

"Judah Blackstone, huh?"

"It's as good a name as any." She turned and headed toward the front porch steps. "I'm going up to say good-night to Eve. Are you coming with me?"

"Yes, I'm coming with you." He followed her onto the porch and into the house. Once inside the foyer, he asked, "Did you have an old boyfriend named Blackstone? Do I need to be jealous?"

Taken off guard by his question, she snapped around and scowled at him.

Judah chuckled. "Don't Raintree have a sense of humor?"

"I don't see anything humorous in our relationship. You and I are enemies who find ourselves temporarily bound together in a common cause—to save our daughter. But once she is no longer in danger…" Mercy walked away from him, heading for the stairs.

He came up behind her and clutched her elbow. She stopped dead still but didn't look back at him. Now, as in the past, his touch heated her blood, warming her as if a fire had been lit deep inside her. She tilted her head and glanced over her shoulder. He was too close, his chest brushing against her back.

He leaned his head low and whispered, "When Eve is no longer in danger, you know that you and I can't share her. She will become either Ansara or Raintree, the outcome decided by which of us kills the other. That's what you were thinking, wasn't it?"

"If you would swear to go away and leave us alone, to never contact Eve again, it wouldn't have to end that way. Eve wouldn't have to grow up knowing her mother killed her father."

"Or that her father killed her mother."

Mercy closed her eyes and took a deep breath. Judah had no qualms about killing her to obtain custody of his child. If only she were as heartless. If only she could kill him without regrets.

"My sweet Mercy." Judah snaked his arm around her waist and jerked her roughly against him, her back to his chest, her buttocks to his erection.

No, this couldn't be. *Fight your feelings,* she told herself. *Don't succumb to the desire eating you alive, screaming inside you to give yourself to him.*

"I find the fact that you are capable of both saving lives and taking them extremely exciting," Judah told her, his breath hot on her neck. "You, my love, are quite the paradox, a healer and a warrior." His lips grazed her neck with a series of seductive kisses. "You love me and you hate me. You want me to live and yet you are willing to kill me to save Eve." His tongue replaced his lips as he painted a damp path from her collarbone to her ear.

Immobilized by her own need, Mercy closed her eyes, savoring this wicked man's touch. His hand crept upward from the front of her waist to her breast. She shuddered as pure electrical sensation shot through her body. While he kneaded her breast through the barriers of her blouse and bra, his fingertips worked against her nipple.

Whimpering, Mercy rested the back of her head against his shoulder.

Put a stop to this now, the sensible part of her brain demanded. But the needs of her woman's body overruled common sense.

While his tongue circled her ear, Judah drove his hand between Mercy's thighs and stroked her intimately through the soft cotton of her slacks and panties. "You belong to me. I own you, Mercy Raintree. You're mine."

Mercy cried out, fighting his hypnotic hold over her and her own wanton needs.

Breaking free, she fled, running away from a temptation almost too powerful to deny.

Midnight. The witching hour. And Mercy *was* bewitched. Entranced by memories of a chance meeting seven years ago. She had never admitted to another soul how those exhilarating hours haunted her, how often, when she was alone at night, the image of Judah Ansara appeared to her. She had never hated anyone the way she hated him. Or loved anyone so deeply and passionately. In all this time, she hadn't been able to reconcile her divided feelings. Love and hate. Fear and longing. Even now, she wanted him. Knowing he was an Ansara. Knowing that he didn't love her, had never loved her. Knowing he planned to fight her—to the death—for Eve.

If only she hadn't insisted on that vacation alone. One week, all to herself, without Dante and Gideon, without Raintree friends guarding her, out from under Sidonia's watchful eye. Had that been too much to ask? Aunt Gillian had thought Mercy's request quite reasonable. As the aged guardian of the sanctuary, she'd known only too well about the great demands on Mercy's time and talents that lay ahead for her when she became the keeper of the home place.

A great empath herself, Gillian had gifted Mercy with the ability not to sense other people's thoughts and emotions on a deep level while on her vacation. Like many other gifts, that one had a nine-day shelf-life.

And so Mercy had gone out into the world alone, ready to experience life without the curse of being bombarded by the thoughts and emotions of everyone around her. For those nine days, she wouldn't be a Raintree princess. She wouldn't be a talented empath. She could enjoy being young and pretty and unguarded.

Mercy had no way of knowing that with her abilities muted, she would be unable to recognize danger when it swept her off her feet. Literally. A waiter by the pool at the resort where she was vacationing had lost his footing and plunged into a guest, who in turn set off a chain reaction, sending tables, drinks, chairs and people flying. From out of nowhere, someone had swooped Mercy up into his arms, saving her from becoming one more domino-effect casualty.

Wearing a bikini for the first time in her life, Mercy had felt naked as her flesh had pressed against the overpoweringly masculine chest belonging to the man who had rescued her. After grabbing him around the neck and clinging to him, she had gazed into his eyes—as cold and gray as a winter sky. He hadn't set her on her feet immediately, but had held her, smiling broadly, the warmth of his big, hard body heating her inside and out.

Pressing her fingertips against her temples, Mercy closed her eyes and huffed loudly. "Get out of my head, damn you, Judah Ansara."

She had tried to erase him from her memory, had even been tempted to use a spell to eliminate all thoughts of him. But she hadn't dared go to such extreme lengths. Only she and Sidonia knew that Eve was half Ansara, and Sidonia alone could not have protected Eve.

Mercy tossed back the sheet and light blanket covering her, then got out of bed, opened the door and crept quietly across the hall. Eve's door, as always, had been left open. Mercy stepped over the threshold and stood there watching her daughter sleep.

If I had never met Judah... If we hadn't been lovers...

Eve wouldn't exist.

She heard Judah's voice inside her head. *Eve was meant to be.*

If she believed nothing else Judah had ever said, she believed that. Their daughter's life was preordained. But for what reason?

The fact that Mercy had conceived during their one night of passionate lovemaking was practically a miracle, what with her having used a temporary sexual protection spell and Judah having been gifted with sexual protection by his cousin. With double protection, conception should have been impossible.

Gifted by his cousin. *Gifted!*

My God! Why hadn't she immediately realized the implication of the word the moment Judah had said "a long-term gift that my cousin Claude and I have been exchanging since we were teenagers"?

In the Raintree clan, only royals had the power to gift charms. Why would it be any different with the Ansara? The ability was ancient, from the time of their eldest ancestors who had lived thousand of years ago, from a time when the Raintree and Ansara had been one.

Was Judah a royal Ansara?

If he was, then she had far more to fear than just a mere Ansara male wanting to claim his child. If Judah was a prince...

No, he couldn't be. The Ansara were no longer a great clan

with a powerful Dranir and Dranira, with a royal family of children, siblings, aunts, uncles and cousins. Perhaps Judah possessed royal blood, and had the Ansara won *The Battle* two hundred years ago, he might today be a mighty prince. That would explain him being able to gift charms and exchange them with a cousin.

But she didn't intend to leave anything to chance. Tomorrow she would confront him with her doubts. For Eve's sake, she had to find out the truth.

Chapter 12

Mercy waited until after breakfast before requesting a private conversation with Judah. To keep Eve occupied and away from the house, she had sent her daughter with Sidonia to take fresh baked goods to the visitors occupying the cabins. Although the kitchens in all the units were well stocked, Sidonia enjoyed sharing her homemade breads, muffins, cakes and pies with their guests. Being a gregarious, curious child, Eve liked nothing better than to meet various members of the Raintree tribe, so this Thursday morning outing with her nanny was a real treat for her.

Alone in the study with Judah, Mercy braced herself for the inevitable magnetic pull that drew her to him. If she denied their sexual connection, she would be lying to herself. What she could and would do was fight that attraction. During the years since she had seen him, she had convinced herself that what she'd felt from him during their brief time together hadn't been as passionately exciting as she remembered. But those moments on the stairs last night had proven otherwise. The extraordinary chemistry between them could still make her weak and vulnerable, two things a Raintree never wanted to be around an Ansara.

"Go ahead. Get it over with." Judah's eyes twinkled with mischievous delight, his expression similar to Eve's when she was up to no good.

Mercy squared her shoulders. "Just what do you think I'm going to say or do?"

"I assume you're going to rip into me about what happened between us last night. So go ahead and tell me that you won't allow it to happen again. Lay down the law. Show me who's boss."

She would like nothing better than to wipe that cocky grin off his face and was tempted to give him a psychic slap. But that would only prove how easily he could rile her. She certainly had no intention of giving him the satisfaction.

Ignoring his deliberate attempt to get a reaction, she asked, "How is it possible that you and your cousin are able to gift charms?"

"What?"

Well, that had wiped the smile off his face, hadn't it? She had surprised him with her question.

"Are you talking about the sexual protection that Claude and I…?"

"I'm talking about the fact that only royals have the power to gift charms. Are you a royal? If so, that means there's an Ansara royal family, right?"

He didn't respond immediately, which bothered her. He was giving serious thought to his reply. Thinking up a plausible lie? she wondered.

"You must know that there's always been a royal Ansara

family. One of the old Dranir's daughter's, Princess Melisande, survived *The Battle,* married, and had children and grandchildren and so forth. To answer your other questions, yes, Claude and I have royal blood, or so our parents told us."

"Are you a prince?"

"No."

Was he lying to her? Did she dare believe him?

"Where is your home?" she asked.

"Why the sudden interest in my personal life? If you're asking for Eve's sake, then I can tell you I'm strong, healthy, mentally sound and possess all the powers of a royal."

"Why are you reluctant to tell me where you live?"

"I live all over the world. I'm an international businessman, an offshore banker, with interests in numerous countries."

"And the other Ansara—how many are there? Where do the Dranir and Dranira reside? Are your people scattered throughout the world as we Raintree are?"

"What few of us there are keep a low profile," Judah told her. "We are not prepared to confront the Raintree and do nothing to call attention to ourselves."

"But you did, didn't you? Seven years ago, you deliberately seduced a Raintree princess. I'd say that's calling attention to yourself."

"But at the time, you didn't know I was Ansara. And if you had not conceived my child, you never would have known."

What he said was true enough and yet a sense of foreboding clenched her stomach muscles, creating a sick feeling in her gut. Was it possible that in only two hundred years, the Ansara had rebuilt their clan enough to actually pose a threat to the Raintree? Surely not. If the Ansara were once again a mighty people, the Raintree would know. One of the Raintrees' many psychics would have sensed the Ansaras' escalating power. Unless... Unless they had deliberately shielded

themselves from detection with a mass protection spell...
But was that even possible?

"What about your Dranir and Dranira?" Mercy asked.

"So many questions." Judah came toward her.

She held her ground, refusing to cower in front of him.

"The Ansara Dranir is single," Judah said. "Some consider him a playboy. He has a villa in the Caribbean and one in Italy, as well as homes and apartments in various places. He owns a yacht and a jet, and women swoon at his feet."

"Sounds like a charming guy," Mercy said sarcastically. "And you're related to him. From what you've said about him, I sense a strong similarity between you two."

"Like two peas in a pod." Judah smirked. "I also manage his money for him."

Mercy wondered why Judah was so forthcoming with information about his Dranir and his people. Either they were, as he had told her, no threat to the Raintree, or he was telling her just enough of the truth to appear open and honest. But why should a Raintree trust an Ansara?

Whenever Judah was this close, their bodies almost touching, Mercy found it difficult to concentrate, and he damn well knew it. *Ignore the fact that your heartbeat has accelerated and your nipples have hardened,* Mercy told herself. *He doesn't know that you're moist with desire, that your body yearns for his.*

"Wouldn't our brief time together be better spent not talking?" Judah leaned over just far enough so that they were nose to nose, mouth to mouth. "As I recall, neither of us needs words to express what we want."

Shivering internally, she barely managed to keep her body from shaking. Her breathing quickened. Her nostrils flared. Her feminine core clenched and unclenched.

"Why does your brother hate you enough to kill you?"

Her question acted as the deterrent she had hoped it would. Judah lifted his head and withdrew from her, at least far enough so that she could take a free breath.

"I told you that Cael's mother killed my mother. There's been bad blood between us all our lives."

"If his mother killed yours, then you should be the one who hates him, the one who wants to kill him. Why is it the other way around?"

"I'm my father's legitimate son. Cael is not. It's as simple as that. An insane mind needs little excuse to act irrationally."

Mercy told herself that she was questioning Judah to acquire needed information about the Ansara, but that was only part of her reason. Curiosity? Perhaps. All she knew was that she felt a great need to know this man, her child's father.

"How old were you when your mother died?" she asked.

Judah's jaw tensed. "My mother was murdered." He tapered his gaze until his eyes slanted almost closed.

Of its own volition, her hand reached over and spread out across the center of his chest, covering his heart. For one millisecond, while emotion made him vulnerable, Mercy absorbed his innermost thoughts. He had been an infant when his mother died, too young to remember her face or the sound of her voice. A small boy's sadness lingered deep inside Judah, both a hunger for a mother's love and a denial that he needed love from anyone.

"I'm very sorry about your mother," Mercy told him. "No child should grow up without a mother to love him unconditionally."

With his mouth twisted in a snarl, his eyes mere slits and tension etched on his features, Judah grabbed her hand and flung it off his chest. "I neither want nor need your sympathy."

Bombarded with his anger and resentment, Mercy gasped for air. The rage boiling inside him spilled over onto her, engulfing her, drowning her in its intensity. This was her fault, not his, she realized. She should have known better than offer him kindness and caring when he understood neither.

And she shouldn't have touched him.

Mercy fought to free herself from the dangerous havoc Judah's fury was creating within her. She had somehow connected to him empathically, and try as she might, she couldn't mange to sever the link. A heaviness bore down on her chest, a weight that robbed her of breath. She gasped for air, struggling for speech to demand that he release her.

Judah grabbed her shoulders. "What's wrong with you?"

She managed to expel a gasping moan.

"Mercy!" He shook her.

She felt herself growing weaker by the minute, her oxygen supply cut off as if she were being smothered. *Help me. Please, Judah, help me.*

Tell me what to do.

Barely conscious, Mercy swayed toward him. *Don't be angry with me. Don't hate me.*

I did this to you?

He caught her as her knees gave way, swooping her up in his arms. "Sweet Mercy."

Closing her eyes, she sank to a level just below consciousness. Judah lowered his head and pressed his cheek against hers as he held her securely. As swiftly as his negative energy had invaded her mind and body, it dissipated, draining from her as it drained from him. She felt a flash of concern and genuine regret before he swiftly placed a protective barrier between them.

Weak from the experience and recovering slowly, Mercy opened her eyes and met Judah's concerned gaze.

"I didn't mean for that to happen," he told her.

"It was my fault," she said. "I let my guard down."

"That's a dangerous thing to do, especially around me."

She nodded. "Would you please put me down now? I'll be all right."

"Are you sure? I could—"

"No, thank you. Just put me on my feet."

He eased her down and out of his arms, slowly, maddeningly, making sure her body skimmed over his. When he released her, she staggered, and he grabbed her upper arms to steady her.

"Should I get Sidonia?" he asked.

"No, I'll be all right. Please…" She wriggled, trying to loosen his secure grip on her arms.

He released her.

"I need to be alone for a while," she told him, then turned her back on him, afraid she would succumb to her weakness for a man who was not only dangerous to her, but to her daughter. Seconds later, the door to her study closed, and she knew Judah had left the room.

After a half hour on the phone with Claude, discussing the fact that Cael had not returned to Terrebonne and had somehow dropped off the Ansara radar, Judah had gone in search of his daughter. He needed to build a strong rapport with Eve as quickly as possible. Only if he bonded with her, if she trusted him completely, would he be able to persuade her to leave the Raintree sanctuary with him. So, he spent hours with her that Thursday morning and afternoon, every moment under the vigilant supervision of Nanny Sidonia. The old woman watched him like a hawk, as if she expected him to sprout horns and a tail. Wouldn't she be shocked if he did just that? he thought. And he could. At least, he could create the illusion of horns and a tail, enough to scare the crap out of the old woman. It would serve her right if he did. But it might frighten Eve and possibly give her the wrong impression of him. He was sure the grumbling old hag had already bad-mouthed him to his child, telling her all sorts of improbable stories about the wicked Ansara.

He supposed there was some grain of truth to it. The good Raintree. The bad Ansara. But all Raintree weren't saints. And not every Ansara was the devil incarnate.

From time immemorial, the Raintree, as a people, had chosen the straight and narrow, taking the high ground, showing an emotional weakness for the welfare of the Ungifted and preferring peace to war. Wizards with far too much conscience.

The Ansara tolerated humankind, manipulated them when they were useful, disregarded them when they were not. Ansara prided themselves on their skills as warriors and defended to the death what was theirs. But they were not monsters, not evil demons. They lived and loved and cherished their families. In that respect, they were no different from the Raintree.

But there were also Ansara like Cael. A few in every generation. Depraved. Evil. True monsters. Often innate sorcerers, they possessed the ability to lure the dregs of Ansara society into their service. They killed for the pleasure of killing. Took great delight in inflicting pain, in torturing others. They were as unlike Judah and his kind as they were unlike the Raintree.

When circumstances required it, Judah had killed. To protect himself and others, or out of necessity, when killing was simply a business decision. He didn't tolerate disobedience or disrespect. As the Dranir, he possessed unequaled power among his people.

He liked power. Respected power.

He used and discarded women as it pleased him, Ansara and human alike. And once, even a Raintree princess.

Eve tugged on his hand, reminding Judah that he was tied to Mercy Raintree through their daughter, a bond that only death could break.

Sidonia's agitated voice called Eve's name.

"Hurry, Daddy, or she'll catch us." Eve urged him to walk faster as they sneaked away from Sidonia on the pretense of playing hide and seek.

Judah swept Eve up into his arms. "Hold tight," he told her.

When she wrapped her arms around his neck, Judah ran, taking his daughter away from unwanted supervision. When they were out of earshot of Sidonia's threats, Judah set Eve on her feet.

"We got away!" Grinning triumphantly, Eve clapped her hands softly. "She doesn't know where we are, and she can't find us."

"So what do you want to do, now that we're on our own?"

"Mmm..." Eve deliberated her choices for a couple of moments, then laughed excitedly. "I want to show you something really special that I can do." She looked up at him, eagerness shimmering in her eyes. Mercy's green eyes.

"Something new?" he asked. "You've already shown me how talented you are."

"It's something I've never tried before, but I know I can do it."

Judah glanced around and noted that they were not near the house or any of the cottages. Open meadow lay north and east of them, a bubbling brook to the south and a wooded area to the west. If Eve tried a new skill and it backfired, she couldn't do much harm way out here. Besides, he was with her to counteract any fallout.

"Go ahead, Princess Eve, test your powers. Try something new. Show me."

Eve smiled broadly, then stood very still and concentrated.

Seconds ticked by. She focused inward, calling forth her power. The ground beneath their feet trembled.

"That's it. Command your power," Judah said. "You're in control."

The fingers on Eve's right hand twitched, moving faster and faster. A tiny circle of energy formed in her palm. An orb of golden light, shimmering like translucent diamond dust, grew larger and larger until it filled her hand.

My God! Eve had created an energy ball, the most powerful and deadliest power in any Ansara's or Raintree's arsenal. No child before had been capable of creating an energy bolt, and only a select number of adults could do it.

"Eve, be careful."

"Isn't it beautiful?"

He zoomed in on the energy bolt his daughter held in her hand, as casually as if she were holding a baseball. "It's very beautiful, but it's extremely dangerous."

"Oh." Eve's eyes widened in surprise, a hint of curiosity in her expression. "What does it do?"

Judah considered his options. He could probably dissolve the ball, but if he did, it might injure Eve's hand. He could ask her to give the ball to him, and then he could dispose of it. Or he could allow her to find out for herself, under his strict supervision, just what such power could do.

"Turn and face the woods," Judah told her. She did. "Now choose a tree."

"That one." She pointed to a towering elm.

"Aim your energy ball at the tree and whirl it through the air."

Eve swung her right arm backward, lifting it over her head, and flung the psychic energy bolt in the direction of the tree she had chosen. She and Judah watched as the blast missed the elm tree entirely, zooming past it and exploding as it hit a stand of twenty-foot pines. A least half a dozen of the evergreens splintered into minuscule shards and rained down in heavy ash particles to the forest floor.

Holy crap! His little girl had just shot one of the most powerful energy bolts Judah had ever seen, taking out not one object but six.

"I missed my tree, Daddy. I missed it." Eve puckered up, her bottom lip quivering.

He knelt down in front of her and tucked his knuckles under her chin, lifting her little face so that she looked directly at him. "You might have missed the elm tree, but look what your blast did. All you need is practice and you'll be able to hit your target every time."

Tears hung on Eve's long, golden lashes, and her eyes shimmered with moisture, but she smiled and threw her arms around Judah's neck.

"I love you, Daddy."

Judah swallowed hard. *I love you, too.*

She hugged him tighter. "Mother's coming."

"It figures."

"Huh?"

"Nothing." Judah gradually eased out of Eve's embrace as he rose to his feet. "Let me handle things, okay? When your mother finds us, she's not going to be happy, so we'll tell her that I'm the one who shot the energy bolt. That way she won't be angry with you."

"But that's lying, Daddy, and lying is wrong."

Judah groaned. Raintree logic. "Actually, it'll just be a little white lie, so you won't get in trouble."

"Mother will know that I did it. She knows everything."

Judah couldn't repress his smile. "Why don't we put her to the test and find out?"

When Eve looked up at him, he winked at her.

She winked back. "Okay."

Exactly five minutes and sixteen seconds later, Judah sensed Mercy coming up from behind as he and Eve sat on the side of the creek, their shoes off, their feet in the cool water. He glanced over his shoulder and spied her a good thirty feet away.

When he turned back around, Eve said, "Mother is very upset."

"Remember, let me do all the talking."

"I think my mother is the one who's going to do all the talking."

When Mercy approached them, Judah and Eve simultaneously turned to face her.

"Hi, Mommy. Daddy and I are just cooling off. It sure is hot today."

Mercy glared at Judah. "What did you let her do?"

Judah shrugged. "Eve didn't do anything. I did. I was showing off a little for my daughter."

"Is that right?" Mercy zeroed in on Eve.

Eve's cheeks blushed bright pink. "Un-huh."

Mercy scanned the area in every direction. When her gaze fell on the empty spot in the woods created by the absence of six large pine trees, she gasped.

Focusing on Eve, she said, "I want the truth, young lady. Did you—" she nodded toward the woods "—do that?"

"Do what?" Eve asked.

Mercy glared at Judah. "Not only did you allow her to do something extremely dangerous, you taught her to lie."

"No, Mother, please. Don't be angry with Daddy." Eve yanked her feet from the creek and hopped up off the ground. "I did it. I zapped a whole bunch of trees. I was aiming at just one, but—" she flopped her hands open on either side of her "—my energy ball kind of went crazy, and all those trees went poof."

"Oh, God, oh, God," Mercy mumbled under her breath, then turned to Judah. "Did you help her create an energy bolt?"

Judah stood up to his full six-two height and settled his gaze on Mercy. "Our daughter didn't need any help. She was perfectly capable of creating an energy bolt all by herself. And in case you haven't realized it, she took out six trees with one bolt."

"She took out—of course she did." Mercy marched over to Judah, nostrils flared, eyes blazing. "And you're proud of her, aren't you?"

"Damn right I am. And you should be, too."

"I *am* proud of Eve, but…she could have been hurt, or hurt someone else."

"I wouldn't have let that happen."

They stood there, glaring at each, a hairsbreadth apart, the tension between them palpable. She was furious with him. He loved that about her, the passion, the fierce, protective mama tiger in her. He wanted nothing more than to take her here and now, and except for Eve's presence, he would have been sorely tempted.

She knew what he was thinking. He could see it in her eyes. And he also sensed her desire. Like animals powerless to resist the mating call, they couldn't break the visual contact or the psychic bond that held them spellbound.

Spellbound his ass! He wasn't some lovesick young fool. And he certainly wasn't in love with Mercy. Once he'd screwed her again, this fever in his blood would cool.

"Mercy!" Sidonia cried as she came across the open field, three people following her. "Is Eve all right? Did that devil…?"

"She's fine," Mercy called.

"I'm getting damn sick and tired of her calling me the devil," Judah said.

"Oh, great. Just great." Mercy heaved a deep, exasperated sigh. "She's got Brenna and Geol and Hugh with her."

"A Raintree lynch party, no doubt." Judah turned to face the approaching hangmen.

"You keep quiet." She gave Judah and Eve stern looks. "Both of you. Let me do all the talking."

Huffing and puffing, Sidonia stopped a couple of feet from Mercy. "I turned my back for two seconds, and he ran off with her."

"It's all right," Mercy said. "It won't happen again. Will it?" She looked from father to daughter.

Eve shook her head, then bowed it in a contrite manner. Totally false regret, of course.

Judah didn't respond.

"What happened over there?" Hugh, a robust, gray-haired Raintree, pointed to the wide bare spot in the nearby woods. "You aren't cutting down timber are you, Mercy?"

"Just a little psychic accident," Mercy said. "I'm completely to blame."

Hugh stepped forward, looked Judah over from head to toe, and held out his hand. "I'm Hugh Sullivan and you're...?"

"This is Judah Blackstone," Mercy said. "Judah and I went to college together. He's visiting for a few days."

Judah hesitated, then took the man's hand and exchanged a cordial shake.

Hugh studied Judah with his green Raintree eyes. "Well, you *are* a handsome devil, all right." Hugh chuckled. "I couldn't figure out why Sidonia kept referring to you as the devil."

"I'm afraid Sidonia and I got off on the wrong foot when I first arrived," Judah said, then looked right at the nanny. "I'm sorry if our little game of hide-and-seek worried you. Eve and I were having so much fun playing that it never entered my head you'd be concerned about her."

"Humph." Sidonia gave him a condemning glare.

Judah glanced at the other man and woman, who seemed as intrigued by his presence as Hugh had been. He nodded to them.

"Hello," the woman said. "I'm Brenna Drummond, a distant cousin of Mercy's."

The other man held up his hand in greeting. "I'm Geol Raintree, a not so distant cousin."

"Forgive us, Mr. Blackstone, for being so curious, but Mercy having an old boyfriend visiting is quite an event." Brenna smiled knowingly at Mercy, apparently giving her approval.

"Judah wasn't my—" Before Mercy could finish her sentence, Judah slipped his arm around her waist. She went stiff as a board.

As if on cue, Eve cuddled up to Judah's other side.

"Well, it looks as if our little Eve likes you, Mr. Blackstone," Hugh said. "It's always a good sign when a woman's child likes you."

"Hugh is grilling trout tonight, and I'm making homemade ice cream," Brenna said. "Why don't all of you come to my cabin for dinner?"

"Thank you, but I'm afraid—"

Once again, Judah cut Mercy off mid-sentence. "We'd love to, wouldn't we?"

"Yippee!" Eve shouted. "Brenna makes the best ice cream in the world."

Mercy forced a smile. After the search party went their separate ways and Mercy sent Eve back to the house with Sidonia, she confronted Judah.

"What did you think you were doing, agreeing to have dinner with my guests?"

"I was making an effort to be polite so they wouldn't suspect there was a wolf among the sheep. Wasn't that what you wanted me to do?"

"What I want you to do is disappear from my life and never return."

"If I left, you'd miss me."

"Like I'd miss the plague."

"I'll be leaving soon enough." *Going home to Terrebonne to fight and kill my brother,* he added silently.

"Once you've taken care of Cael, please don't come back here. Leave us alone. You're bad for Eve. You must know that."

"As a Raintree princess, you may be accustomed to issuing orders and having them obeyed, but I'm not one of your loyal subjects. Between us, I'm the master. And you're my willing slave."

"When hell freezes over!"

Chapter 13

Friday Afternoon,
Cael Ansara's Compound in North Carolina

Cael had tried unsuccessfully to crack the shield surrounding Eve Raintree's mind. All protective devices, no matter how strong, could be breached. It was simply a matter of finding the key. Every spell had a reversal spell. Every charm could be destroyed. Every power could be deflected. Given enough time, he could find a way into Eve's thoughts so he could influence her thinking, but time was one thing he didn't have. In two days he would lead his troops against the Raintree sanctuary. In two days he would kill his brother and become the Ansara Dranir. Only one thing stood in his way: little Princess Eve. She, too, had to die—along with her parents.

But the child was an unknown. Half Ansara, half Raintree.

Such children possessed the talents of each parent. With Eve's parents both royals, the girl's capabilities could be uniquely powerful.

Cael laughed at his own foolishness. Eve was six. No matter what abilities she had inherited, they would be immature and untutored. Her supernatural skills couldn't possibly be a threat to him. But her being Judah's daughter could.

Projecting his thoughts, Cael directed his message to one recipient. *Can you hear me, little Eve? Are you listening? I'm your uncle Cael. Don't you want to talk to me?*

Silence.

Talk to me, child. Tell me why I shouldn't kill your father. I'll listen to whatever you have to say. Perhaps you can change my mind.

No response.

You want to help Judah, don't you? If you'll talk to me, I'll listen.

A boom of psychic energy thundered inside Cael's head, the sound deafening in its intensity as it radiated through his body and brought him to his knees. As he doubled over in pain there on the rough wooden floor of his private compound quarters, an outraged voice issued a warning.

Stay away from my daughter, Judah said. *She is off-limits to you. Don't try to contact her again.*

The pain stopped as quickly as it had hit him. Cael staggered to his feet, thrust his fist into the air and cursed his brother.

Get ready. I'm coming for you. Do you hear me, Judah? And when you die, our people will rejoice that they have a true Ansara leader, one who can return them to the old days when we ruled the world.

Judah heard Cael's threats like a distant echo as he shut out his half brother's ranting. Cael had finally crossed that thin line between instability and full-blown insanity. He wasn't surprised. It had always been a matter of when, never if.

Knowing that, sooner or later, Cael would force his hand, Judah had put off killing Cael all these years for one reason only: his father's dying request.

"Do all you can to save your brother. Kill him only if you must."

In his own way, their father had loved Cael and had chosen to overlook his many faults. But in his heart of hearts, he had known that the seeds of insanity needed very little nourishment to burst open, bloom and ripen.

Kill him only if you must.

I must, Father, to save the Ansara. To save Eve.

Daddy?

No, Eve. Don't use your thoughts to speak to me.

I'm sorry. It's just that bad man tried to—

Shh... I'll come to you.

Undoubtedly Eve had heard Cael's threats. Damn his brother! Damn him to hell! Hurrying downstairs, Judah took the steps two at a time.

He found Eve alone in the living room, sitting on the floor amid an array of colorful construction paper, crayons scattered all around her. She glanced up at Judah when he entered but didn't rise to meet him.

"I saw him, Daddy," Eve said. "I drew a picture of him and of where he was when he tried to talk to me. Come see."

Judah walked across the room, stood directly behind Eve and looked down at her artwork. His muscles tightened when he saw the remarkable likeness of Cael that she had sketched in crayon. She had depicted his brother standing, his fist in the air, an expression of sheer madness on his handsome face. The background appeared to be gray cinder block walls, rough wooden flooring and outdated metal furniture. Interesting. He had never known Cael to rough it, not when it came to accommodations. His brother preferred luxury above all else.

"Amazing," Judah said, awed by his daughter's talent. "You're a remarkably gifted artist."

Eve looked up at him, smiled and laid down the yellow crayon she had used to shade Cael's hair. "Am I, Daddy? Mother says the same thing. But she told me that she has no idea where I got such talent, because she and Uncle Dante and Uncle Gideon can't draw pictures like I do."

"My mother was a renowned Ansara artist," Judah said. "The pala—" He caught himself before the word "palace" escaped his lips. "My home is filled with her paintings."

"She wasn't your brother's mommy," Eve said with certainty. "His mother was bad, just like he's bad."

"Yes, Nusi was a very bad woman."

Eve stood and looked up at Judah. "Don't worry. I won't let him hurt my mother the way Nusi hurt my grandma Seana."

Judah stared at his child, amazed anew at her keen insight. Her abilities were not only unnaturally strong for one so young, but far more numerous than those of even the most powerful members of either clan. "How did you know about what happened to my mother?"

Eve laid her left hand over her heart. "I know in here. That's all. I just know."

"What do you know?" Mercy stood in the open doorway, her features etched with concern.

Eve ran over to her mother. "Guess what? I know where I got my talent for drawing such good pictures." She beamed her radiant smile at Judah. "I got it from my grandma Seana."

Mercy shot Judah a questioning glare.

"My mother was a gifted artist," Judah said. Seana Ansara

had been the most talented Ansara artist in generations. Not only had Nusi's bitter jealousy robbed Judah of his mother and Hadar of his beloved wife, but the world of an artistic genius.

"Did you draw something for Daddy?" Mercy entered the room, Eve at her side.

"I drew a picture of that bad man, Daddy's brother." Eve rushed over, picked up her drawing and held it in front of her to show Mercy.

"When did you see this bad man?" Mercy asked, staring at the remarkably accurate portrait of Cael's madness. Judah realized she was doing her best not to reveal just how upset she was.

"He tried to talk to me again," Eve said. "He keeps calling my name and saying if I'll talk to him, he'll listen." Frowning, she threw the picture on the floor, then stomped on it. "But I didn't talk to him, and my daddy told him he'd better not ever bother me again or he'd be sorry. Didn't you, Daddy?"

Judah cleared his throat. "There's no way Cael can invade Eve's thoughts unless she willingly allows him in. The shield you've put around her will protect her."

"Yes, I know." Mercy motioned to Eve. "Come along, sweetie. Sidonia has lunch ready. Your favorite—macaroni and cheese. With fresh peaches and whipped cream for dessert."

Eve eyed her drawings, and the paper and crayons lying on the floor. "Don't I need to pick up first?"

"You can do that after lunch." Mercy exchanged a we-need-to-talk look with Judah, then gave Eve a nudge toward the door. "You run along and tell Sidonia that Judah and I will be there in just a minute."

Eve hesitated, glanced from one parent to the other, and said, "You're not going to fuss at each other again, are you?"

"No, we're not," Mercy promised.

"I hope not." Eve slumped her shoulders, sighed and ambled slowly out into the foyer.

Judah didn't wait for Mercy to attack. "He's going to come for me. Soon."

"I see." She took several steps back and closed the pocket doors. "I suppose Eve overheard him say this to you."

"She didn't tell me she heard him, but, yes, I assume she did."

"When he comes, you can't fight him here on Raintree ground."

Judah nodded. "I understand your concerns. But if he finds a way to breach the shield around the sanctuary, I'll have no choice."

"Only someone with power equal to mine or my brother Dante's—"

"Before you ask—no, Cael is not the Ansara Dranir," Judah said. "But he *is* a powerful sorcerer, with an arsenal of black magic tricks."

"When he comes here to the sanctuary and calls you out, Eve will be aware of his presence, and she'll want to do something to help you."

"We can't allow her anywhere near Cael. Somehow we have to make her understand that the fight must be between my brother and me."

"She'll listen to what we say, but whether or not she'll obey us is another thing altogether."

"I'll find a way to make her understand."

"You can certainly try."

"When the time comes, I'll need you to stay with Eve," Judah said. "If I'm distracted by trying to protect her…"

"You need to talk to Eve and explain on a level she will understand how important it is for her not to interfere."

"Would you allow me time alone with her, without her guard dog?"

"Yes. I'll tell Sidonia that you're allowed to take Eve for a walk this afternoon while I'm working."

Judah noted Mercy's frown and the weariness she couldn't hide.

"You've been gone all morning, and Sidonia refused to tell me where you were, but Eve mentioned that you were making sick people well."

"It's no secret that I'm a healer," Mercy said. "This morning, I was with two Raintree seers who can no longer see clearly into the future."

"And were you able to restore their powers?"

"No. Not yet. This happens sometimes, especially when a talent is overused or… I believe with rest and meditation, they'll be fine."

"And what will you be doing this afternoon?"

"We had a new arrival yesterday, someone who lost her husband and both children in a horrific car accident six months ago. She's in agonizing emotional pain."

"And you're going to take her pain into yourself. How can you stand it? Why put yourself through such torment when you don't have to?"

"Because it's wrong not to use the talents with which we're blessed. I'm an empathic healer. It's not just what I do, it's who I am."

"Yes, you're right. It *is* who you are. I understand." Judah wondered if Mercy would understand that their daughter had been born to save his people?

Judah spoke with Claude every morning and every evening, using secure cell phones, despite their advanced telepathic abilities. Telephone communication was more difficult for Cael to intercept.

"He hasn't returned to Terrebonne," Claude said.

"Then where the hell is he?"

"I have no idea. It's as if he's vanished off the face of the earth. Even Sidra can't locate him. He's undoubtedly shielding his whereabouts."

"Eve drew a picture of him today, after he tried to talk to her."

"Could she locate him for us?"

"She might be able to," Judah said. "But I can't risk her getting that close to him. He could capture her thoughts and hypnotize her, or enter her dreams and make her deathly sick."

"Wherever he is and whatever he's doing, he's up to no good."

"What about the warriors who left Terrebonne with him? Have they returned?"

"No, and several others are unaccounted for."

"Then it's begun, hasn't it? He's gradually amassing his army."

"Let him." Claude emitted a grunting huff. "He's a fool if he believes that a few dozen renegade warriors make an army."

"He told me that he's coming for me soon."

"And when he does, you'll kill him."

"We should be there on Terrebonne for the Death Duel," Judah said. "But that could well be what he expects me to do—return home and leave Eve unprotected."

"She has protection. Her mother and—"

"Raintree protection. It's not enough for a child such as Eve."

"Then do what you have to do. Kill Cael on Raintree ground, then bring your daughter home to Terrebonne where she belongs."

After dinner with his daughter and the ever-watchful Sidonia, Judah told Eve that he was going for a walk and would see her before bedtime to say good-night. They had spent hours alone together today, and he felt he had convinced her that she could be of more help to him by not interfering in his fight with Cael than if she injected herself into the situation. He needed to find Mercy and assure her that Eve had listened to him, and that when the time came, she would obey their orders.

As he headed out the back door, Eve called, "I wish you'd go see about my mother. She's almost always home for supper, and she wasn't tonight. Meta must be terribly sick for Mommy to spend so much time with her."

"Your mother's fine." Sidonia gave Judah a warning glare. "She doesn't need anything from him. When she's done her job, she'll come home."

"Don't worry about your mother," Judah said. "I'm sure Sidonia's right and your mother's fine."

"No, she's not, Daddy. I think she needs you."

Once outside, with the sun low in the west and a warm breeze blowing, Judah thought about Eve's concern for Mercy. He had wondered what would keep Mercy from dinner with her daughter, and suspected that Eve's take on the problem was accurate. Undoubtedly the woman—Eve had called her Meta—that Mercy was counseling was seriously ill. Was this Meta the woman Mercy had told him about, the one who had lost her husband and children six months ago?

Had Mercy become so engrossed in easing this woman's pain that she had taken too much of the agony into herself and was in such bad shape that she either couldn't return home or didn't want Eve to see her in her weakened condition? Was Eve right—did Mercy need him?

Hell. What difference did it make? Why should he care if Mercy was writhing in pain, or perhaps unconscious and tortured by the suffering that rightfully belonged to someone else?

Don't think about Mercy. Think about Cael. About finally meeting him in combat.

Think about Eve. About keeping her safe and taking her home to Terrebonne.

But he couldn't help himself, and his thoughts returned to the past and the promise he'd once made.

I'm sorry, Father. I've done all I can, tried everything possible. Cael can't be saved. He is as insane as Nusi was. Even in death, her hold on him is too strong. Forgive me, but I have no choice but to kill my brother.

Less than an hour into his solitary walk, Judah ran into Brenna and Geol taking an evening stroll. By the way they held hands and from the mating vibes he picked up from them, he suspected that if they were not already lovers, they soon would be.

"You're out all alone?" Geol asked. "Where's Mercy?"

"She's with a new arrival to the sanctuary," Judah replied. "A woman named Meta."

"Oh, yes. Poor Meta." Brenna shook her head sadly. "She should have come to Mercy months ago. I'm afraid it may be too late for her now."

"What do you mean, 'too late'?" Judah asked.

"Did Mercy not tell you? Meta tried to kill herself and will probably try again."

"No, she didn't tell me."

"We've all been taking turns," Brenna said, then lowered her voice to a whisper. "A suicide watch."

"Where is Meta's cabin?" Judah asked, then quickly added, "I thought I'd meet Mercy and walk her home."

Brenna smiled. Lovers always assumed the whole world was in love. Brenna was young, her mind an open book, so he could read her romantic thoughts quite easily. She suspected that Judah Blackstone, Mercy's old boyfriend from college, might possibly be Eve's father, and she hoped they would rekindle their romance.

Without hesitation, she gave Judah directions; then she and Geol disappeared, arm in arm, into the advancing twilight. The sky to the west radiated with the remainder of the day's light, spreading red and orange and deep pink layers of color across the horizon.

Meta's cabin was about a quarter of a mile away, one of three structures built along the mountainside. The topmost cabin overlooked a small waterfall that trickled steadily over worn-smooth boulders, until it reached one of the creeks that ran through the Raintree property not far from the main house.

When Judah approached Meta's cabin, he noticed that the door and windows were all open, a misty green light escaping from them. Pausing to watch the unusual sight, he tried to recall if he'd ever witnessed anything similar. He hadn't. Although there were a few Ansara empaths, only two or three had actually cultivated the healing aspects of their personalities. It took a great deal of selflessness to devote your life to healing.

He had heard stories of how, in centuries past, many royal Ansara had kept empathic healers caged for the sole purpose of emptying their pain into these women as if they were waste receptacles. He could well believe that someone like Cael was capable of such an atrocity and would even take great pleasure in inflicting such torture.

Judah moved cautiously toward the open front door but stopped dead still when he saw Mercy standing over a woman sitting on the floor, each woman with her arms outstretched as if welcoming a lover into her embrace. The eerie green light came from Mercy. It surrounded her, enveloped her, poured from her like water from a free-flowing fountain. The black-haired woman Judah assumed was Meta had her eyes closed, and tears streamed down her face.

Mercy spoke softly, her words in an alien tongue. Judah, as the Dranir, possessed the unique talent of zenoglossy, the rare ability to speak and understand any language. The gift of tongues. He listened to her soothing voice as she beseeched any remaining unbearable pain to leave Meta's heart and mind and enter hers. Wisps of green vapor floated from the woman's fingertips and entered Mercy's body through her fingers.

When Mercy cried out and cursed the pain, Judah tensed. And when she moaned, shivering, writhing in agony, it took all Judah's resolve not to rush into the room and stop her. But the moment passed, and the green mist filtered through Mercy and into the air, leaving behind a tranquil turquoise glow inside the cabin. Judah heaved a deep, groaning sigh.

Mercy reached down, took Meta's outstretched hands and pulled her to her feet. Speaking in the ancient tongue once again, Mercy bestowed tranquility on Meta's mind, solace on her heart and peace on her soul, a white light passing from Mercy's body into Meta's.

Judah watched and waited.

Finally Mercy released Meta's hands and said, "Rest now. Tomorrow you will prepare to move into the next phase of your life."

"Thank you." Meta wiped the moisture from her damp cheeks. "If you hadn't... I can never repay you for what you've done."

"Repay me by living a long and full life."

Judah could tell by how whisper soft Mercy's voice was, and by the way she wavered slightly, that she was near exhaustion. When she turned and walked toward the door, she moved slowly, as if her feet were bound with heavy weights. Judah backed out of the doorway and waited for her outside. When she stepped out into the fresh night air, she staggered and grabbed the doorframe to steady herself. As the moment of weakness passed, she closed the door behind her. Then she saw Judah.

"What are you doing here?"

"Waiting for you, to walk you home."

She glared at him.

"That was quite remarkable, what you did in there," he told her.

"How long have you been here?"

"Only a few minutes, but long enough to see what you were doing. She's going to be all right now, isn't she? She won't try to kill herself again."

"How did…? Who told you about Meta?"

"I ran into Brenna and Geol. Brenna told me about Meta, and also how to find her cabin. Did you know that Brenna thinks we were lovers and that I'm Eve's father?"

Mercy rubbed her forehead. "I'm too tired to worry about what Brenna thinks. As long as she doesn't suspect that you're Ansara…"

"She doesn't."

Mercy nodded. "Good. Now I need to go home and rest. I'm very tired. If you wanted to talk to me about something in particular, it will have to wait a few hours until I've rested."

"I really did come here just to walk you home."

She eyed him suspiciously, then started moving away from the cabin. Judah fell into step beside her but didn't say anything else. They walked a good forty yards or so in silence, the only sounds the nocturnal rural symphony coming slowly to life all around them.

Suddenly Mercy stopped. "Judah?"

"Yes?"

"I—I don't think—"

She wavered unsteadily, then spiraled downward in a slow whirl to the ground. Judah called her name as she lay at his feet, a serene angel who had spent her last ounce of energy. He knelt and lifted her into his arms; then glanced up at the mountainside cabin nestled above the waterfall.

Waking suddenly, Mercy shot straight up, gasping for air, feeling disoriented and strangely frightened. Where was she? Not at home. She patted the surface around her. She was in a bed, just not her bed.

"How do you feel?" Judah asked.

Judah?

She turned to follow the sound of his voice. He was standing halfway across the room, near the windows, moonlight highlighting his tall, muscular body.

"Where are we?" she asked.

"In the cabin near the waterfall."

"What happened?" She held up a restraining hand. "No, it's all right. I remember. I felt faint and… Why did you bring me here instead of taking me home?"

He moved toward her. She scooted to the edge of the bed and stood to face him.

"I thought we needed some time alone. Without Sidonia. Without Eve."

"Eve will be concerned that we haven't come home."

"I let her know that you're all right and we're together. She's asleep now."

"I'm not staying here." Mercy took several weak, tentative steps, then faltered.

Judah reached out and caught her before she fell, keeping her on her feet as he wrapped his arms around her. "Why should we fight the inevitable? I want you, and you want me."

When she tried to free herself from his tenacious embrace, he held fast.

Tilting her head so that she could look him right in the eyes, Mercy said, "You are Ansara. I am Raintree. We hate each other. When you have killed your brother, then you and I will fight for Eve, and I will kill you."

He lowered his head, his lips hovering over hers. She tried again to break free, but without success.

"And it will bother you to have sex with me and then try to kill me. How deliciously naive you still are, sweet Mercy."

"Don't call me that."

"Why? Because that's what I called you the night you conceived Eve, the night we couldn't get enough of each other?"

"Let me go. Don't do this. Don't make me fight you tonight."

"I don't want to fight."

She struggled against his superior physical strength but couldn't overpower him. "Do you intend to try to rape me?"

He loosened his hold on her, and she pulled free, managing to make it to the door before her knees weakened. As she stumbled, she reached out and broke her fall, managing to stay upright only by leaning against the door. Judah came up behind her and gently pressed himself against her, trapping her between his muscular body and the wood. When she felt his warm breath on her neck, she trembled.

"I haven't even touched you, and you're falling apart," he told her, his voice a sensual rasp.

"I hate you."

"Hate me all you want."

Judah eased his hand across and down her shoulder, over her waist, and then he cupped her butt. Even through the cotton of her summer dress and panties, she felt the heat of his touch. And, God help her, she wanted him. All of him.

When he reached down, grasped the edge of her skirt and slowly bunched it in his hand, she closed her eyes and whimpered. His fingertips moved upward beneath the dress and over her panties.

She managed to say one word. "Don't."

"Shh…" he hissed into her ear as his fingers found the small of her back, that ultrasensitive spot just above her buttocks. "Relax, sweet Mercy. Let me pleasure you."

Judah, please…please…

He rubbed his index finger over her sacrum, faster and faster, harder and harder. Mercy held her breath as sensation built inside her. Suddenly a zap of electrical energy shot from Judah's fingers directly into the vertebrae in the small of her back.

Jerking uncontrollably, Mercy cried out as she climaxed.

Chapter 14

How could she have let this happen? She could have escaped. She could have stopped him. Why hadn't she?

Because you wanted this. Because you want him.

Judah eased his hand out from under her dress, letting the skirt fall back down over her legs, the hem brushing against her calves. But he kept her pinned against the cabin door, her back to his chest, his erection throbbing against her buttocks.

As the aftershocks of her orgasm faded away, Mercy fought an inner battle, her heart versus her mind. Her heart whispered soft, passionate yearnings, but every logical thought commanded her to flee.

Fight your desires.

Fight Judah. Don't let him do this to you.

"Let me go," she pleaded. "You don't want me this way, taking me against my will."

"I'll take you any way I can." He murmured the words

against her neck. "And make no mistake, sweet Mercy, I intend to have you. Tonight." He shoved himself against her, grinding his erect penis against the cheeks of her ass.

Calling forth what strength the recent hours of sleep had regenerated within her, Mercy focused on overpowering Judah and gaining her release. She needed only a moment of forceful energy to take him off guard and free herself. As he ran his hands over her, his breath hot against her neck, she shot a jolt of electrical pressure from her body into his. He bellowed in pain as the shock waves hit his nerve endings.

She broke away from him, grasped the doorknob and yanked open the door.

Run. Fast. Get away while you can.

If only she possessed the ability to levitate, she could fly away from danger.

With her energy once again greatly depleted, Mercy made it only ten feet from the cabin before Judah caught her and whirled her around to face him. Hardened with rage over what she'd done, he focused his frigid glare on her body, raking over her from neck to toes. She felt the intensity of his gaze, a sensation of hot and then cold sliding downward, between her breasts, across her belly, between her thighs. Her dress split apart where his gaze moved over it, as did her bra and panties beneath.

Judah released her, then stepped back to view his handiwork.

Calling on what energy she had left to form a countermove, she sent a mental blast straight toward him, but he caught it mid-flight and crushed it as it were nothing more than spun glass. Her only hope was conjuring a spell. But did she have enough strength? And should it be a defensive or an offensive spell?

When Judah smiled, thinking himself the victor in their battle, she remained perfectly still, as if she were unable to move. But all the while she worked frantically, mentally reciting the ancient words in the tongue of her ancestors, casting a powerfully dangerous spell that would instantly infuse her with enough strength to defend herself.

Judah stopped abruptly, his big body rigid. *Do you know what you're doing? In your weakened condition, such a spell could kill you once its effects wear off.*

How did he know what she was trying to do?

He was inside her head, listening!

How do you know the language of my ancestors? Mercy demanded.

Because they were my ancestors, too, and just as your elders taught you the language, my elders taught me.

"Doesn't knowing to what lengths I'm willing to go to escape from you tell you anything?" she shouted.

Judah didn't reply.

Suddenly she felt him probing her mind. No! He was trying to erase the mystical connections she had been creating. One by one, the words disappeared. She struggled to replace them, but he worked faster than she did, removing more than she recreated, until the magic of the words exploded inside her, shattering the last of her energy and leaving her completely vulnerable.

He came toward her again, determination in every step.

"You're an animal! A brute!" She inched backward, intending to turn and run, but he was on her before she realized it, swooping down over her like a giant bird of prey capturing his quarry.

She struggled, beating her fists against his face and chest, flailing like a fish on a hook. While physically fighting him, she delved deeply inside herself, seeking the core of her strength. She might be weak and exhausted, but the essence of her powers remained. Always.

When Judah manacled her wrists in one hand and twisted her arms behind her back with the other, she kicked at him, hitting his ankles and calves. He thrust his left knee between her thighs and slid his leg around and behind hers, causing her to lose her balance. They fell together onto the ground, Mercy on her back, the wind knocked out of her, and Judah sprawled on top of her.

She gasped for breath, her chest aching as her lungs struggled for air.

He rose up just enough so that she could catch her breath, but before she had a chance to renew their sparring match, Judah plunged his hand between her thighs and ripped the torn fragments of her panties from her body. Mercy bucked up, trying to stop him, but inadvertently drew his exploring fingers into her feminine folds. He stroked his thumb across her nub as he delved two fingers inside her.

She keened softly as pure sensation spiraled through her.

He lowered his head and nudged the tattered edges of her bodice and bra apart to reveal her left breast. He lapped her nipple with the tip of his tongue, the action eliciting soft whimpers from her throat. While his thumb worked her nub and his fingers explored, his mouth covered her nipple and areola, sucking greedily.

Mercy lifted her arms and pushed against his chest, her movements weak and ineffectual. Not because she no longer had the strength to fight him, but because she no longer had the will to fight herself. She wanted Judah as much as she had wanted him seven years ago when she hadn't known he was Ansara. No, that wasn't quite true. She wanted him even more now than she had then.

She brought her right arm up and around his neck. Her fingers forked through his long, black hair, cupping the back of his head, holding him to her breast. She slipped her left hand between them and rubbed her open palm over his erection.

Judah growled like the aroused beast he was, and flung her hand aside to open his trousers and free his straining sex. When he withdrew his hand from between her thighs and lifted his head from her breast, she whimpered.

He looked down at her; their gazes locked. Passion ignited between them, shooting sparks of energy all around their bodies. While she draped her left arm across his back and yanked his shirt free of his slacks, he shoved his hands under her hips and lifted her up to meet his swift, hard push into her body. He took her with relentless force, battering her repeatedly, completely out of control. Clinging to him, she gladly took all that he gave her, as wildly hungry for him as he was for her. For every thrust, she countered. For every hot, tongue-dueling kiss, she reciprocated. For every earthy, erotic word he uttered, she replied in kind.

A passion that intense had to burn itself out quickly, otherwise it would have destroyed them. Mercy came first, spinning apart, unraveling with a pleasure that bordered on pain, a sensation she wished could go on forever. While she trembled beneath him, gasping and moaning, he climaxed so fiercely that his release caused the earth beneath them to tremble. Judah sank into her, his large, lean body a heavy weight that she held close, longing to capture this one perfect moment while they were one, their bodies still joined.

He lifted his head and gazed down at her. "Sweet, sweet Mercy."

She caressed his cheek.

He rolled off her and onto the ground beside her. When she glanced at him, she noticed that he was staring up at the starry night sky. She didn't know what to say or how to act. Had what just happened between them meant anything more to him than a sexual conquest? Now that he'd had her, would he not want her again?

"Judah?"

He didn't respond.

She lay there on the ground for several minutes, then sat up and pulled her tattered dress together, holding it at the waist. She rose to her feet, then glanced down at Judah and saw her ripped panties lying beside him. She turned from him and walked away, not caring in which direction she went.

When she reached the waterfall, she crept down the rough pathway that led to the small cave behind it. After removing the remnants of her dress and bra, she stepped beneath the cascading water and let the cool, clean spray rinse away the scent of Judah Ansara from her body.

Loving a man should bring a woman joy, not sorrow. The aftermath of lovemaking should be a time for togetherness. How could she love Judah so completely, so desperately, when he was an Ansara? How could she yearn to be with him, to lie with him, to be his woman forever, when she meant nothing to him?

Where was her pride? Her strength? Her common sense?

Without warning, Judah intruded on her shower. Totally naked, he stood under the waterfall in front of her, tilted his head and tossed his hair back over his bare shoulders. There in the moonlight, beneath the crisp, roaring water, he reached for her. She went into his arms willingly, unable to resist. He took her mouth in a kiss that spoke more distinctly than any words could have, telling her that he wanted her again, that he was far from finished with her. The kiss deepened as their desire revived, hot and overpowering. He lifted her up, his big hands cradling her buttocks. She straddled his hips as he walked them out from under the waterfall and against the boulder behind it. Balancing her against the rock surface, he buried himself inside. She gasped with the sheer pleasure of being filled so completely. He hammered into her as she clung to him, and within moments they came simultaneously. Judah eased her down and onto her feet, her naked body grazing over his slowly, his mouth on her lips, her cheeks, in her hair, on her neck, devouring her.

"I can't get enough of you." He growled the words, resentment in his tone.

"I know," she whispered, unable to move away from him. "I feel the same way. What are we going to do?"

He cupped her face with both hands. "For the rest of the night, we're going to forget who we are. You aren't Princess Mercy Raintree, and I'm not Judah Ansara. We're just a man and a woman, with no past and no future."

"And come morning?"

He didn't respond. But she knew the answer to her question. In the morning they would be enemies again, warriors in an eternal battle, tribe against tribe, Raintree against Ansara.

Judah roused at dawn, the sound of his cousin Claude's voice a wake-up call inside his head. He rolled over and felt the soft, naked body lying beside him, her arm draped across his waist. Mercy. His sweet Mercy. They had spent the night having sex again and again until they were spent. And yet just the sight of her aroused him, strengthening his morning hard-on.

Judah, answer me, Claude called.

What do you want?

Why aren't you answering your phone?

His phone? Damn, where was his phone?

Give me a minute.

Judah eased out of bed, careful not to wake Mercy, and spied his slacks lying on the floor where he'd tossed his clothes when he and Mercy had returned to the cabin after their tryst at the waterfall. He walked quietly across the room, bent over, picked up his pants and delved into the pocket to check for his phone. It was still there, vibrating away, signaling an incoming call. After slipping into his pants, he left the bedroom and went into the living room.

He put the phone to his ear. "Claude?"

"About damn time you answered."

"What's going on?" Judah asked, keeping his voice low.

"I've been trying to reach you for the past hour, and finally gave up and used telepathy, despite the risks."

"Do you know what time it is? It's not even daylight here."

"You should know I wouldn't bother you if it wasn't urgent. We've got big trouble here in Terrebonne."

"Hold on."

Judah glanced back at the open bedroom door. Mercy still slept. Moving silently so he wouldn't disturb her, he went outside and made his way a good thirty feet from the cabin.

"Okay, now tell me what's going on."

"Cael's minions have been quite busy throughout Terrebonne, spreading a rumor that Dranir Judah has sired a half-Raintree child."

"Son of a bitch," Judah cursed. "How widespread is the rumor?"

"It's just begun, but it's spreading like wildfire. By daybreak, half the island will know. By lunchtime, the other half will have heard the news. You have to know that Cael is hoping this will incite a rebellion."

"We need to do damage control right away. Call an emergency council meeting. Tell Sidra that I need her to address the people this evening and tell them about her prophecy."

"You have to come home, Judah. You need to be at Sidra's side when she confirms the rumor that you have a mixed-breed daughter."

"I can't leave Eve," Judah said. "Cael expects me to rush home when I learn of the rumors about Eve's existence. One of the reasons he's done this is to lure me back to Terrebonne, to leave Eve unprotected."

"If it comes down to a choice between Eve and your people…"

"There is no choice. Sidra has prophesied that Eve's existence is necessary for the continuation of the Ansara tribe. She told me that if I am to save my people, I must protect Eve."

"I don't know how well Sidra's prophecy will be received. She has said that Eve will be the mother of a new clan, that she will transform the Ansara."

"The people know that in her ninety years of life, Sidra's prophecies have provided us with unerring truths about the future. The Ansara revere her and believe in her prophecies."

Claude remained silent for several long moments. Judah simply waited, knowing his cousin would speak his mind after giving Judah's words more thought.

"If you feel you must stay there and protect your daughter, then I will stand at Sidra's side tonight when she addresses the Ansara kingdom," Claude said. "Since you can't return in person to Terrebonne, may I make a suggestion, my lord?"

Claude did not have to explain to Judah what he must do. He knew. "You want me to make a psychic connection to you and speak through you to my people."

"I will contact you later when our plans are finalized and the time is set for Sidra's address." Claude hesitated for a moment, then added, "These are dangerous times for the Ansara. It would be unwise to let your guard down, especially around anyone who is Raintree."

Claude hung up, leaving Judah to decipher his cryptic message. Claude could be referring to Eve, since she was half

Raintree. But he suspected that the Raintree Claude believed he would be most susceptible to was Princess Mercy.

When Mercy woke at dawn to find herself alone in the cabin, she considered it a blessing. How could she have faced Judah in the cold light of day and accepted the fact that they were no longer lovers but once again bitter enemies? She crawled out of bed, dragging the top sheet with her to cover her naked body and protect her from the early morning chill. As she made her way to the bathroom, she stepped on the dress that Judah had sliced half in two last night.

She would have to mend it.

As she picked up the tattered garment, just the feel of it beneath her fingertips set off her empathic powers. The cotton material held fragments of her own energy and all the emotions she had experienced when Judah's cold, penetrating glare had cut her clothes apart. Anger. Fear. Desire.

She hugged the fabric to her and buried her face in its softness as she relived the experience of Judah overpowering her and taking her savagely on the hard ground.

Carrying the dress with her, Mercy went into the bathroom, where she relieved herself, then washed her hands and splattered cold water in her face. She had the look of a woman who had spent the night making love.

Stop thinking about Judah, about the hours of pleasure you shared, about how much you love him.

Mercy lifted her dress from the hook on the back of the door, where she'd left it, closed the commode lid, readjusted the sheet around her chest and sat down. Fixing her gaze on the repair job at hand, she concentrated on using the heat she could generate with the touch of her hands to fuse the material together.

She had almost completed her task when she heard footsteps beyond the bathroom door. Her hand stilled. Her heart-beat accelerated.

Judah?

She flung the dress aside and opened the door. Wearing only his wrinkled trousers, Judah stood in the middle of the bedroom. They looked at each other for one heart-stopping moment; then he moved steadily, purposefully, toward her. She waited for him there in the bathroom doorway. When he reached her, he grasped the edge of the sheet where she'd tucked it across her chest, gave it a strong tug and peeled it from her body.

"It's dawn," she said.

"Then we'd better not wait. It'll be full daylight before long."

He lifted her into his arms and carried her back to bed, then stripped off his slacks and joined her. They mated with the same fury they had shared the first time they made love last night.

Would this be the final time? she wondered. Would she never lie in his arms again, never belong to him again, never possess and be possessed with such passion?

They had walked halfway back to the house together, then Mercy had gone on ahead and managed to sneak up the back-stairs without getting caught. She had showered and dressed before she heard Sidonia stirring, then started her day as if everything were normal. Although Sidonia hadn't questioned her about why she hadn't returned home last night, she *had* given her several damning looks during the day, especially whenever Judah was nearby.

And to complicate matters even more, Eve apparently thought that her parents were now a couple. She was too young to understand anything about sex between adults, but she was intuitive enough, possessing some of Mercy's empathic talents as well as both her parents' basic psychic gifts, to know that things had changed between Mercy and Judah. Even if Judah didn't love her, Mercy accepted the fact that she did love him and always would. A Raintree mating with an Ansara was as improbable as a hawk mating with a tiger. But not impossible. What did seem impossible was that a Raintree truly loved an Ansara.

How would she ever be able to explain her feelings for Judah to Dante and Gideon? God help her, how would they react when she told them that Eve was half Ansara?

Dante could be stern and unforgiving, but he was always logical and usually fair. As with most people born into a position of supreme authority, he had grown up with a sense of entitlement, expecting to make all the decisions for his younger siblings. For the most part Gideon had followed in his big brother's footsteps until they grew to manhood; then he had become his own person, not always agreeing with Dante and occasionally locking horns with him.

When Mercy had told them she was pregnant, both Dante and Gideon had demanded the name of Eve's father. The fact that she had refused to name the man had enraged both her brothers, but in time they had let the subject drop. She knew that they assumed Eve's father was one of the Ungifted, or maybe a "stray," as Dante referred to humans who had developed gifts independently but were neither Raintree nor Ansara. Only with Sidonia's help had Mercy been able to keep Eve's unusually powerful abilities hidden and the truth of her paternity a secret.

But this was one secret that couldn't be hidden for much longer. Once Judah had dealt with Cael, he would try to take Eve.

No matter how much she loved Judah, she couldn't give him their child. And there was only one way to stop him.

But could she kill him?

* * *

After dinner that evening, Judah left the house without any explanation. He chose an isolated area more than a mile from the house and far from any of the guest cottages. Standing alone and insulated from all that was Raintree, he telepathically linked with Claude. He could hear what his cousin heard and see what he saw. He listened as Sidra addressed the assembled council, the highest ranking officers and many of the nobility, all congregated in the great hall at the palace. Through closed-circuit television, her message was carried to every home in Terrebonne.

"I have seen a child with golden hair and golden eyes. She has been born for her father's people, to transform the Ansara from darkness into light. Seven thousand years of Ansara and Raintree noble blood runs through her veins."

Gasps and grumbles and cries of outrage rose from the audience.

Judah spoke through Claude. "Do you dare question Sidra's visions? Do you doubt her love for our people? Has my brother's madness infected all of you?"

Nine tenths of those assembled rose to their feet. Their shouts of faith in Sidra and allegiance to Judah completely overshadowed the handful of dissenters.

Sidra spoke again, her words of wisdom reassuring the Ansara that Judah's mixed-breed child was unlike any child ever born. "Eve is the child of our ancestors, the seed of a united people. She is more than Ansara, more than Raintree. Our fate is in her hands. Her life is more precious to me than my own."

The assembly listened with reverence, and through Claude, Judah sensed their doubts and concerns, but also their acceptance and hope.

A single request came from numerous Ansara, all wanting

to know if, when Judah returned to Terrebonne, he would bring the Princess Eve home to her people.

"Princess Eve will come to Terrebonne when the time is right for her to take her place as your future Dranira," Judah replied through Claude.

When the cheers died down, a lone woman stepped forward and posed one simple question. "What of the child's mother?" Alexandria Ansara asked. "Are we to believe that Princess Mercy will simply give her daughter to you?"

A deafening silence fell over the assembly as they waited for Judah's reply.

You must answer them, my lord, Claude told Judah.

As he contemplated his response, Judah felt Sidra's hand on Claude's arm and sensed that she wanted to speak to him through his cousin.

Your fate is tied to hers. Your future is her future, your life, her life. If you die, she dies. If she dies, you die.

Every muscle in Judah's body tensed, every nerve charged with electrical energy. He understood that if Sidra could have explained further, she would have. Her prophecy was open to interpretation, but Judah knew that she spoke of Mercy, not Eve, and if he and Mercy fought over possession of their child, whichever one of them survived would die a thousand deaths during their lifetime.

"When the time comes, I will do what must be done," Judah told his people.

Sunset colored the evening sky as Mercy searched for Judah. He had left the house shortly after supper and had not returned. While she had been giving Eve her bath, Eve had stopped splashing her array of tub toys in the waist-deep, lukewarm water and grasped Mercy's hand.

"It's Daddy. Something's wrong. He's very sad."

"Are you talking to your father? Didn't he tell you not to—"

"I'm not talking to him," Eve said. "I promise."

"Then how do you know that he's sad?"

"I just know." She placed her hand over her heart. "In here. The way I sometimes just know things. He needs you, Mother. Go to him."

So here she was, sent off by her daughter on a quest of compassion. But when she found Judah, would he accept her comfort, or would he turn her away?

There was no point in wasting time taking useless routes that wouldn't lead her to Judah. She used all her senses to home in on his location. Once she picked up on his presence, she followed the energy trail left by his powerful aura.

She found him alone and lost in his own thoughts, sitting on one of several stone boulders in an isolated clearing deep within the woods.

"Judah?"

He turned his head and looked at her, but said nothing.

She took several hesitant steps toward him. "Are you all right?" she asked.

"Why are you here?"

"Eve sent me. She's concerned about you. She said you were sad."

"Go back to the house. Tell Eve that I'm fine."

"But you're not. Eve is right, something is wrong, and—"

Using a psychic thrust, Judah shoved Mercy backward, just enough to warn her off but not knock her down. She staggered for only a second.

"I get the message," she told him.

"Then leave me alone."

"Is it Cael? Has something happened? If you'll tell me, I can help."

"Leave me!" Judah shot up off the boulder, hell's fury in

his eyes. "I don't want you." As he came toward her, he pinned her to the spot, and she didn't try to break through the invisible bonds that kept her from moving. "I don't need you. Damn you, Mercy Raintree!"

Judah grabbed her shoulders and shook her as frustration and anger and passion drove him hard. She felt what he felt and realized that he hated her for making him care.

"My poor Judah."

He clutched her face between his open palms and ravaged her with a possessive kiss. Swept up by the passion neither of them could deny, Mercy surrendered herself. Heart. Mind. Body.

And soul.

Chapter 15

Sunday, 11:08 a.m.
The Summer Solstice

Eve bounced onto the foot of Mercy's bed and whispered loudly, "I've been up for hours, Mommy. Are you and Daddy going to sleep all day?"

Mercy's eyes flew open. Startled by her daughter's cheerful greeting, she woke from a deep, sated sleep. "Eve?"

Wiggling around, making her way up the bed to position herself between Mercy and Judah, Eve spoke a bit louder now that she had roused her mother. "Sidonia told me not to disturb you, but I got tired of waiting, so I sneaked up the backstairs when she wasn't looking."

"What the hell?" Judah cracked open one eye and then the other. "Eve?" He shot straight up in bed, exposing his naked chest.

As Mercy lifted herself into a sitting position, the sheet covering her slipped, and she suddenly remembered that she was as naked as Judah. She grabbed the edge of the sheet and yanked it up to cover her breasts.

"Hi, Daddy."

"Hello, Eve." Judah glanced at Mercy, as if asking her how they were going to handle this rather awkward situation.

"You're not going to stay in bed the rest of the day, are you?" Eve looked from one parent to the other.

"No, we…er…uh…" Mercy stammered. "Why don't you go to your room or back downstairs with Sidonia, and Daddy and I will—"

Sidonia's voice bellowed, "Eve Raintree, I thought I told you not to disturb your mother. Come here right this min—" Sidonia stopped abruptly in the doorway, her eyes round and her mouth agape as she stared at the threesome in Mercy's bed. "This won't do," she muttered. "This just will not do." She shook her head disapprovingly.

"Eve, go with Sidonia," Mercy told her daughter.

Eve eyed her mother from tousled hair to bare shoulders. "Why aren't you wearing your gown?" She turned her gaze on Judah. "Daddy, are you naked, too?"

Judah cleared his throat but couldn't disguise the tilt of his lips.

How dare he find this amusing! Mercy glowered at him. He smiled.

"Come along, child." Sidonia held out her hand. "It's already summertime weather, and no doubt your mother got hot last night and removed her gown so she could cool off." If looks alone could kill, Sidonia's outraged glower would have zapped Judah. Thank goodness her old nanny didn't have the ability to shoot psychic bolts.

Making no move to leave her parents, Eve asked, "Did you get hot, too, Daddy?"

"Uh, yeah, something like that," Judah replied.

"Eve, go with Sidonia," Mercy said. "*Now.*"

Puckering up as if she were on the verge of tears, Eve scooted back down to the foot of the bed, then slid off and onto her feet. " I woke you up because I needed to tell you that something's going on. I thought you and Daddy would want to know."

"Whatever it is, it can wait for a few minutes," Mercy said.

When Eve dawdled, her shoulders slumped, her head hung low, Sidonia grabbed her hand and marched her toward the door. Dragging her feet at the threshold, Eve balked. Glancing back over her shoulder, she said, "I'm going. But can I ask Daddy one question first?"

"What do you want to ask me?" Judah focused on Eve.

"Well, actually, it's two questions," Eve admitted.

When Sidonia jerked on Eve's hand, she issued her nanny a stern, warning glare.

"Ask your questions," Judah said.

"Uncle Dante doesn't have a crown even though he's a Dranir." Eve's eyes sparkled with anticipation. "I was just wondering if you have a crown?"

What? Huh? Mercy's mind couldn't quite comprehend her daughter's comment and question. "Eve, why would your father have a—"

"Actually, I just wanted to know if, since I'm a Raintree princess and an Ansara princess, do I get to wear two crowns? Maybe a solid gold crown and another one that's all sparkly diamonds. Or maybe just one really big crown."

Mercy snapped around and stared at Judah, who had gone deadly still. "What's she talking about?"

Unclenching his jaw, Judah ignored Mercy and answered

his daughter. "I don't have a crown. But if you want a crown or two crowns or half a dozen, I'll get them for you."

Lifting her shoulders, tilting her chin and smiling like the proverbial cat that ate the canary, Eve turned around and all but pulled a stunned Sidonia out of the room.

Mercy got out of bed, found her robe lying on the floor, snatched it up and slipped into it hurriedly. Then she confronted Judah, who had gotten up, found his discarded slacks and was in the process of zipping the fly when Mercy headed toward him. She marched up to him and looked him right in the eyes.

"Why would Eve think you might have a crown, and why would she think she's an Ansara princess?"

He shrugged. "Who knows what puts ideas in a child's head?"

"Uh-uh, mister. That's not going to work with me."

"I'm starving. What about you? After the workout we had last night…all night—" he tried using that cocky, aren't-I-sexy? grin on her "—I need to rebuild my strength."

Mercy grabbed Judah's arm. "Answer my question. And so help me, you'd better tell me the truth."

He didn't try to veil his thoughts completely, allowing Mercy to momentarily use her empathic ability.

What is the truth between us? We have a child we can't share. A life we can't share. I have never wanted another woman the way I want you, have never known such pain or such pleasure. If it were within my power to change the way things are, I would. But I cannot betray my people.

Mercy jerked her hand away, her gaze glued to his face. "You lied to me. You *are* the Ansara Dranir."

"Yes, I am, and Eve is an Ansara princess, heir to the throne. According to our great seer, Sidra Ansara, Eve was born for my people. That's why I rescinded the ancient decree to kill all mixed-breed children—to protect my daughter."

"No! Eve is my daughter. My baby. She's a Raintree."

Eve's words echoed inside Mercy's head. *I was born for the Ansara.* "Only a few dozen Ansara were left alive after *The Battle*. Just how many Ansara are there now? Thousands? Hundreds of thousands?"

"Don't do this," Judah told her. "It serves no purpose, and it changes nothing."

"My God, how can you say that? The Raintree have believed that the Ansara were scattered over the earth and—no, no!"

She backed away from him, her eyes bright with fear. "I worried about how my giving birth to a half Ansara child would affect me, but when I saw no visible signs all these years, I assumed I was for the most part unaffected, but now..."

"You're wondering how much if any Ansara there might be in you, since you gave birth to the Ansara Dranir's child. I don't know, but my guess is none. You seem to have remained totally Raintree."

"But it's possible I was somehow affected and I'm not aware of it. When a Raintree woman takes a human mate, he does not become Raintree, but when a woman gives birth to a Raintree child, she becomes Raintree. It stands to reason that when a woman gives birth to an Ansara child, especially the child of the Dranir, it would somehow change her."

Mercy knew that she could no longer keep Eve's paternity a secret. If she had even suspected that Judah was the Ansara Dranir, she would have gone to Dante and told him the truth years ago. Was it too late now? It couldn't be coincidence that the Ansara Dranir had come to the sanctuary and saved her from one of his own. One of Cael's followers had tried to kill her, but Judah had stopped him. Why? Not because he loved her.

"Cael wants to be Dranir," Mercy said. "That's why he intends to kill you. And Eve. He can't allow your daughter to live, because even if she is half Raintree, she threatens his claim on the throne. My God, it all makes sense now. My child is at the center of an Ansara civil war."

"Don't do anything rash," Judah said. "I swear to you that keeping Eve safe is my number one priority. I won't let Cael hurt her."

"You've brought this evil here to us!" Mercy screamed. "If you'd never come to the sanctuary, if you'd stayed away…"

"You would be dead," Judah told her. "Greynell would have killed you."

"Why did you stop him from killing me?"

Judah hesitated, a look of anguish in his cold, gray eyes. "No other Ansara has the right to kill you."

Mercy couldn't breathe. Her pulse pounded in her head, and for a millisecond she thought she might faint. "I understand. Dranir Judah had already claimed me as his kill."

Sidonia's screams echoed up the stairs, down the hall and through the open door to Mercy's bedroom.

"Eve!" Mercy cried as she ran past Judah on her way out of the room.

Judah followed her down the backstairs. When they entered the kitchen, they instantly saw what had frightened Sidonia. Levitating several feet off the floor in the middle of the kitchen, Eve hung in midair, her mouth open, her little body stiff, and rotating slowly around and around. Her long, willowy hair floated straight up, parting in the back to reveal a glimpse of the blue crescent moon birthmark that branded her an Ansara. Her eyes faded from Raintree green to shimmering yellow-brown, then back to green. Soft, golden light twinkled on each of her fingertips.

Mercy rushed toward her daughter but couldn't touch her. A barrier of some kind protected Eve, sealing her off completely from everything around her.

Judah shoved Mercy out of the way, and he, too, tried to breach the shield around Eve. "It's impenetrable."

"This has never happened to her before," Mercy said. "Is Cael doing this? Are you doing it?"

"No, I don't think this is Cael's handiwork. And I swear to you that I'm not doing it." He stared at their child, who was deep in the throes of some unknown type of transformation. "Maybe it has something to do with Sidra's prophecy."

Grabbing Judah's arm, Mercy demanded, "What about the prophecy?"

"He's trying to change her." Sidonia pointed a bony finger at Judah. "He's drawing the Raintree out of her. You see the way her eyes are going from green to gold."

"Hush, Sidonia." Mercy looked at Judah, her gaze imploring him.

"Sidra says that Eve is a child of light, born for the Ansara." Judah focused completely on Eve. "As her father, I'd die to protect her. And as the Dranir, I am sworn to protect her for the sake of my people's future."

Mercy wasn't sure what to believe. Was Judah telling her the truth, or at least a half-truth? Or was he lying to her? "We have to do something to stop this." She tried again to penetrate the force field surrounding Eve but was thrown backward from an electrical charge the shield emitted. "There has to be a way to break the barrier."

"I don't think that will be necessary," Judah said. "Look at her. She seems to be returning to normal."

Eve floated down to the floor, landing easily on her feet. Her hair fell about her shoulders, and the light on her fingertips disappeared. She glanced from Judah to Mercy, her eyes once again completely Raintree green.

"Eve? Eve, are you all right?" Mercy asked, choking back tears.

Eve ran to Mercy, her arms outstretched. Mercy lifted her daughter into her arms and held her possessively. Resting her head on Mercy's shoulder, Eve clung to her mother. When Judah approached, Mercy gave him a warning glare, all but snarling in her protective mother mode.

Suddenly Eve lifted her head and gasped. "Oh, shit!"

"What?" Mercy and Judah asked in unison.

"Where did you ever hear such an ugly word?" Sidonia, ever the grandmotherly nanny, scolded.

Eve looked at Sidonia. "I heard Uncle Dante say it. And Uncle Gideon."

Mercy grasped Eve's chin to gain her attention. "When did you hear your uncles—"

"Just a minute ago," Eve said. "I heard them both say it. Uncle Dante said it when he found out that the bad Ansara caused the fire at his casino. And Uncle Gideon said it when he found out that the person who killed Echo's friend was a very bad Ansara."

"How do you know about the fire?" Mercy asked. "And Echo's roommate?" She hadn't told Eve anything about either incident.

"I heard what Uncle Dante and Uncle Gideon were thinking when they said 'oh, shit' right before I said it."

If Eve had heard her uncles' thoughts correctly, then that meant only one thing. "They're trying to kill us." Mercy realized the horrible truth. "The Ansara went after each of us—Dante and Gideon and me and...oh, God—Echo!" Holding Eve tightly, she started moving backward, away from Judah. "You knew what was happening, didn't you? Has it all been a lie? Are you and your brother really allies?"

"Don't jump to conclusions," Judah said. "Everything I've told you about Cael is the truth."

"Just like everything you told me about *you* was the truth?"

Judah took several steps toward her.

"Stop!" Mercy shouted. "I mean it. Don't come near me or Eve."

"Mommy, don't be mad at my daddy." Eve gazed into Mercy's eyes.

Suddenly the telephone rang.

"Answer it, Sidonia," Mercy said.

Sidonia scurried across the room and picked up the portable phone from the charger base. "Hello." She sighed. "Thank God, it's you. Yes, she's here." Sidonia brought the telephone to Mercy, all the while glaring at Judah as if she thought her evil stare could keep him at bay. "It's Dante."

"Dante?" Mercy said as she took the phone.

"Don't talk, just listen," he told her. "We're under attack from the Ansara. They were behind the fire here at the casino, and behind the attempt on Echo's life. Don't ask me any particulars. Just believe me when I say that I know it's only a matter of time before they strike the sanctuary. It'll be soon. Today would be my guess since—"

"Today is Alban Heruin." *Light of the Shore*, the summer solstice, lying between *Light of the Earth* and *Light of the Water*, the equinoctial celebrations. "The height of the sun's power."

"I've just boarded the jet, and we're leaving Reno. I'm on my way home. Gideon has already left Wilmington. We should both be there by late this afternoon."

"Dante, there's something I need to tell you." How could she explain to him that this was all her fault?

"Whatever it is, it'll have to wait."

"Please—"

"Just hold things together until we get there. Understand?"

"I understand."

"And if a woman named Lorna tries to contact you—she's mine."

The dial tone hummed in Mercy's ear. "Dante?" She flung the phone down on the kitchen counter, then turned to confront Judah.

"Daddy's gone," Eve said.

Mercy visually scanned the room. Judah *was* gone. When had he left, and where was he now?

A couple of seconds after Dante called Mercy, Judah heard Claude's telepathic message. *You're not answering your cell phone again. Damn it, Judah, all hell's broken loose and you've left me no choice but to—*

All hell's broken loose here, too, Judah told his cousin. *Mercy knows that I'm the Dranir.*

That's the least of our problems right now.

Judah ran up the backstairs. *Look, if you're about to tell me that Cael not only sent someone after Mercy but after her brothers and her cousin Echo, too, don't bother. Dante just called Mercy, and I listened in on their conversation.*

Then they figured it out just about the same time the council did, Claude said.

Don't say anything else. Give me a minute. My phone's upstairs.

We don't have a minute to waste.

Judah rushed into Mercy's bedroom and searched for his cell phone. He finally found it lying on the floor next to his shirt, covered with one of his socks. He picked it up and called Claude.

"What do you know that I don't?" Judah asked.

"We received information that Cael is somewhere in North Carolina," Claude said.

"That's no surprise."

"We suspect that he has up to a hundred warriors with him, and they're somewhere between Asheville and the Raintree sanctuary."

"A hundred! How the hell did he—crap! He's been recruiting these people for quite some time, hasn't he? Which isn't really a surprise."

"Well, this *will* surprise you—according to our informant, Cael is planning an all-out attack on the sanctuary sometime within the next twelve hours."

"Damn! What does Sidra say? Why didn't she see this coming?"

"She's not sure, but she suspects that Cael has somehow cloaked the details of his plan so that none of our Ansara seers were able to clearly foresee it. And he's probably put some kind of spell on all the Raintree seers, as well."

"We can't let this happen," Judah said.

"We can't stop it."

"We can try. Call in the Select Guard. Have as many as will fit on the jet come with you immediately. Have the rest follow as soon as possible. Bring them here to North Carolina. Fly into Asheville. Civilian dress for everyone. Understand?"

"Yes, my lord. We need to be as inconspicuous as possible. They can change into uniform on the way to the sanctuary."

"I'll arrange ground transportation for you, and when you arrive outside the sanctuary boundary, I'll be waiting for you," Judah said. "Contact me when you're close. In the meantime, once I'm certain Mercy can safeguard Eve during the battle, I'll make plans of my own."

"I know your first priority is to protect Princess Eve. But once she's no longer in harm's way, it will be too late to turn back. It will be all-out war between the Ansara and the Raintree. Cael has left us no choice but to fight now."

"Then we'll fight," Judah said.

"Where's my daddy?" Eve asked as Mercy knelt in front of her daughter. "Where did he go?"

"I don't know," Mercy lied. She suspected Judah had either left to join Cael or was making plans to do so. "But you mustn't worry about your father." She cupped Eve's beautiful little face with her open palms. "Listen to me, sweetheart, and do exactly what I tell you to do."

"All right," Eve said, her voice shaky. "Something really bad is wrong, isn't it?"

'Yes, something really bad is wrong. Your father's brother is going to come here and bring some other very bad men with him. So I'm going to send you with Sidonia to the Caves of Awenasa, and I'm going to invoke a cloaking spell to keep you and Sidonia safe."

"I need to be here," Eve said. "With you and Daddy. You'll need me."

Mercy choked with emotion. "You can't stay here. Your father and I can't do what we have to do if you're here. I'll be—*we'll* be too concerned about you. Please, Eve, go with Sidonia and stay there until I or Uncle Dante or Uncle Gideon comes and gets you."

Eve stared at Mercy, a soulful expression in her true Raintree green eyes.

"Tell me that you understand and that you'll do as I ask," Mercy said.

Eve put her arms around Mercy's neck and hugged her. "I'll go with Sidonia to the caves. You can go ahead and do the cloaking spell. I won't try to stop you."

Mercy heaved a deep sigh of relief. "Thank you, my sweet baby girl." She hugged Eve with the fierceness of a warrior facing possible death, knowing she might never see her child again.

When Mercy finally released Eve, she stood and turned to Sidonia. "I'm trusting you with the most precious thing in the world to me."

"You know that I'll guard her with my life."

Eve went to Sidonia and took her hand. The two waited while Mercy spoke the ancient words, invoking the most powerful cloaking spell she knew of, one that would make it difficult—hopefully impossible—for anyone to track and find Eve.

Mercy stood at the kitchen door, and watched while Sidonia led Eve across the open field and toward the higher mountain range. The Caves of Awenasa were over three miles away, deep in the forest that covered the far western mountainside. Within minutes, both Sidonia and Eve disappeared, the cloaking spell in full effect now, protecting them from detection, guarding them from harm.

Believing that Eve was safe and that she would instantly know if anyone had penetrated the cloaking spell, Mercy hurried upstairs to dress and make preparations for what was to come: battle—perhaps the final battle—with the Ansara.

Fifteen minutes later, dressed in black pants, knee-high black boots and a crimson blouse, Mercy came down the front stairs and headed for her study. Dante would contact all Raintree within driving distance first, and then word would go out to Raintree around the world. How many could actually make it to the sanctuary before the Ansara attack, she didn't know. There were only a handful visiting the home place right now—less than twenty in all, and some of them not at full strength. And her guess was that another twenty-five or so could be here within a few hours.

She also had no way of knowing how many Ansara comprised the forces Judah and Cael would bring down on the sanctuary, or exactly when the first attack would take place. Soon, certainly. Within a few hours? Before sunset?

After entering her study, she picked up the phone and dialed Hugh's cabin. He answered on the third ring. "Hugh, it's Mercy. I need you to gather up all the Raintree visiting here at the sanctuary and bring them to the house. Do this as quickly as possible."

"All right," he replied. "Can you tell me what this is about?"

"I'll tell all of you as soon as you get here."

Mercy could hardly believe what was happening. She felt like such a fool—for the second time in her life. Both times thanks to Judah Ansara. How much of what he'd told her had been lies? Part of it? All of it? One thing she didn't doubt: he wanted Eve and was willing to kill Mercy to get her.

And she also believed that he had killed one of his own people to stop the man from killing her. Because Judah had claimed her as his kill and wouldn't allow anyone else the honor of taking the Raintree princess's life. No doubt Dante was also Judah's kill. And perhaps Gideon, too.

How was it possible that she loved Judah, loved him as much as she hated him? Why had she let down her defenses, even for a few days, a few hours, a few moments?

All the while Judah had proclaimed Eve was in life-threatening danger from his brother, had it simply been a ruse, a plot the brothers had concocted together? Had Judah's purpose in staying at the sanctuary been to keep Mercy distracted?

No, it wasn't possible that he had fooled her so completely.

Then where is he? Why isn't he here explaining himself to me?

Damn you, Judah. Damn you!

Reno, Nevada, 9:15 a.m.(Reno time)

Lorna hadn't taken the time to make any calls while she'd still been at Dante's house; instead, she'd grabbed his address book, checked to see that both Mercy and Gideon were listed, then run for her old Corolla. While she was on the way to the airport, she put her cell phone to use. She knew she didn't have time to fly commercial, but she didn't know how to go about renting a jet. She had a pocket full of cash and one credit card with a five-thousand-dollar limit. If that wasn't enough money, she didn't know what she would do.

The only person she knew in Reno who might be able to help her was Al Franklin, Dante's chief of security. He wasn't exactly on her favorites list, but Dante not only liked him, he trusted him—and this was an emergency.

Thank God, thank God. Al's number was listed, too. She'd been afraid Dante would have all his numbers stored on his cell phone, which he had with him. Swiftly, keeping one eye on the twisting road, she punched in the numbers.

"'Lo?"

The sleepy voice reminded her that it was—she glanced at the dashboard clock—not yet ten o'clock on a Sunday morning.

"This is Lorna Clay!" she half yelled. "Dante's gone— there's trouble at Sanctuary—he might get killed! I have to get there. How do I hire a jet?"

"Whoa! Wait—what did you say?"

"Sanctuary. There's trouble at Sanctuary. I need a jet!"

"How is Dante getting there?"

"I don't know!" Why was he playing twenty questions? Why didn't he answer *her* questions? "He just ran out. I'm about half an hour behind him, I think."

"Go to the airport," Al said swiftly. "He has two corporate jets. He'll take the bigger, faster one. I'll call and have the smaller one fueled and ready. It'll take longer— you'll have to put down somewhere for fuel—but you still won't be more than an hour, hour and a half, behind him."

"Thank you," she said, almost sobbing with relief. "I didn't think—"

"You didn't think I'd help? You said the magic word."

"'Please'?" She didn't know if she'd said 'please,' but she'd definitely said 'thank you.'"

"Sanctuary," he said.

Wilmington, North Carolina, 1:00 p.m.

Hope Malory paced the kitchen nervously as she waited for the phone to ring. Gideon hadn't been gone much more than an hour, so she really shouldn't expect his call so soon, but still…she was anxious. He owed her a *serious* explanation.

When the phone finally did ring, she lurched forward and grabbed the receiver. "Hello?"

She held her breath as she waited for Gideon's calming, reasonable voice on the other end of the line. Her first clue that it wasn't Gideon was the lack of static.

A woman's smooth voice caused Hope's heart to drop. "Is this the Gideon Raintree residence?"

Great. An old girlfriend. A wannabe girlfriend. Maybe a telemarketer. "Yes, but he's not—"

"Not there, I know," the woman said, not quite so smoothly this time. There was an almost undetectable hint of panic in her voice. "There's no time for a proper explanation, but—"

That was the *wrong* thing to say. "I don't know who you are, but 'no time for a proper explanation' isn't going to earn you any points with me today."

Before Hope could hang up the phone, the woman laughed in a nervous but friendly way that caught her attention. "I can only imagine. I'll make this brief, then. My name is Lorna Clay. Dante and Gideon need us. I'm coming your way on a jet that's scheduled to land at Fairmont Executive Airport just west of Asheville shortly before six this evening. If you can pick me up, I'll explain all that I can while we're on our way to the Raintree home place."

Hope glanced at the clock on the kitchen wall and did some mental math, taking into account the horsepower in Gideon's Challenger. "I'll be there."

During the early afternoon, Mercy spoke to the eighteen Raintree visiting the home place, and together they began making preparations for the attack. By mid-afternoon, ten Raintree who lived within easy driving distance had arrived, including Echo, who had come flying in, tires screeching and horn honking. Her psychic abilities were powerful, but she had not yet mastered them, making her predictions a hodge-podge of sights and sounds and feelings. Mercy knew that one day soon, Echo would fulfill all the promise she now showed, including a latent empathic ability.

The moment Echo stormed into the house, she began calling Mercy's name as she ran from room to room. She shoved open the door to the study. Wild-eyed and frantic, she rushed toward Mercy and grasped her hand. "I've been going nuts all the way here. Seeing things. Hearing things. Help me, please." Echo clutched her head. "It won't stop. I had to pull off to the side of the road twice on the way here."

Mercy grasped Echo's trembling hands.

Bloody sunset. Silent twilight. Death and destruction. Mercy saw what Echo was seeing and understood the girl's panic. Working hurriedly, Mercy drew the fear and confusion from her young cousin's mind, and infused her with calmness and a sense of purpose. But Echo's mind fought what her subconscious perceived as interference and control.

Mercy clutched Echo by the shoulders and gave her a gentle shake. "Calm down. Now. We need you. I want you to concentrate. Can you do that?"

Echo quieted. "I—I can try."

"Good girl. Concentrate on the Ansara, think about the warriors who will soon attack the sanctuary. Try to find them."

"You mean…"

"I mean go deep and search for the Ansara who are close enough to reach the sanctuary before sunset." Mercy squeezed Eve's shoulders. "I'll be right with you every step of the way. I'll feel and see what you do."

Echo closed her eyes. "I'll do my best."

Mercy gave her shoulders another reassuring squeeze. "Concentrate on the name Cael Ansara. He's the Ansara Dranir's brother."

Echo nodded and closed her eyes again.

Mercy followed Echo, her mind and her cousin's separate and yet connected. Echo went deep within herself, while Mercy stood guard as she gently guided her cousin on a single, focused path.

A convoy of trucks filled with men, flanked front and back by jeeps, rolled along the highway. Cael Ansara, dressed all in black, rode in the first jeep.

Suddenly Echo saw only darkness and heard the screams of the dying. She fought to emerge from the vision, but Mercy urged her to fight her fear and follow through until the end. As if in accelerated motion, Echo's sight flashed over the faces of the Ansara warriors inside the trucks, and with Mercy's assistance, she absorbed minute traces of their emotions. The overwhelming hatred and savage bloodlust Echo sensed frightened her, and Mercy could no longer keep her focused. Realizing it was best not to force the matter, she helped Echo pull back from the vision as she took all the Ansara emotions from Echo and into herself.

"Crap!" Echo's eyes flew open, and she jerked away from Mercy. "There were at least a hundred of them. And they were all thinking about coming here, killing every Raintree in sight and capturing the home place."

Mercy staggered slightly as she struggled to dissolve the evil emotions trapped inside her. She could hear Echo talking to her, then felt her cousin shaking her, but she couldn't respond, couldn't return to the here and now, until she had disposed of the last particle of negative energy.

Several minutes later she slumped over, weak from the inner battle. Echo caught her before she hit the floor.

"Damn, that scares me," Echo said. "I've seen you do it before, but it's not an easy thing to watch."

Mercy offered her cousin a weak smile. "I'm all right."

"You saw what I saw, didn't you? There are so many of them, and they're heading here today."

"I know. We have to be as prepared for them as we can be. Dante and Gideon are on their way. I expect them to arrive sometime between five and six."

"How many Raintree do we have already here or that can make it here by the time Dante and Gideon arrive?" Echo asked.

"Not enough," Mercy said. "Not nearly enough."

5:40 p.m.

By late afternoon on the day of the summer solstice, a small band of Raintree were ready to go into battle to defend the sanctuary.

The clear blue sky slowly darkened with rain clouds moving in to obscure the sunlight. The rumble of distant thunder announced a brewing storm. But Mercy knew that Mother Nature had not created the impending tempest. Cael Ansara's forces had breached the protective shield around the Raintree sanctuary and were at this very moment charging toward the handful of Raintree prepared to defend their home place.

She had sent out Helene and Frederick as scouts, because of the few Raintree under her command, they possessed the strongest telepathic abilities and therefore could send her instant reports on the positions and movements of Cael's troops.

In times past, when the Raintree went into battle, their empathic healers were called upon to fight, but their primary purpose on the battlefield had been to attend to the wounded. Today Mercy had no choice but to be all warrior. Until Dante and Gideon arrived, she would lead her people against the Ansara, and then she would fight beside her brothers, a united royal front with combined powers. Temporarily outnumbered more than two to one, the Raintree had to hold out against the invaders by any means necessary.

Reinforcements from the nearest towns and cities had joined the others who were visiting at the sanctuary, giving Mercy forty-five fighters to combat over a hundred renegade Ansara. The odds were not in their favor, but those odds would improve as more and more Raintree arrived at the home place.

Standing alone in her study, she bowed her head, closed her eyes and mediated for a few brief moments, focusing on the challenge she faced. Not only was the sanctuary threatened, but so was her daughter's life.

Mercy reached above the fireplace mantel and ran her hand over Ancelin's sword, the one the Dranira had carried on the day of *The Battle* two hundred years ago. According to legend the sword was much older, thousands of years old, and enchanted with an eternal magic spell. Only a royal empath could wield this powerful weapon, and only against great evil. If Raintree lore was correct, once Mercy used the weapon, it would then be known as Mercy's sword to future generations.

Using both hands to lift the heavy weapon from its resting place, Mercy recited the words of honor that Gillian had taught her. Once in her possession, the sword's weight lightened immediately, enabling Mercy to hold it easily in either hand.

Knowing that Eve was safely hidden in the Caves of Awenasa, protected by a cloaking spell and guarded by Sidonia, Mercy concentrated solely on leading her people against the Ansara.

Now, prepared in every possible way, she went to join her troops. When she emerged from the house, she was met with rousing shouts from those assembled, a show of respect and confidence. Twenty men and women stood before her, and the others were already strategically placed in and around the battlefield Mercy had chosen. The western meadow was protected by high mountains on all sides, and it was miles away from the Caves of Awenasa. The dozen Raintree who lay in hiding were ready to attack as Cael's troops drove farther into the sanctuary.

Mercy lifted her sword high into the air and keened the ancient battle cry. Following her lead, the others yelled in unison. The sound of their combined voices rang out across the sanctuary and mated with the late afternoon wind, carrying the Raintree call to arms far and wide.

Chapter 16

The hills rumbled with the clatter of battle, physical force united with psychic power, resulting in bloody bodies ripped, mangled and near death, as well as minds numbed or destroyed. The ashes of many disintegrated Raintree and Ansara covered the ground. spread across the meadow and into the hills by the force of the wind. Less than an hour since Cael's forces had set foot within the Raintree sanctuary and Mercy had lost a fourth of her people. Her only consolation was that they had destroyed more than an equal number of Ansara.

In the struggle, she had not seen Cael Ansara, nor had she caught sight of Judah. Had the brothers sent their troops into the fray while they bided their time until more Ansara could join them? She couldn't imagine Judah standing back and watching as his warriors fought and died. If she knew anything at all about Judah, she knew that he would do as she had done—take the lead and charge into battle.

So where was he?

She shouldn't be concerning herself with thoughts of Judah. He was the enemy. It was inevitable that they would meet on the battlefield and one of them would die. It didn't matter that he was Eve's father or her own lover. She couldn't allow her personal feelings to influence her, not where the Ansara Dranir was concerned.

During the battle, Mercy had employed psychic bolts sparingly, since they required a great deal of energy and she wanted to conserve as much as possible. Luckily she had encountered only two Ansara capable of the feat, and she had been able to deflect their bolts with Ancelin's sword. One of the sword's most potent magical properties was its ability to protect the woman who wielded it from all attacks, including psychic blasts, thus making her practically invincible.

Standing alone on a rock formation that jutted out of the ground, Mercy applied her telepathic powers to induce the illusion of a dozen green-eyed warriors on either side of her, battle ready and protective of their princess. To keep her magical guard in place, she would have to renew the illusion periodically or replace it with another.

As two male Ansara warriors approached, she concentrated on sending out paralyzing energy strong enough to permanently incapacitate them. Once she had dispensed with the males, she turned to the redheaded female Ansara coming toward her from the left. Mercy projected a mind-numbing mental bolt that caught the woman by surprise; she froze to the spot, then dropped into a crumpled heap. Sensing an immediate threat from her right, Mercy whirled around and swung her sword, landing a fatal blow to her attacker, a tracker with keen animal senses. Ashes to ashes. Dust to dust. As so often happened to those who died on hallowed Raintree land, his splintered body instantly returned to the earth.

Mercy noted Brenna in a fierce struggle near the creek, barely able to keep two Ansara at bay—a huge, black-bearded man and a tall, willowy blonde. After dissipating her troop of fading shadow soldiers, Mercy ran across the field, rushing to Brenna's aid. She took on the more dangerous of the two Ansara—the woman, who Mercy sensed possessed far more power than the male. The blonde turned and lifted her hand, showing Mercy the glistening energy ball floating in her palm. She smiled wickedly as she released the psychic bolt, but when she realized that Mercy's sword deflected the energy and sent it back toward her, she scrambled to get out of its path. She lunged for safety, but Mercy swooped down on her, plunging the sword through her heart. As Mercy withdrew her blade, the dripping blood vanished drop by drop, leaving the weapon shimmering and pure.

Brenna managed to take out her opponent, but not before he had pierced his poisoned dagger into her body several inches beneath her left arm. Mercy stepped over the dying blonde warrior in her haste to reach Brenna, who clutched her wounded side as blood seeped through her fingers. Mercy leaned down, lifted Brenna's hand away from the jagged slash and brushed her own fingertips over the torn flesh. The blood slowed to a trickle, then stopped altogether. Within minutes the cut would seal, and by tomorrow the wound would be completely healed.

As the pain and infection from the poison she had taken from Brenna flooded Mercy's mind and body, she doubled over in pain. She fought the agony within her, and it slowly drained away on a green mist of recycled energy carried off by the wind.

Mercy suddenly lifted her bowed head and looked due east. Her brothers were close. She sensed their nearness. For the first time since she was a child—except when they joined together yearly to renew the shield around the sanctuary—Dante and Gideon had opened their minds to her, connecting with her to give her infusions of their strength and power. The Raintree royal triad possessed an unequaled combined energy. Together, they could accomplish the impossible. They had to. The alternative was too unbearable to even consider.

More than twenty minutes later, as the battle escalated, Mercy caught her first glimpse of Dante, and shortly after that she spied Gideon. Within an hour of her brothers' arrival, more Raintree joined them, fighting alongside Dante and Judah and Mercy. Still outnumbered, but holding their own, they called upon every resource available.

And then the moment she had anticipated and feared arrived. Cael Ansara appeared out of nowhere, his ice-cold eyes reminding her that he was indeed Judah's brother. Their gazes met across the battlefield, and Mercy heard his warning.

Death to Dranir Dante. Death to Prince Gideon. Death to Princess Mercy. Death to all Raintree!

Gideon shot a thin sapphire bolt of lightning at the most threatening of the three Ansara who surrounded him. Electricity danced on his skin, coloring his body and everything near him blue in the evening light, and deflecting almost all the attacks that came his way. He held a sword in his right hand, while he used his left to deliver deadly jolts of electricity.

None of these three were capable of sending psychic bolts his way, so Gideon conserved that special energy and fought with the power that was so much a part of him that it didn't require intense concentration. He would need to use psychic bolts again before the battle was over, he was sure, but he didn't need them now. The electricity he wielded was more than powerful enough for most of those he fought.

A long-haired burly Ansara whose gift was apparently one of extraordinary physical strength had twice penetrated the electrical field surrounding Gideon, leaving a deep, jagged cut on his shoulder from the small knife he'd tossed. Gideon's left thigh was sore from being slammed with a good-sized rock that had easily broken through the streams of electricity and almost knocked him down. But both injuries were healing as he fought.

The big man dropped to the ground as the lightning hit him square in the chest, but Gideon realized the bastard wasn't dead. This Ansara warrior's brute strength made it difficult to kill him with one shot, but knocking him down at least bought a little time. Gideon turned to face the other two.

These three—two men and one woman—had led him away from the others, obviously working to separate him from the siblings who gave him enhanced power. What they didn't realize was that, physically separated or not, the strength of his brother and sister remained in him, and would until the battle was over.

The female Ansara had short black hair and a gift for robbing the air of heat. She carried a sword, and had swung it at Gideon's head and neck more than once, only to have it deflected by a stream of electricity or by his own sword. The blade that had sliced his shoulder had not been poisoned, since the brutish soldier relied more on his extraordinary strength than anything as common as poison, but he suspected this woman's blade might be tainted. She'd also tried to freeze him by sucking the natural heat from the air that surrounded him, but he was generating so much energy at the moment that freezing him was impossible.

The redheaded man at her side most likely had some sort of mental power. He carried a sword in one hand and a small knife in the other but had displayed no outwardly threatening magical abilities. As he was the least menacing, Gideon turned his attention to the female Ansara, who had the audacity to smile. There had been a time when he would have hesitated to kill a woman, even an Ansara soldier, but after tangling with Tabby, he had not a single doubt about sending a deadly bolt of lightning, the strongest he could muster, into her forehead. Her head snapped back, she gasped loudly and dropped her sword. Dead, she was instantly frozen, taken by her own gift.

Her companion, the only one of the three standing at the moment, did not smile as Gideon turned to face him. The hesitant soldier lifted the sword in his hand, and Gideon did the same. He needed a moment to recharge, after putting down the more powerful two, and the remaining soldier did not look to be an immediate threat. In fact, he looked damned scared. Still, the redheaded Ansara before him had a chance to run but did not. Brave, but it sealed his fate.

There was great concentration on the Ansara's face, a wrinkling of the brow and a narrowing of eyes, and Gideon imagined the man was trying to affect him mentally in some way. Was he trying to push thoughts or emotions into Gideon's mind, or was he perhaps attempting to muster a pathetic bolt of psychic energy? Whatever he was trying didn't work, and as Gideon stepped toward him, sword in hand, the man swallowed hard.

Gideon was about to swing the sword when a sound stopped him cold. Someone called his name in a loud, frightened, familiar voice. *Hope.*

He deflected his opponent's blade, then turned his head toward the voice that had broken through the sounds of battle and claimed his attention. Hope appeared, cresting the hill at a run, her gun in one hand, her eyes wide with shock and revulsion and all the horrors he did not want for her.

Out of the corner of his eye, Gideon saw the large, unnaturally strong warrior stand and shake off the electrical surge that should have killed him. Long brown hair fell across the Ansara soldier's face, and the muscles in his arms and chest seemed to ripple, to harden. Then the Ansara lifted his head and tossed his hair back, and his gaze fell on Hope.

"Kill her!" the man who fought Gideon screamed as he swung wildly with his sword again. "She is *his*."

Gideon quickly killed the redheaded man, a dark psychic of some sort who had identified Hope as his woman, with a blade through the gut. He withdrew his sword smoothly and let the body fall, then spun to see the one remaining warrior running toward Hope.

Hope and Emma. They were his future, his soul, his home—and he would not allow the Ansara to take them away.

The enemy who now focused on Hope was closer to her than Gideon was. He could slow the big bastard down with another jolt, but would it be enough to stop him? Or would it be too little, too late? The Ansara warrior was too far away for Gideon to take him down with a psychic bolt, too far away for the accuracy and strength he needed. The incredibly high stakes of this battle crept higher.

"Shoot him!" Gideon screamed as he ran up the hill. "Now, Hope. Shoot!"

In getting this far, Hope had seen enough of the battleground to know that his order was a serious one. Before the long-haired brute reached her, she lifted her weapon and fired. Twice.

Her bullets didn't stop the Ansara, but they did slow him down. The enemy soldier staggered, looked down at the blood staining his massive chest, and appeared to be very annoyed by this unexpected resistance from a mortal woman—and Gideon knew he would now realize that she was mortal, since she'd been able to fire a gun. No Ansara or Raintree would have been able to make the weapon work on sanctuary land, and Hope wouldn't become Raintree until she gave birth to Emma.

Gideon continued to run, until at last he was close enough to do what had to be done. He formed and projected a psychic bolt, a bolt very unlike the lightning that was in his blood. Gold and glittering, it smacked into the Ansara, and in an instant, the threat to Hope was over as the Ansara warrior turned to dust.

Hope rushed toward Gideon. He let his electrical shield fall, and she threw herself into his arms.

"What the…?" she began breathlessly, her heart pounded against him. "This is not… Oh, my God… He just…" She took a deep breath and regained a bit of composure, then said, in a breathless voice, "You're bleeding again, dammit."

There was no time to explain as two Ansara warriors came into sight, rushing toward them with deadly intent. One held a sword in each hand, and the other displayed a weak flame of unnatural fire on his open palm. The firebug would have to go first.

"Stay with me," Gideon ordered as he placed Hope behind him.

As he raised his own sword and erected a barricade of protective electricity that surrounded them both, she muttered, "I'm not going anywhere."

Dante whirled away from a psychic bolt of energy, and it shattered the tree trunk behind him. He threw himself as far away from the tree as he could, not even daring to look back, because if one of those massive limbs hit him, he would be dead. As he ran, he threw a bolt in retaliation, hoping to keep the Ansara ducking for cover until he himself could find a handy boulder to duck behind.

He'd lost track of Gideon and Mercy in the fierce battle,

but he could still sense them there, pooling their strength with his. Together the whole was greater than the sum of the three parts, and they needed every scintilla of power they could muster. There were enough Ansara that they could almost team up three to each one of the Raintree.

An Ansara woman sprang from behind a tree and expertly threw a chain at his ankles. The chains weren't deadly, but if one wrapped around his legs he would fall, almost as helpless as a turtle on its back, and then the Ansara would make mincemeat of him. The chain flashed toward him, and less than two seconds after the weapon had left the Ansara's hand, he leaped as high as he could, drawing his legs up like an athlete on a trampoline. With silver fire the chain passed beneath him, whipping into the face of a groggy Ansara who had been trying to get to his feet. The man's face exploded in a mist of blood.

Dante threw a bolt at the woman, but she was as fast as a cheetah and bounded behind a tree.

He was tiring somewhat, taking a little longer to recharge between bolts. The Ansara had to be tiring, too, but there were more of them.

When had they gotten so strong? How could they have rebuilt the clan undetected? Had an unusually strong Ansara escaped, two hundred years ago and somehow successfully shielded the clan from the Raintree sentinels? They must have established a home place somewhere and used it to feed their power. On a vortex, all things were possible.

Three Ansara erupted from cover, thirty yards to his left, charging him. He spun to face them and shot a bolt at the biggest one; the blast of energy hit the man in the middle of the chest, and he disintegrated from the force, but the other two raced on, and Dante didn't have time to rebuild enough energy to take both of them down.

Alarm prickled the back of his neck. He didn't stop to

think, didn't wonder what was behind him; instinctively, he ducked and rolled to the right, coming back to his feet as a six-foot sword hacked the air where he'd been. A woman who had to be at least seven feet tall was wielding the sword as if it were a toothpick. Her lips pulled back in a snarl as she swung it again. He leaped back once more, but the tip sliced him diagonally from the left side of his rib cage and across his abdomen, and down to his hip.

The cut hurt like hell, but it wasn't mortal. She was too close for him to hit her with a bolt without getting caught in the back-blast, and the other two were only ten yards away now. Desperately he lowered some of the mental shields with which he held back his fire and sent a long tongue of flame licking at her. She fell backward in her haste to escape the hungry red beast. He turned his head toward the other two attackers, and they split up, going in opposite directions, flanking him but keeping a wary distance.

Fire was too dangerous to use on a battlefield. Any battle was chaotic, uncontrolled. He could send out a wall of fire at any time, but with the Raintree engaging the enemy all over the battlefield, he would be killing his own people, too. The larger the fire, the more power and energy it took to control. The risk was very real that, distracted at every turn, he would loose a monster he couldn't control. No one used fire in a battle.

The tall woman slowly got to her feet, grinning. Holding the sword in a two-handed grip, she began circling him, joining the other two as they looked for an opening.

His ass was likely dead, but he intended to take all three of them with him.

He didn't want to leave Lorna. The thought pierced him like a lance. He wished he'd told her again that he loved her, told her what to do in case he didn't make it back. She might be pregnant. The chance was small, but it existed. He would never know. He remembered the sound of her voice, full of outrage, yelling, "Where are you going?" and wished he could hear it again.

He heard her, actually heard her, so hard did he wish it.

Except she was yelling, *"What the hell are you doing?"*

Every hair on his body stood up in alarm. Aghast, he dared a quick look around and almost passed out in sheer terror. She was running headlong across the field toward him, not looking right or left, her hair flying like a dark flame. A body lay in her path, and she hurdled it without pause. "Fry their asses!" she bellowed, evidently wondering why he wasn't using his greatest gift.

He had recharged enough of the enormous energy needed for a psychic bolt, and without warning, he shot it at the tall woman. She turned, instinctively bringing up her sword to deflect the bolt as if it were another blade. The blast hit the big blade broadside, shattering it, driving needle-sharp shards of steel into her. She screamed, pierced in a hundred places from her head to her knees. One long shard protruded from her right eye. Shrieking nonstop, she instinctively put her hand to her eye and hit the shard, driving it deeper. She dropped to her knees and toppled over, much as the tree had done.

Dante spared her no more than a glance as he danced in a circle, trying to keep Lorna behind him and out of the kill zone, trying to keep the remaining two Ansara where he could see them. If he could hold them off until his energy rebuilt...

Without warning, one shot a psychic blast at him. Not all warriors could muster enough energy to wield this most powerful of gifts; most used more physical weapons, like the swords, which might be gifted with different powers but were still essentially used in traditional moves. This bastard had been hiding his light under a bushel, as it were. If their tactic

had been to let Dante bleed his energy level down before un-
leashing their own blasts, the ploy had worked.

Lorna never stopped moving, stooping as she ran to pick
up a fist-sized rock. "Fire!" she kept screaming. "Use your
fire!" She was only twenty yards away, rushing headlong
into the circle of death. His blood froze in his veins.

"Yeah, Raintree, use your fire!" one of the Ansara
taunted, knowing he wouldn't. Then the man turned and
shot a bolt at Lorna.

He miscalculated, not taking enough time to anticipate
her speed. She made a furious sound and heaved her rock at
the Ansara, making him duck. "Amateur," Dante muttered,
firing a blast at the bastard—or trying to. He was too tired;
he didn't have enough energy left.

The Ansara wolves circled closer, grinning, enjoying his
helplessness as they waited for their own energy to rebuild.
They had used far less than he had; it would take only seconds
more.

"Link with me!" Lorna screamed. "Link with me!"

His heart almost stopped. She *knew* what it would do to
her, *knew* the agony....

There was no time for careful preparation, the gradual
meshing of minds and energies. There was time only for
smashing his way into her mind and tapping the deep pool
of power. It fed him like water crashing into a valley after a
dam collapsed, a deluge of energy that shot from both his
hands in simultaneous bolts. Linked to him as they were,
Mercy and Gideon both felt the enormous surge and were
fed in turn.

Dante furiously fired bolt after bolt. Tears burned his eyes
but never fell, the moisture evaporated by the cascade of
energy running through him. *Lorna!* He could see her on the
ground, lying motionless, but her power still poured into him

as if there were no limit to it. He didn't need time to rebuild; the energy was there immediately, flying off his fingertips in white-hot blasts.

Faced with the killing machine he'd become, the Ansara retreated, drawing back to regroup. Agonized, Dante broke the link with Lorna's mind and charged to where she lay unmoving, her face paper white. There were bodies all around her, testament to how close the Ansara had come. If she hadn't been lying so still that they must have thought she was already dead, they would surely have killed her.

If he hadn't done the job for them, Dante thought with an inner howl of savage pain. He fell to his knees beside her, yanking her into his arms.

"Lorna!"

She managed to open her eyes a little; then her lids drooped shut again as if she didn't have the energy to hold them open.

He had drained her, turned her mind to mush. She had recovered before—but would she recover this time? Mercy and Gideon, not knowing what they did, had also been siphoning power from her. He couldn't predict the effects on her brain, because what he'd done to her—twice, now—simply hadn't been done before.

He looked up, looked around for help. The Ansara were retreating, disengaging from the battle. He felt numb, unable to make sense of everything that was happening around him. He needed Mercy. If anyone could heal Lorna, she could.

Lorna jerked in his arms, batting at him with a limp hand, and he realized he was crushing her to his chest. His heart leaped, almost choking him. Gently he laid her back on the ground, hoping against hope as he watched her swallow and try several times to speak.

"Are you okay?" he asked, but she didn't answer.

He picked up her hand and cradled it against his cheek,

willing her to speak. If he could hear her talk, he would know her brain was recovering.

"Lorna, do you know who I am?"

She swallowed, nodded.

"Can you talk?"

She held up her hand like a traffic cop, telling him to slow down, to stop peppering her with questions. Slowly, laboriously, she rolled to the side and began trying to sit up. Silently he supported her, kept her from falling, as he watched her efforts. Finally she could sit, her head hanging down as she took in deep breaths. Dante rubbed her back, her arms, and asked again, "Can you talk?"

She blinked at him, then nodded, the movement as ponderous as if her head weighed fifty pounds.

Thinking she could and actually doing it were two different things. He waited for a sentence, a single word, anything, but she was silent.

In just a few minutes she got to her feet. She stood weaving, staring around her at the carnage, the sprawled bodies. He would have done anything to spare her seeing this. War was ugly, and war between the gifted clans was brutal. No one went to war and came out of it unmarked.

"Honey, please," he begged softly. "If you can, say something."

She blinked at him some more, frowning a little; then her gaze wandered back to the bodies around her. She took a deep breath, let it out, and said, "This looks like Jonestown, without the Kool-Aid."

During the relentless fighting, Mercy lost track of Cael and feared he had gone to find either Dante or Gideon, neither of whom she had seen in quite some time. But now that Dante led the Raintree, she could both fight and heal, as the situation demanded. Both were her right and her duty. She sensed Geol nearby, severely wounded and dying. If she could find him, she could save him. Following the flicker of energy left inside him, Mercy searched the ash-strewn meadow where the bloody bodies and dust particles of dead Raintree and Ansara mingled together, once again united— in death if not in life.

A large, muscular Ansara, his silver hair secured in a shoulder-length ponytail, lifted his sword in both hands as he charged toward Geol, who lay helpless on the ground. Instantly calling forth the power from deep within her, Mercy created a psychic bolt and hurled it into the attacking warrior's back. The blast exploded through him, shattering his body into dust fragments. She hurried to Geol, knelt down and laid her hands on him, drawing out his pain, healing his wounds. But as with every healing, Mercy paid a high price. Once the process of experiencing another's suffering and converting it into positive energy ended, she released that energy back into the universe, allowing it to escape from her in vapor form, a mist as green as her Raintree eyes.

When she rose from her knees, weak but revived enough to continue, Mercy sensed someone trying to connect with her. Then, without warning, she heard Eve's voice.

Daddy's coming.

Eve?

A thunderous roar shook the ground beneath her feet as hundreds of warriors in blue uniforms stormed into the vast meadow, quickly taking over the battleground. Mercy gasped in horror when she saw the man leading the massive force. Judah Ansara. He had brought reinforcements. Hundreds of Ansara men and women, armed and prepared to fight. There was no way that the Raintree who were united together here at the sanctuary could overcome such a mighty force. But they could and would figure out a way to hold out as long as possible, until more Raintree arrived to continue the battle. Tonight. Tomorrow. They would fight to their dying breaths, every man and woman defending the sacred Raintree sanctuary. This land could never belong to the Ansara.

The fighting slowed and then gradually stopped altogether. Cael reappeared, and his warriors lifted him up and onto their shoulders. He flung his arm high into the air, his sword silver bright and dripping with fresh Raintree blood.

Judah's troops formed a semicircle around their Dranir, a blue crescent moon of Ansara power. Then an elderly woman, at least as old as Sidonia, appeared at Judah's side, apparently having teleported herself into the battle, which meant she possessed a rare and powerful ability. Mercy immediately sensed a wave of respect and awe surround the woman and knew that this was Sidra, the great Ansara seer.

The battle weary Raintree followed Dante and Gideon, congregating on the opposite end of the meadow. To wait. To watch. To prepare. Mercy made her way to her brothers as quickly as possible. Knowing their thoughts, she assured them that Eve was safe.

A reverent silence fell over the valley as Raintree faced Ansara on the battlefield.

Mercy stood between Dante and Gideon. The two women with her brothers—Lorna and Hope, she had learned from reading their thoughts—stayed a good ten feet behind them. Mercy could not deny her fear. She might die today, but she feared far more for Eve than for herself. If she and her brothers did not survive this battle…

Dante made no move to initiate an attack. The Raintree continued waiting and watching, mentally preparing, psyching themselves up for what lay ahead.

Cael gestured for his men to lower him to his feet. Once

on the ground, he marched toward Judah like a cocky little bantam rooster, at least four inches shorter than the Ansara Dranir. Brother faced brother.

"Hail, Dranir Judah," Cael shouted.

Cael's followers repeated his shout. Judah's warriors stood at silent attention.

"We fight together today, my brother," Cael said. "To avenge our ancestors."

Sidra laid her hand on Judah's arm, her eyes beseeching his permission to speak. With his gaze unwaveringly linked to his brother's, Judah nodded.

"Choose this day whom you will serve." Sidra's voice rang out with loud clarity, as if amplified a hundred times over, her words heard by every Ansara and Raintree within the boundaries of the sanctuary. The old seer lifted her hand and pointed at Cael. "Do you choose Cael, the son of the evil sorceress Nusi? If so, you follow him straight to hell."

When Cael lunged toward Sidra, Judah raised his arm in warning. Cael halted.

"Or do you choose Dranir Judah, son of Seana and father of Eve, the child of light, born to the Raintree princess and yet born for the Ansara tribe to provide us with the gift of transformation?"

Though Cael bristled and cursed, Mercy barely heard him over her own heartbeat, which drummed maddeningly in her ears. Sidra had shared Mercy's deepest, most carefully guarded secret with Ansara and Raintree alike—with Dante and Gideon. Her brothers glared at her, shock on Gideon's face, rage on Dante's.

"Tell me this isn't true," Dante demanded.

"I can't," Mercy replied.

"Eve is half Ansara, the daughter of their Dranir?" Gideon asked.

"Yes." Mercy answered Gideon, but her gaze never left Dante's face. "When I met him, I didn't know who he was."

"How long have you known?" Dante asked.

"That he was Ansara? Since the moment I conceived his child."

"Why didn't you tell me...tell us?"

The sound of Sidra's voice echoed off the mountains, spreading like seeds in the wind, capturing the attention of all who heard her.

"It is your choice," she said. "To live and die with honor at your Dranir's side, or be destroyed along with this madman who claims a throne that is not his!"

Shouts of allegiance rang out as the Ansara chose sides. Not one blue uniformed warrior broke formation, and only a handful of Cael's troops deserted him to join his brother's army.

"What's going on with the old Ansara seer?" Dante asked. "It's as if she's instigating war between the brothers." He looked to Mercy. "You don't seem surprised, which leads me to believe that you know what's happening, why the Ansara created this lull in the battle to iron out family differences."

Mercy realized that she did know, at least to some extent, what was occurring within the Ansara camps. "The brothers and their warriors are probably going to fight to the death."

"And you know this how?"

"How I know doesn't matter," she said. "All that matters is that we have to be prepared to fight the winner."

Within minutes, Mercy realized she had underestimated Cael's madness. The vision of brother battling against brother, Ansara renegade warriors against the Ansara army, that she had expected altered dramatically when Cael commanded his forces to attack the Raintree instead.

Taken off guard, Dante quickly recovered and started

issuing orders, first to Mercy and then to his warriors. He told Mercy to search, find and heal as many of their wounded as possible, then send them back into the battle.

"If we have any hope of holding the sanctuary until reinforcements arrive, we'll need every Raintree warrior left alive," Dante said.

As the battle raged around her, Mercy, who occasionally had to use her sword for both protection and attack, combed the battleground, searching for Raintree wounded. In all she found nine, including Echo, who had been frozen in place, and Meta, whose left arm had been hacked off. With the heat from her healing hands, Mercy thawed Echo slowly and drew the frostbite from her body. Before Mercy recovered from the healing, Echo left, rushing back into the battle.

Mercy managed to save eight of the nine wounded, including Meta, whose arm Mercy reattached, but she warned her not to use it during the battle.

"It won't be completely healed for at least twenty-four hours," Mercy cautioned.

After expending enough energy to work her healing magic on nine people, Mercy's strength was greatly depleted, so much so that she could barely stand. She desperately needed rest, hours of recuperative sleep. But there was no time.

As she continued her search, her legs grew weaker and her arms felt as if they weighed fifty pounds each. Her hands trembled. She staggered, then fell to her knees. She clutched her sword tightly but felt her grip softening.

Hold on to Ancelin's sword! Don't let it go!

Try as she might, she couldn't keep her eyes open, couldn't fight her body's urgent need for rest.

She toppled facedown onto the ground, Ancelin's sword slipping from her fingers. She could hear the clatter of battle and smell the scent of death all around her as she lay there in her half-conscious state, drained and defenseless.

She had to find cover, a place to hide away until she could re-energize. Forcing her eyes open, she reached to her side until her fingers encountered her sword. Clasping it loosely, she dragged it with her as she crawled toward a stand of trees less than fifteen feet in front of her. She made it halfway there before a booted foot knocked Ancelin's sword from her grasp, then stomped on her hand, flattening it against the ground. As pain radiated from her hand, along her arm and through her body, Mercy gazed up into a set of cold gray eyes.

Cael Ansara's eyes.

He lifted his foot from her broken hand, then grabbed her hair and yanked her to her feet. Realizing that in her condition she wouldn't be able to fight him, she sent out a psychic scream for help. It was all she could do.

Pressing her back against his chest, he slid a dagger beneath her chin, resting the sharp blade across her throat. He pushed his cheek against hers, and his hot, foul breath raked across her face as he laughed.

"Judah's beautiful Raintree princess." Cael licked her neck.

Mercy cringed.

"Too bad we don't have time for me to show you that I'm superior to my brother in every way." He thrust his semi-erect sex against her buttocks.

If only she could muster enough strength to command Ancelin's sword to come to her, she might be able to—

"Release her!" The commanding voice came from behind them.

Before Cael managed to turn around, the hand he held to her throat sprung open, and his dagger fell out and dropped to the ground. Startled by the appearance of a man who had been nowhere near them only seconds before, Cael momentarily focused on Mercy's rescuer and not her. While Cael was distracted, she directed her core of inner strength on one objective —freeing herself from his tenacious hold.

Just as she managed to break away from Cael, Judah reached out, grabbed Mercy's arm and pulled her to him. Cael growled with rage as Judah shoved Mercy behind him.

Where had Judah come from, and how had he gotten here so quickly? Mercy asked herself. The only explanation was teleportation, an ability she hadn't realized he possessed. But why had he appeared, and not Dante, whom she had beckoned with her silent screams?

As Judah faced Cael, he spoke telepathically to Mercy. *It wasn't Dante's name you called,* he told her. *It was mine.*

Had she actually screamed for Judah to save her and not Dante?

How did you...?

Eve transported me, Judah said. *She also heard your screams for help, so she sent me to you.*

"How touching." Cael's lips curved in a mocking smile. "You actually called for my brother to help you. You must be a fool, Princess Mercy. Don't you know the only reason he's here to fight me is because he doesn't want me to have the pleasure of killing you? That's a treat he wants for himself."

Judah didn't deny his brother's accusations. In fact, he ignored them completely. Instead he instructed Mercy to lay her hand on his shoulder. When she hesitated, he said, "Trust your instincts."

She did, and laid her hand on his shoulder. Immediately she felt a surge of Judah's strength transported into her. Not much, but enough to keep her standing, and enough to enable her to call Ancelin's sword up from the ground and into her hand.

Cael sent the first wave of mind-numbing mental bolts

toward Judah, who deflected them effortlessly, then returned fire. Mercy moved backward, away from Judah, and knew he understood that she could now protect herself with the ancient power of Ancelin's sword, which left him free to concentrate completely on the Death Duel with his brother.

Cael used every weapon in his arsenal of powers and black magic to attack Judah and to counteract Judah's superior abilities. Mercy watched while the brothers fought, bloodying each other, exchanging energy bolts and optic blasts, pulverizing trees and brush and boulders within a hundred-foot radius all around them. And then they charged each other, coming together in mortal physical combat, sword against sword, might against might.

Mercy held her breath when Cael pierced Judah's side, ripping apart his shirt and slicing into the flesh beneath. Judah cursed, but the wound didn't affect his agile maneuvers as he backed Cael up farther and farther, until he managed to chop off Cael's sword hand. Howling in pain as his sword fell to the ground along with his severed hand, Cael reared up and, using all his energy, conjured a psychic bolt. Judah deflected the bolt, sending it back toward Cael, who barely managed to escape. As he hit the ground and rolled, Judah strode toward him. Before Cael could rebound and come up fighting, Judah swooped over him and plunged his sword through his half brother's heart. Cael screeched like a banshee. Judah yanked the sword from Cael's heart, and with one swift, deadly strike took off Cael's head.

Cael's body shattered, splintering into dust. Judah stood there silent and unmoving, his brother's blood coating the blade of his sword. Mercy rushed to him, her only thought to comfort and heal Judah. Holding Ancelin's sword in her left hand, she ran the fingers of her right hand over Judah's wound, then realized his body had already begun healing itself.

Judah pulled Mercy to him and slid his arm around her waist, each of them still holding their battle swords.

"Judah Ansara!" Dante Raintree called.

Gasping, Mercy lifted her gaze until it collided with her brother's.

"Release her," Dante said. "This fight is between the two of us."

Judah tightened his hold about Mercy's waist. "Do you think I intend to kill her?"

In that moment Mercy understood that Judah had no intention of harming her. He wouldn't have given her the strength to retrieve Ancelin's sword if he hadn't wanted her to live.

"He saved me from Cael when I was too weak to fight," Mercy said.

"Only to save you for himself," Dante told her. "Have you forgotten that we are at war with the Ansara?"

"Only with Cael's warriors," Judah corrected. "Or have you been too busy fighting to realize that my army was killing more of Cael's soldiers than you Raintree were? I brought my army here to defeat Cael and to save my daughter…and her mother."

Mercy's gaze met Judah's, and their minds melded for a brief moment, long enough for her to realize that Judah was telling the truth.

Dante narrowed his gaze until his eyes were mere slits. "You're lying."

Mercy sensed that her brother was not going to back down from this fight, that he had every intention of engaging Judah in battle, Raintree Dranir against Ansara Dranir. To the death. When Dante stepped forward, sword drawn, gauntlet dropped, Judah shoved Mercy aside and confronted his enemy.

"No, Dante, don't! I—I love him!" Mercy cried. When he

disregarded her completely, she turned to Judah. "Please, don't do this. He's my brother."

Both men ignored her. If only her powers hadn't been depleted to such a great extent, she might have been able to stop them, but as it stood...

As suddenly and mysteriously as Judah had appeared from out of nowhere in time to save Mercy from Cael, a bright light formed in the space between Judah and Dante. Both men froze, transfixed by the sight.

When the light dimmed, Eve was revealed, hovering several inches off the ground, her body glowing, her hair flowing high into the air, her eyes glistening a brilliant topaz gold. And her Ansara crescent moon birthmark had disappeared.

"My God!" Dante stared at his niece.

"I am Eve, daughter of Mercy and Judah, born to my mother's clan, born for my father's people. I am Rainsara."

An unnatural hush fell over the meadow, the last battlefield of an age-old war, once thought to be eternal. Raintree and Ansara alike laid down their weapons and ceased fighting, then one by one made their way to the area where Eve awaited them.

When the warriors assembled, Raintree behind Dante and Ansara behind Judah, Eve stretched out her arms on either side of her shimmering body and levitated each of her parents upward from where they stood, then brought them to her.

Judah and Mercy looked at each other and recognized the truth. Judah was no longer Ansara. His eyes were as golden as his daughter's. Mercy was no longer Raintree; her eyes, too, were burnished gold.

Eve's gaze traveled the expanse of the vast meadow, shadowing all the warriors with her light. As she passed over the Ansara first, at least twenty of them disintegrated in puffs of sparkling dust, and all the others transformed, their eyes as golden as their Dranir's, and just as he was no longer Ansara, neither were they. When Eve turned her attention to the Raintree, a handful of them, including Sidonia, Meta and Hugh, also transformed. They were no longer Raintree.

"The Ansara are no more," Eve said. "And from this day forward, the Rainsara and Raintree will be allies."

Dante and Judah glared at each other, neither prepared to sign a peace treaty, both wise enough to know the choice was no longer theirs.

"My father is now the Dranir of the Rainsara and my mother the Dranira," Eve said. "We will go home to Terrebonne and build a new nation." She turned to her uncles. "Uncle Dante, you will rule the Raintree for many years, and your son after you. And Uncle Gideon, you won't ever have to be the Dranir."

Eve brought her parents down with her to stand on solid ground; then she led her father to her uncle and said, "The war is over, now and forever."

Neither man moved or spoke.

Simultaneously Mercy took Judah's hand and stood at his side as Lorna moved forward and grasped Dante's hand.

Judah extended his other hand. Tensing, Dante glared at Judah's hand. He hesitated for a full minute, then shook hands with his former enemy.

A reverent hush fell over the last battlefield.

Send our people home, Judah issued the telepathic message to his cousin. *Ask Sidra and the other council members to remain here for now. We will need to meet with Dranir Dante and his brother. In a few days, I will take my Dranira and our daughter to Terrebonne. Mercy and Eve will need time to say their goodbyes, but our people will need the royal Rainsara family to guide them through the transition period and into the future.*

Claude issued orders hurriedly. The new Rainsara clan

began their exodus from the sanctuary, heads held high, as the Raintree rallied around Dante, Lorna, Gideon and Hope.

Judah lifted Eve off her feet and settled her on his hip, then slipped his arm around Mercy's waist. "If you need more time…" Judah said.

"No," Mercy replied. "I heard what you said to Claude. You're right. Our people need us—you and me and Eve."

Epilogue

Eve walked over to Hope and placed her hand on Hope's flat stomach. "Hello, Emma. I'm your cousin, Eve. You're going to like being Uncle Gideon's little princess."

The adults watched in utter fascination as Eve communicated with Gideon and Hope's unborn daughter. From hearing Eve's side of the exchange, they all realized that Eve and Emma were having quite a conversation.

Mercy had accepted the fact that her six-year-old was undoubtedly the most powerful being on earth, and that she and Judah had their work cut out for them. But they would have Sidonia and Sidra to help guide them. The two old women were already acting like rival grandmothers.

Eve gazed up at Gideon, and they smiled at each other. "It's a good thing that I got in a lot of practice with you," he said. "I just hope Emma isn't half the handful you've been."

"She won't be. I promise. Emma is going to be the

Guardian of the Sanctuary," Eve announced, then settled her gaze on Echo. "But until Emma is old enough to take over, you're going to be the keeper."

"Who, me?" Echo's eyes widened in surprise.

Eve laughed. "You really are going to have to work on controlling your abilities. You should have known that you're going to be the new keeper."

"I'm no good at seeing my own future."

Sidra placed her hand on Echo's shoulder. "Nor am I, my dear. And I count that a blessing."

In the two days since the final battle between the Ansara and the Raintree, Judah and the high council had met with Dante, Gideon, Mercy and the highest ranking Raintree in the clan. Word had come in from around the world that numerous Ansara had perished in the cleansing, but many more had been transformed, becoming members of the new clan—the Rainsara, allies of the Raintree.

There had also been another meeting, this one between Mercy and her future sisters-in-law. She had immediately liked both women and sensed that Lorna was Dante's perfect mate, as Hope was Gideon's. Mercy knew that when she left the sanctuary, she left it in Echo's capable hands. Even if the young seer questioned her ability to handle such an enormous responsibility, Mercy had no doubts. One day Echo's empathic talents would equal her abilities as a prophet. Mercy also knew that she left her brothers in the capable hands of the women they loved and who loved them. She was free to enter her new life with Judah without guilt or remorse.

"It will be some time before I'll see my brothers again," Mercy told Hope and Lorna. "At best, Dante and Gideon tolerate Judah and he them. I don't expect they'll ever be friends, but..." Mercy cleared her throat. "Our children will be friends as well as cousins, and then the Raintree and Rainsara will truly be united."

At day's end, shortly before leaving the sanctuary, Mercy tried to return her battle sword to its place of honor above the fireplace in the study, but it fell off the wall and back into her hand. The same thing occurred with her second and third attempts.

"It is now Mercy's sword," Gideon told her.

"Take it with you," Dante said. "And pray you never have to use it again."

Reaching out from where she stood behind Dante, Lorna laid her hand on his shoulder. She didn't say anything. She didn't have to. Mercy saw the immediate change in her brother, a gentling of his spirit.

Judah placed his arm possessively around Mercy's shoulders. "Are you ready to go?"

With tears glistening in her eyes and a lump of emotion caught in her throat, Mercy nodded.

When they turned to leave, Dante said, "Take good care of them."

Without looking back, Judah tightened his hold on Mercy and replied, "You have my solemn promise."

Hours later, as Judah's personal jet flew the new Rainsara royal family from Asheville, North Carolina, to Beauport, Terrebonne, in the Caribbean, Eve slept peacefully, Sidonia snoring at her side. In the quiet stillness, high above the earth, Judah took Mercy into his arms and kissed her.

"You know that I love you," she said. "I've loved you since we first met. Through all these years and everything that has happened...I never stopped loving you."

He traced his fingertips over her lips as his gaze all but

worshiped her. But he didn't speak. Mercy laid her hand over his heart and connected with him.

I won't allow you to read my thoughts, nor do I want to read yours, he told her.

But look inside me now and know how I feel.

When she turned, curled up beside him and took his hand in hers, he wrapped his arms about her and held her close.

You are mine. And I am yours. Now and forever. I need you the way I need the air I breathe. I love you, my sweet Mercy.

* * * * *

**Every Life Has More
Than One Chapter**

Award-winning author Stevi Mittman delivers another
hysterical mystery, featuring Teddi Bayer, an irrepress-
ible heroine, and her to-die-for hero, Detective Drew
Scoones. After all, life on Long Island can be murder!

*Turn the page for a sneak peek
at the warm and funny fourth book,
WHOSE NUMBER IS UP, ANYWAY?
in the Teddi Bayer series
by STEVI MITTMAN.
On sale August 7*

"Before redecorating a room, I always advise my clients to empty it of everything but one chair. Then I suggest they move that chair from place to place, sitting in it, until the placement feels right. Trust your instincts when deciding on furniture placement. Your room should "feel right."
—TipsFromTeddi.com

Gut feelings. You know, that gnawing in the pit of your stomach that warns you that you are about to do the absolute stupidest thing you could do? Something that will ruin life as you know it?

I've got one now, standing at the butcher counter in King Kullen, the grocery store in the same strip mall as L. I. Lanes, the bowling alley cum billiard parlor I'm in the process of re-decorating for its "Grand Opening."

I realize being in the wrong supermarket probably doesn't sound exactly dire to you, but you aren't the one buying your father a brisket at a store your mother will somehow know isn't Waldbaum's.

And then, June Bayer isn't your mother.

The woman behind the counter has agreed to go into the freezer to find a brisket for me, since there aren't any in the case. There are packages of pork tenderloin, piles of spareribs and rolls of sausage, but no briskets.

Warning Number Two, right? I should be so out of here.

But no, I'm still in the same spot when she comes back out, brisketless, her face ashen. She opens her mouth as if she is going to scream, but only a gurgle comes out.

And then she pinballs out from behind the counter, knocking bottles of Peter Luger Steak Sauce to the floor on her way, now hitting the tower of cans at the end of the prepared foods aisle and sending them sprawling, now making her way down the aisle, careening from side to side as she goes.

Finally, from a distance, I hear her shout, "He's deeeeeeaaaad! Joey's deeeeeeaaaad."

My first thought is *You should always trust your gut.*

My second thought is that now, somehow, my mother will know I was in King Kullen. For weeks I will have to hear "What did you expect?" as though whenever you go to King Kullen someone turns up dead. And if the detective investigating the case turns out to be Detective Drew Scoones… well, I'll never hear the end of that from her, either.

She still suspects I murdered the guy who was found dead on my doorstep last Halloween just to get Drew back into my life.

Several people head for the butcher's freezer and I position myself to block them. If there's one thing I've learned from finding people dead—and the guy on my doorstep wasn't the first one—it's that the police get very testy when you mess with their murder scenes.

"You can't go in there until the police get here," I say, stationing myself at the end of the butcher's counter and in front of the Employees Only door, acting as if I'm some sort of authority. "You'll contaminate the evidence if it turns out to be murder."

Shouts and chaos. You'd think I'd know better than to

throw the word *murder* around. Cell phones are flipping open and tongues are wagging.

I amend my statement quickly. "Which, of course, it probably isn't. Murder, I mean. People die all the time, and it's not always in hospitals or their own beds, or…" I babble when I'm nervous, and the idea of someone dead on the other side of the freezer door makes me very nervous.

So does the idea of seeing Drew Scoones again. Drew and I have this on-again, off-again sort of thing…that I kind of turned off.

Who knew he'd take it so personally when he tried to get serious and I responded by saying we could talk about *us* tomorrow—and then caught a plane to my parents' condo in Boca the next day? In July. In the middle of a job.

For some crazy reason, he took that to mean that I was avoiding him and the subject of *us*.

That was three months ago. I haven't seen him since.

The manager, who identifies himself and points to his nameplate in case I don't believe him, says he has to go into *his cooler*. "Maybe Joey's not dead," he says. "Maybe he can be saved, and you're letting him die in there. Did you ever think of that?"

In fact, I hadn't. But I had thought that the murderer might try to go back in to make sure his tracks were covered, so I say that I will go in and check.

Which means that the manager and I couple up and go in together while everyone pushes against the doorway to peer in, erasing any chance of finding clean prints on that Employee Only door.

I expect to find carcasses of dead animals hanging from hooks, and maybe Joey hanging from one, too. I think it's going to be very creepy and I steel myself, only to find a rather benign series of shelves with large slabs of meat laid out carefully on them, along with boxes and boxes marked simply Chicken.

Nothing scary here, unless you count the body of a middle-aged man with graying hair sprawled faceup on the floor. His eyes are wide open and unblinking. His shirt is stiff. His pants are stiff. His body is stiff. And his expression, you should forgive the pun—is frozen. Bill-the-manager crosses himself and stands mute while I pronounce the guy dead in a sort of *happy now?* tone.

"We should not be in here," I say, and he nods his head emphatically and helps me push people out of the doorway just in time to hear the police sirens and see the cop cars pull up outside the big store windows.

Bobbie Lyons, my partner in Teddi Bayer Interior Designs (and also my neighbor, my best friend and my private fashion police), and Mark, our carpenter (and my dogsitter, confidant, and ego booster), rush in from next door. They beat the cops by a half step and shout out my name. People point in my direction.

After all the publicity that followed the unfortunate incident during which I shot my ex-husband, Rio Gallo, and then the subsequent murder of my first client—which I solved, I might add—it seems like the whole world, or at least all of Long Island, knows who I am.

Mark asks if I'm all right. (Did I remember to mention that the man is drop-dead-gorgeous-but-a-decade-too-young-for-me-yet-too-old-for-my-daughter-thank-god?) I don't get a chance to answer him because the police are quickly closing in on the store manager and me.

"The woman—" I begin telling the police. Then I have to pause for the manager to fill in her name, which he does: *Fran*.

I continue. "Right. Fran. Fran went into the freezer to get a brisket. A moment later she came out and screamed that Joey was dead. So I'd say she was the one who discovered the body."

"And you are…?" the cop asks me. It comes out a bit like who do I *think* I am, rather than who am I really?

"An innocent bystander," Bobbie, hair perfect, makeup just right, says, carefully placing her body between the cop and me.

"And she was just leaving," Mark adds. They each take one of my arms.

Fran comes into the inner circle surrounding the cops. In case it isn't obvious from the hairnet and bloodstained white apron with Fran embroidered on it, I explain that she was the butcher who was going for the brisket. Mark and Bobbie take that as a signal that I've done my job and they can now get me out of there. They twist around, with me in the middle, as if we're a Rockettes line, until we are facing away from the butcher counter. They've managed to propel me a few steps toward the exit when disaster—in the form of a Mazda RX7 pulling up at the loading curb—strikes.

Mark's grip on my arm tightens like a vise. "Too late," he says.

Bobbie's expletive is unprintable. "Maybe there's a back door," she suggests, but Mark is right. It's too late.

I've laid my eyes on Detective Scoones. And while my gut is trying to warn me that my heart shouldn't go there, regions farther south are melting at just the sight of him.

"Walk," Bobbie orders me.

And I try to. Really.

Walk, I tell my feet. *Just put one foot in front of the other.*

I can do this because I know, in my heart of hearts, that if Drew Scoones was still interested in me, he'd have gotten in touch with me after I returned from Boca. And he didn't.

Since he's a detective, Drew doesn't have to wear one of

those dark blue Nassau County Police uniforms. Instead, he's got on jeans, a tight-fitting T-shirt and a tweedy sports jacket. If you think that sounds good, you should see him. Chiseled features, cleft chin, brown hair that's naturally a little sandy in the front, a smile that…well, that doesn't matter. He isn't smiling now.

He walks up to me, tucks his sunglasses into his breast pocket and looks me over from head to toe.

"Well, if it isn't Miss Cut and Run," he says. "Aren't you supposed to be somewhere in Florida or something?" He looks at Mark accusingly, as if he was covering for me when he told Drew I was gone.

"Detective Scoones?" one of the uniforms says. "The stiff's in the cooler and the woman who found him is over there." He jerks his head in Fran's direction.

Drew continues to stare at me.

You know how when you were young, your mother always told you to wear clean underwear in case you were in an accident? And how, a little farther on, she told you not to go out in hair rollers because you never knew who you might see—or who might see you? And how now your best friend says she wouldn't be caught dead without makeup and suggests you shouldn't either?

Okay, today, *finally,* in my overalls and Converse sneakers, I get it.

I brush my hair out of my eyes. "Well, I'm back," I say. As if he hasn't known my exact whereabouts. The man is a detective, for heaven's sake. "Been back awhile."

Bobbie has watched the exchange and apparently decided she's given Drew all the time he deserves. "And we've got work to do, so…" she says, grabbing my arm and giving Drew a little two-fingered wave goodbye.

As I back up a foot or two, the store manager sees his

chance and places himself in front of Drew, trying to get his attention. Maybe what makes Drew such a good detective is his ability to focus.

Only what he's focusing on is me.

"Phone broken? Carrier pigeon died?" he asks me, taking in Fran, the manager, the meat counter and that Employees Only door, all without taking his eyes off me.

Mark tries to break the spell. "We've got work to do there, you've got work to do here, Scoones," Mark says to him, gesturing toward next door. "So it's back to the alley for us."

Drew's lip twitches. "You working the alley now?" he says.

"If you'd like to follow me," Bill-the-manager, clearly exasperated, says to Drew—who doesn't respond. It's as if waiting for my answer is all he has to do.

So, fine. "You knew I was back," I say.

The man has known my whereabouts every hour of the day for as long as I've known him. And my mother's not the only one who won't buy that he "just happened" to answer this particular call. In fact, I'm willing to bet my children's lunch money that he's taken every call within ten miles of my home since the day I got back.

And now he's gotten lucky.

"*You* could have called *me*," I say.

"You're the one who said *tomorrow* for our talk and then flew the coop, chickie," he says. "I figured the ball was in your court."

"Detective?" the uniform says. "There's something you ought to see in here."

Drew gives me a look that amounts to *in or out?*

He could be talking about the investigation, or about our relationship.

Bobbie tries to steer me away. Mark's fists are balled. Drew waits me out, knowing I won't be able to resist what might be a murder investigation.

Finally he turns and heads for the cooler.

And, like a puppy dog, I follow.

Bobbie grabs the back of my shirt and pulls me to a halt.

"I'm just going to show him something," I say, yanking away.

"Yeah," Bobbie says, pointedly looking at the buttons on my blouse. The two at breast level have popped. "That's what I'm afraid of."

REASONS FOR REVENGE

A brand-new provocative miniseries by *USA TODAY* bestselling author **Maureen Child** begins with

SCORNED BY THE BOSS

Jefferson Lyon is a man used to having his own way. He runs his shipping empire from California, and his admin Caitlyn Monroe runs the rest of his world. When Caitlin decides she's had enough and needs new scenery, Jefferson devises a plan to get her back. Jefferson *never* loses, but little does he know that he's in a competition....

Don't miss any of the other titles from the REASONS FOR REVENGE trilogy by *USA TODAY* bestselling author **Maureen Child.**

SCORNED BY THE BOSS #1816
Available August 2007

SEDUCED BY THE RICH MAN #1820
Available September 2007

CAPTURED BY THE BILLIONAIRE #1826
Available October 2007

Only from Silhouette Desire!

REQUEST YOUR FREE BOOKS!

2 FREE NOVELS PLUS 2 FREE GIFTS!

Silhouette®

n o c t u r n e™

Dramatic and Sensual Tales of Paranormal Romance.

SN07

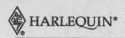

n o c t u r n e™

COMING NEXT MONTH

#21 FAMILIAR STRANGER • Michele Hauf
Dark Enchantments (Book 1 of 4)

P-Cell agent Jack Harris was recruited to fight the
Cadre—instead, he fell in love with their most free-
spirited member, the girl with the green cat eyes,
Mersey Bane. Their joining leads to a whirlwind of
passion and adventure that will deliver them deep
into a world of danger.

#22 DAMNED • Lisa Childs
Witch Hunt (Book 3 of 3)

Ty McIntyre saw Irina Cooper's murder before it ever
happened. But with a witch killer on the hunt, Ty has to
put his disbelief in his newfound abilities on hold so he
can save Irina—and end the Cooper family curse—before
it's too late.